a note of madness

The International School of Amsterdam

www.kidsatrandomhouse.co.uk

a note of madness
tabitha suzuma

DEFINITIONS

A Note of Madness
A DEFINITIONS BOOK 978 0 099 48753 1

First published in Great Britain by The Bodley Head,
an imprint of Random House Children's Books

The Bodley Head edition published 2006
Definitions edition published 2007

3 5 7 9 10 8 6 4 2

Papers used by Random House Children's Books are natural, recyclable
products made from wood grown in sustainable forests.
The manufacturing processes conform to the environmental regulations
of the country of origin.

Set in New Baskerville

Definitions are published by Random House Children's Books,
61–63 Uxbridge Road, London W5 5SA,
a division of The Random House Group Ltd,
in Australia by Random House Australia (Pty) Ltd,
20 Alfred Street, Milsons Point, Sydney, NSW 2061, Australia,
in New Zealand by Random House New Zealand Ltd,
18 Poland Road, Glenfield, Auckland 10, New Zealand,
in South Africa by Random House (Pty) Ltd,
Isle of Houghton, Corner Boundary Road & Carse O'Gowrie,
Houghton 2198, South Africa,
and in India by Random House India Pvt Ltd,
301 World Trade Tower, Hotel Intercontinental Grand Complex,
Barakhamba Lane, New Delhi 110001, India

THE RANDOM HOUSE GROUP Limited Reg. No. 954009
www.**kids**at**randomhouse**.co.uk

A CIP catalogue record for this book is available from the British Library.

Printed and bound in Great Britain by
CPI Bookmarque Ltd, Croydon, Surrey

To Dilly, Nori, Tadashi, Tansy, Thalia
and, of course, Tiggy

Acknowledgements

My deepest thanks go to: my mother for all her time and hard work, Tiggy Suzuma and Tristan Back for quotes from *Backuma's Revised Musical Dictionary*, Thalia Suzuma for her wit, Brendan Davis for the leap of faith and Charlie Sheppard and Lucy Walker for their invaluable edits.

a note of madness

PROLOGUE

It was impossible to say how it had all begun.

Shoulders pressed against the back of a hard chair, wintry sunlight streaking through steel blinds across a grey carpet, gazing at the sharp-cheeked woman at the cluttered desk, there was nothing to say. How did any madness begin? It could either creep up on you, like a slow, degenerative disease, or there could be a sudden, dramatic impact, like slamming into a brick wall and being told you were clinically insane. And how did you know when the impact actually hit? You could be walking around, getting on with life as normal one minute, and then find yourself on a window ledge four storeys up the next. Or the line between what was commonly perceived as normal and abnormal behaviour would gradually begin to blur until you found yourself, barely perceptibly, moving towards the wrong side.

Some people seemed to manage to live their whole lives just on the edge of that line, never actually crossing it. That line – always close but never enough to touch, never consciously present, yet for ever lurking some-where in the subconscious, making itself known.

1

Whereas others somehow drifted over, never any deliberate stepping onto it or over it, but suddenly it just seemed to disappear, leaving nothing but a cluttered office, here in the hospital, and a bedroom like a cell to which one didn't have the key.

The woman with the unmemorable name levelled her steady gaze, pen poised. 'Let's start with your childhood. What was life like when you were growing up?'

A look at her. Her gaze unfaltering. But there really wasn't much to say. A childhood that had been normal, if that meant anything any more – no traumas, no abuse, she wasn't going to find anything of interest there. Unlike the other patients, there was no reason for being here. Physical war-scars like burns and cuts or weird, paranoid behaviour stemming from some terrible incident were all around them. But there was nothing to talk about – nothing that was going to lead them any closer to finding out what was wrong, if indeed anything *was* wrong. Life had been normal and then it wasn't any more and that was all there was to say about it. No startling day awaking with madness, nor madness cunningly creeping up. It was just that somehow, sometime, somewhere down the road, things had changed, and why or when that had happened was impossible to tell.

Ten years was a long time. He had just been a student, back then. No real pressures, no real responsibility, no real reason to go off the rails. His mind might drift briefly back over a dozen or more fragmented shards but it wasn't able to fit them together, as with pieces of a jigsaw, to form a coherent picture. A professor at a desk, running over muddy grass, the chipped beech piano in the living room, you're breathing too quickly. Mum's greying hair, notes flowing like torrents, hands unable to keep up, you're playing too fast. Smoking on a picnic bench, manuscript scrawls on a grubby floor, feet thudding on a deserted path, stop running for goodness' sake. A grey university building, Rachmaninov's Third, Jennah's green eyes, a gilded concert hall. It didn't really make any sense. So he looked at the psychiatrist and smiled.

CHAPTER ONE

It was nearly spring. The air was still raw and sharp and the sky an icy blue. The first leaves on the trees, fresh and pungent, sprinkled sequins of sunlight across the street.

Flynn let the heavy door slam as he left the Royal College of Music and headed across the road towards Hyde Park, bag slung over his shoulder. As he went in through the gates, he caught sight of a familiar back ahead and broke into a jog.

'Hey!' He elbowed Harry in the side as he drew level.

'Flynn. Don't tell me you're going running again.'

'Thinking about it.' Flynn jogged backwards along the wide path. 'Want to join me?'

'Christ, no. Did you hear what Myers said in HS? Two weeks, just two weeks to hand the bloody thing in.'

'Yes, loads of time.'

'Ha ha.' Harry didn't smile. 'I still haven't finished the last one. He's given me an extension but a fat lot of good that does me now we've got another one.'

'You worry too much, Harry, that's your problem.'

'Not everyone reels them off like you do. I'm going

to get myself a sandwich. I've got a lecture in twenty minutes. Coming?'

'No, I'm going for a run.'

Harry rolled his eyes. 'See you later.' He returned to the path, shoulders hunched against the chill air.

Flynn set off at a fast jog. No lectures for him this afternoon; he was as free as the chill, swirling wind, and the quiet, empty park before him spread itself out, enticing and desolate.

Flynn had come to England with his family when he was four. He remembered little of Helsinki now except for building snowmen in the dark and his brother, Rami, pulling him along in a sledge made out of a tray and a length of rope. He had missed his bike and the wide-open spaces and remembered hating England for a very long time.

But one day he had discovered a piano, a dusty upright at the back of the local church hall. Two notes in the bottom octave stuck and the keys were a dirty yellow. While his mother ran Sunday bake-sales, Flynn would tentatively work out nursery rhymes with two fingers. Sometimes an older child would come along and dazzle him with 'The Entertainer' or 'Für Elise'. And when they had wandered off again, Flynn would painstakingly try to find the notes himself. For his fifth birthday, his parents had given him a toy piano. It was made out of plastic, ran on batteries and could be made to play as eight different instruments which all sounded the same. And Flynn had cried because it wasn't real. After that they had let him have piano lessons.

At school in Sussex he had been a big fish in a small pond. He had been the star of every school concert, the one that other kids' parents talked about. Whenever there had been an important school event, they had brought him out to play the piano. It had been a shock to arrive at the Royal College of Music here in London and find himself surrounded by students who practised as hard as he did, if not harder. Students who had spent their childhood at music school, sometimes hundreds of miles away from their families, just in order to play their instrument. Students destined to become professional musicians since they were born, starting on the Suzuki method at two, playing in concerts and winning competitions around the country when still at primary school. Sons and daughters of famous parents who toured the world and played at the Royal Festival Hall. There were even students here who had already begun to make a name for themselves, who had won prestigious competitions and had been written about in the press. Here things were very different. You had to fight to stay on top and there was always, always, someone just that bit better than you.

Still, London life suited Flynn. He liked the grey sky-line, the huge parks, the bustling streets, the overfull buses and the endless traffic. He liked the way no one knew each other, no one really mattered. In a sprawling and impersonal city like this, there was such a mixture

7

of backgrounds, races and nationalities that everyone just blended in and nothing and no one could look out of place.

Flynn ran out of the park, cut across the main road and headed home. Harry's flat in Bayswater, loaned to him by his parents who were living in Brussels, had been home to Flynn for almost six months now. It was on the fourth floor of a tall, white house on a long tree-lined street behind the tube station. When you came in the front door, the first thing you did was trip over the collection of trainers and a massive accumulation of junk mail in the narrow hallway. The kitchen was white and fitted, although one of the cupboard doors was held together with masking tape, and the small wooden table against the wall was covered with university papers, half-opened envelopes, dog-eared textbooks and bills. Above the table, a small, hopelessly cluttered noticeboard held a collection of papers almost an inch thick, bearing notices such as 'Your mum phoned' and 'Your mum phoned again' and 'PHONE YOUR MUM!' On the fridge door, a magnet in the form of a treble clef held a photo of Harry, Jennah and Flynn during their inter-railing holiday last summer, all white smiles, burned noses and blue sky.

The living room housed a large, sagging brown couch, a matching brown armchair and a coffee table. There was a dusty television sitting on top of a small cupboard stuffed full of DVDs, and an old side table against the wall. Next to the window was a chipped, black upright that Harry's mum had bought for Harry's dad as an engagement present twenty-odd years ago. On top of the upright teetered several piles of music books, scores and manuscript pads as well as two metronomes and some kind of dying plant in a cracked pot. The music stand held several Rachmaninov scores, the top one opened at a well-thumbed page with a great many pencil scribblings between the staves. In the corner of the room was a dent in the yellow carpet where Harry's cello usually stood, more piles of music, a top-heavy music stand and a cello bow in need of rehairing.

At the end of the hallway were the two bedrooms. Flynn's contained a small, cluttered desk, his keyboard, a PC that only occasionally worked, his stereo, an unmade bed and a burgundy rug that Rami had brought back from Taiwan. Harry's contained a slightly larger desk, an executive-style chair, a complicated hi-fi system, Picasso prints on the walls and a cupboard with sliding doors. Flynn had grown fond of this flat. It was nice and comfortable, and it certainly beat university halls.

As he emerged from a steaming shower, the phone began to ring. Padding into the kitchen, stepping over a pile of washing in front of the machine, he answered, swearing mildly as his towel slipped off him.

'Hang on,' he said down the phone, and readjusted himself. 'Hello?'

It was Jennah. 'Flynn, don't tell me you've just woken up again!'

'I had lectures all morning, I'll have you know! Doctor Swift talking about subsidiary harmony notes, suspensions and appoggiaturas. I could practically see my whole life flash in front of my eyes.'

Laughter. 'I can imagine. Swifty's classes always make me lose the will to live. Is Harry in?'

'No, he doesn't finish till four.'

'Oh. Well I was only calling to remind the two of you about tonight.'

Flynn paused. 'Tonight?'

'The concert! At the Queen Elizabeth Hall?'

'Oh yes, of course.' *That* concert.

Jennah's muse, the elusive Professor Miguel, conducting Beethoven and Wagner. She had got them all tickets months ago. A concert was always exciting, although the prospect of this one in particular left Flynn with mixed feelings. One of his fellow students in keyboard, André Kolov, would be playing. Flynn never particularly relished listening to André play the piano – he was too good.

'You'd forgotten!'

'No, of course not!'

'Yeah right! Meet you in the foyer at seven. Ask Harry to wear something smart.'

'I can try.'

Harry and Jennah were Flynn's oldest friends. They had met at music camp seven years ago. Harry had been a tall, dark, mature-looking twelve-year-old, sauntering around the car park on the first day, hands in his

10

pockets, checking out the new arrivals. Flynn had been a small, blond, hyperactive eleven-year-old and the pair had found themselves sharing a room together. After the first few days they had adopted Jennah, a tomboy with dirty fingernails and messy hair who laughed at their jokes and knew some good ones herself. Together they climbed up scaffolding, played practical jokes on unsuspecting music teachers and generally caused chaos.

The following year they had got into so much trouble that Harry and Flynn weren't allowed to share a room. The year after that, Harry's voice had broken, Jennah no longer had messy hair and things had changed. The practical jokes stopped. Harry and Jennah continued to tease each other but Flynn only felt relaxed with Harry and hadn't been sure how to treat Jennah any more. Although she hadn't changed from her usual chatty, friendly self and they still got on well, deep down something seemed to have changed within Flynn. Things were somehow difficult, and very different.

'Jennah wants you to wear something smart.' Seated on the kitchen counter, Flynn greeted Harry with this the moment he stepped in. The last hour of practice had been particularly frustrating and as a result Flynn now felt bored and impatient, drumming his heels against the cupboard doors.

Harry's outraged expression was amusing. 'What on earth for?'

'Miguel's concert. Tonight.'

Harry swore. 'I forgot about that! I wanted to get my essay finished tonight and I'm knackered! She wants me to wear something smart? Forget it. No wonder Charlie's as henpecked as he is. What is it – Beethoven? Piano, isn't it? All right for you.' Still muttering to himself, Harry disappeared into his bedroom.

The District line was packed as usual. Flynn glanced across at Harry, hanging onto the rail opposite him. They made an unlikely pair. Harry was tall and lanky, unruly black curls hanging over a permanently tanned face. Flynn was almost a head shorter, with blond hair that tended to stick up at crazy angles and pale skin that betrayed his every emotion. Harry always wore the same half-amused expression and was down-to-earth and sensible, whereas Flynn had once been described as eccentric and was renowned at college for being very intense. Harry's family was posh, but although he entertained a liking for corduroys and velvet jackets, these usually looked as if they had been unearthed from Oxfam, adorned as they were with patches over the knees and elbows. Flynn couldn't knock Harry's dress sense too much, though – he was hardly a fashion statement himself, tending to live in checked shirts and holey jeans.

Flynn turned to Harry. 'Have you got the tickets?'

Harry jumped. 'No – what the hell? She gave them to you—'

Grinning, Flynn pulled them out of his pocket.

'Bastard! Although at least it would have got us off the hook.' Harry took his ticket and peered down at it short-sightedly. 'Ho, the lovely André, is it?'

'Shut up.'

'No wonder you're looking so excited. Going to learn a thing or two off the real maestro?'

Flynn pulled a face. 'I'll make sure I've got my sick bag.'

'That'll come in handy when you start turning green!' Harry almost choked with laughter at his own wit, and Flynn thumped him.

Jennah had dressed up, Flynn noticed. She was wearing a long black skirt and a peach-coloured top. She looked painfully pretty. And she actually had make-up on. That had to be a first. Jennah never normally wore make-up. She obviously had it pretty bad. Hard to understand really. Professor Miguel had to be in his forties, at least, and was short with a receding hairline. And Jennah's boyfriend, Charlie, was tall, fresh-faced, and an undergrad at the London School of Economics. Unfortunately, he wasn't into classical music. Very unfortunate, really, considering Jennah was a talented flautist and singer.

Outside the Queen Elizabeth Hall, Jennah kissed Flynn and Harry on the cheek, hopped up and down a couple of times saying how excited she was, and led them into the thick, warm fug of the foyer.

13

'So, what have you done with Charles?' Harry asked her as they took their seats.

'He's at home watching *Match of the Day*. One concert a term is about all I can drag him to.' Jennah glanced up and waved at some fellow students from their Stylistic Studies class who were looking for their places.

'God, has Miguel persuaded the whole of the department to come along?' Harry asked, noticing.

'Don't be mean. We were lucky to get tickets – the concert's sold out,' Jennah replied.

'I hope you realize that I'm sacrificing my Time and Transcendence essay to be here.'

Jennah laughed and elbowed him playfully. 'Oh, Harry, are you still on that one? That was due in weeks ago.'

'I know, that's why I'm so stressed out! I'm barely halfway through. I just can't find any more bloody examples of time and transcendence in twentieth-century music.'

'You can find examples of time and transcendence anywhere if you try,' Jennah said, smiling. 'Why don't I give you a copy of my essay for you to plagiarize – intelligently, mind you.'

'Really?' Harry was as eager as a puppy after a bone.

'If it means you'll shut up about it, then yes.'

Harry grabbed her shoulder and planted a big kiss on her cheek. 'You're a star.'

'Yes, I know.' Jennah took a deep breath and exhaled

slowly. 'Why is it always overheated in here? I'll come in a summer dress next time. Flynn's very quiet tonight.'

'What?' Flynn reluctantly pulled his eyes away from the gleaming Steinway on the stage.

Harry and Jennah laughed together. 'Flynn's preparing to give André the evil eye,' said Harry.

'What's wrong with André?' Jennah looked outraged, then caught Harry's eye. She caught her breath suddenly. 'Oh, I forgot.'

'Stop!' Flynn said to Harry. 'I have only praise and admiration for André.' He tried not to smile. 'I wish that he'd develop gangrene and his hands would drop off, but that's all.'

Jennah laughed and then pulled an apologetic face. 'Sorry.'

Flynn shrugged, smiling a little. 'Doesn't matter. I gather he's a *fairly* good pianist.'

They all laughed and started to clap as the orchestra filed onto the stage.

André made his entrance once the orchestra was seated, greeted by heavy applause. Although he was only eighteen like them, his stride was purposeful, his chin tilted upwards and everything about him exuded the kind of confidence that only touring five countries and winning the BBC Young Musician of the Year contest could bestow. Flynn knew him only from a distance, but had absorbed a fair bit about him from Professor Kaiser, who taught them both. Despite being head of the keyboard

15

department, Professor Kaiser had only two individual students. In Flynn's mind that was his tough luck because no one could ever measure up to André Kolov. If it weren't for André . . . But it was difficult to imagine what life would be like if it weren't for André. Realistically, although perhaps not very modestly, Flynn suspected that if it weren't for André he would be the Royal College's top pianist. He had no other real rival at the moment, although the competition in the strings department was fiercer. If only André played something else – that was another thought that frequently went through Flynn's mind.

The Royal College gave out a handful of scholarships each year, one for each instrumental category, which entitled its receiver to a weighty financial award, coupled with considerable prestige. Of course, with André competing in the same category as himself, Flynn hadn't stood a chance, although Professor Kaiser had gone a bit funny when Flynn had shared this thought with him. The professor had actually gone as far as insisting that this was not the case – probably just to try to get Flynn to work harder. Well, as it turned out, André got the award anyway, just as Flynn had expected. Ironic really, considering that André's family was loaded and the money meant nothing to him.

It hurt, though. Professor Kaiser actually seemed genuinely disappointed – presumably that Flynn hadn't risen to the challenge.

'You didn't try,' he told him. 'You gave up before

you even went on,' he continued, referring to the performance that each of the candidates had been required to give. 'You didn't believe in yourself. That's your biggest problem, Flynn. You don't understand your full potential.' Whatever that meant.

Six months later, Flynn still remembered the moment well. The audience had been made up almost entirely of students and music staff, the judges sitting in the front row. André had played just before him, with that self-assured, almost cocky manner with which he was playing now. The tilt of the head, the half-smile, the shoulders moving confidently with the music. Each little mannerism that screamed, *I know I'm damn good!* His playing looked effortless and what he lacked in emotion he certainly made up for in technical ability. Every piece, every note was precision perfect. Flynn knew he was out of the game before he even began. And, of course, he was right. He lost the flow in the first piece. The second piece sounded methodical and cold, even to his own ears. By the third, he was thinking about the notes, which obviously only spelled disaster.

Professor Kaiser was outraged. 'You never let yourself go!' he exclaimed heatedly the next day. 'You went through the whole audition like a robot, thinking only of the notes, never the feeling behind them! That was not the pianist I have in my study every day!'

All in all, the whole experience had not been particularly pleasant. Flynn had gone out of his way to avoid maestro André after that. And now, that swaying

17

head, that tilted chin, the packed concert hall reminded Flynn of everything that he was not. He pulled his eyes away and gazed dully at the back of the conductor's red neck instead. And, blissfully unaware, André played on.

Harry bought them drinks in the lobby during the interval. He was the only one who wasn't broke, so they let him. Jennah vanished into the throng to talk to a couple of friends. It was hot, too hot. Flynn found the atmosphere oppressive.

The second half was even longer than the first. André played Beethoven's Third Piano Concerto. Flynn knew it well. He had been learning it for the past year and still struggled with the third movement. There was a standing ovation at the end. Jennah looked across at Flynn and gave him a sympathetic grin as he reluctantly got to his feet.

'Wasn't Professor Miguel's conducting majestic?' Jennah's eyes were bright as they climbed up the steps of the Hungerford Bridge.

'Majestic? You've been reading too many reviews,' Harry said.

'Well, what did *you* think?'

'It was nice.'

'Nice?' Jennah snorted. 'You can't go round calling Beethoven nice, Harry.'

'How's soporific then?'

'*What?*'

'The last one was. I've always thought that piece was too long.'

Flynn thought that Jennah might explode. But she only gave Harry a playful shove. He launched into an exaggerated stagger and leaned over the side of the bridge, arms dangling. Flynn and Jennah flanked him as the stream of people thinned, heading towards the station entrance on the other side of the river.

Harry straightened up and leaned back, holding onto the rail and inhaling deeply. 'Wow, look at that. London really is a beautiful city.'

St Paul's, the Gherkin and Tate Modern were lit up in pink and orange against an inky black sky. Flynn loved this bridge. The bright white light, the smooth walkway, the tall crisscrossing white posts reaching up into the darkness, making you feel as if you were aboard some luxury yacht. He had lost count of the times he had just stood here and looked out, at night, across the multi-coloured city.

When he had first moved to London six months ago, standing here had overwhelmed him completely, had made him believe that anything was possible. He had turned to face the Royal Festival Hall and whispered, 'One day, one day I will play there. Rachmaninov's Third Piano Concerto with the Philharmonic. I will. Wait and see.'

'Did *you* enjoy it, Flynn?' Jennah asked him a touch tentatively, elbows resting on the rail.

He looked at her. The wind was whipping her hair

19

across her face and her eyes were very bright. 'Yes,' he said.

'Please don't tell me you thought it was nice.'

'No, it was—' He stopped. His true feelings would only sound fake. André's playing had been exquisite beyond words.

Harry and Jennah were both looking at him. The heat rose to his cheeks as he faltered.

'Tell me, why does André keep rolling his head around?' Harry stepped in effortlessly. 'Does that help him keep tempo or something? You don't play like that.'

Jennah grinned. 'No, Flynn just rolls his eyes.'

'That's at Professor Kaiser's barking, though, not at the music,' Harry said.

Flynn forced a smile.

'Let's go,' Harry said. 'I'm getting cold.'

At the other side of the ticket barriers Harry tried to tempt Jennah back to the flat with the offer of coffee.

'No, I really should have an early night.'

'Hot chocolate then? Ovaltine?'

Jennah shook her head, smiling, and gave them each a kiss before departing for her platform. 'Don't talk to any strange men!' Harry called after her.

'You mean stranger than you?'

They went down to their platform in companionable silence. Harry waved at Jennah, waiting alone on the other side. Her burgundy scarf was wrapped tightly around her neck, and her arms were crossed against her black jacket. Even all dressed up, Jennah still had a childlike, windswept look about her, with her tousled brown hair and overgrown fringe. She was so petite, she looked a lot younger than eighteen and still got asked for ID in bars. She often appeared wide-eyed and innocent – big green eyes set against a pale complexion, a small up-turned nose and naturally dark red lips. And when she smiled . . . her nose did this little crinkly thing and her eyes grew really bright and her teeth were very white . . . Flynn was sure she used that smile to keep Charlie wrapped around her little finger, because it was a smile you couldn't say no to, a smile that made you feel really strange inside.

As she stood gazing up at the train information, Flynn watched her covertly until a train came hurtling through. He glanced away as she waved at Harry through the window. When he looked back, the platform was bare.

Flynn made coffee while Harry set up his battered laptop on the living-room carpet.

'You're not going to do that now, are you?' Flynn asked in disbelief.

'I'm going to try. I'm going to stress about it all night otherwise.'

'I thought Jennah was going to give you hers to copy.'

Harry glanced up as Flynn handed him his cup. 'Do you think she meant it?'

'Course she did. Jennah would do anything for you.' Flynn sat down against the wall on one of the carpet cushions and glanced surreptitiously at Harry, who showed little emotion as the computer bleeped and lit his bespectacled face with an eerie, pale blue glow.

For a moment, Flynn wondered if Harry had even heard, but then he said, 'Yes, she's very sweet.'

A long silence stretched out between them, and Harry fiddled with the mouse as Flynn sipped his too-hot coffee. He wasn't sure what had prompted his last comment and now felt more than a little embarrassed about it, but could hardly take it back. Jennah had been going out with Charlie since the summer holidays and in recent weeks Harry had started going out with Kate, a serious-looking violinist from their Musicianship class. But there had always been this thing between Jennah and Harry. It was hard to pinpoint. A gentle warmth. Shared jokes, joint secrets, an extremely similar sense of humour. They had an affinity, like brother and sister, that Flynn was unable to share, and it was only with varying degrees of success that he managed not to feel left out.

Harry always seemed so at ease around everyone, even girls. Especially girls. He was good-looking, but in an unusual sort of way, with the slow gait of a gentle giant. Yet he had a sophistication, a maturity in his demeanour that commanded a certain respect. He was Flynn's closest friend. Yet sometimes he hated him. Around Jennah, he made Flynn feel like a tongue-tied fool.

'Are you going to practise?' Harry's voice made him jump.

'No, I did enough this morning.' He stretched out his legs. 'Think I'll go to bed.'

He got as far as the doorway when Harry's voice stopped him. 'You OK?'

Flynn half turned, coffee cup still full in his hand.

Harry was regarding him placidly, his face still eerily glowing.

'Yeah, why?'

'You were kind of quiet again this evening.'

Flynn resented the 'again'. Just because Harry talked for England didn't mean that everyone found it so easy. He gave a small shrug. 'Just tired.'

'Sleep well then.'

'You too. Don't work too late.'

CHAPTER TWO

When his alarm went off at seven the next morning, Flynn thought it had to be a cruel joke. Every morning for the last week he had been getting up and going for a run in the park before lectures. Some days – yesterday, for example – even managing a run after class. Today, the very thought of it was horrifying. He felt as if he had only just gone to bed and a crushing torpor seemed to have taken hold of his limbs. Even reaching out to turn off the alarm before it woke Harry didn't seem worth the effort. With great difficulty, he opened his eyes and blinked dully at the pale morning light filtering in through the curtains. The thought of lectures this morning sickened him.

'I can't believe you skipped Historical Studies again.' Sick of canteen mush, Harry had returned home to gaze into the empty fridge. 'What's the matter with you? Are you ill?'

Still in the T-shirt and jogging bottoms which served as pyjamas, Flynn surveyed him from his usual place among the crumbs on the kitchen counter. 'No.'

'I knew last night you were going to go all mono-syllabic again,' Harry said matter-of-factly, buttering two slices of bread for a sandwich. 'Want half?'

'No.'

'Have you got Kaiser this afternoon?'

'Of course.'

'Oh well, cheer up. At least you're not me with two essays to do in as many days! Jen's given me hers, by the way – what a star.'

'Good for you.'

Harry shrugged good-naturedly. 'What else are friends for, hey? Are you ready?'

'No.'

'Well get dressed and let's go. It's nearly one already.'

The Royal College was one of those places where you just weren't allowed to feel tired. From the moment you stepped off the Kensington street, through the heavy doors and into the grand entrance hall with its marble floor and huge, sweeping staircase, you were enveloped by an aura of purpose, of hard graft, of dedication. Sometimes, if the orchestra was rehearsing, the corridors would be deserted and music would explode from the double doors at the end of the hall. Occasionally there would be a concert on and students and professors alike would be hurrying from one place to another, carrying sheet music, stands and instruments, a palpable feeling of urgency in the air. Or it would just be lunch time, with the faint strains of

25

practice coming from the music rooms, and the few students who actually believed in stopping for lunch standing around and chatting, or drifting in small groups towards the canteen with tempered, controlled enthusiasm. It was an impeccably well-oiled establishment, in which there was always something you should be doing and always a feeling you hadn't done quite enough.

'What is the matter?' Professor Kaiser greeted him. 'Have you not slept?'

Jesus Christ! What was it with everyone today? 'I'm OK.'

'You don't look "OK",' Professor Kaiser said in his clipped German accent. 'You look like someone who has not had so much sleep. I warned you, did I not, about going out during the week?'

'We went to Professor Miguel's concert,' Flynn said to shut him up.

'I see.' There was a pause. 'Well that should not have kept you up so very late. But you must make sure to get enough sleep. Remember the other week we wasted much time.'

Flynn had a dim recollection of feeling almost equally crap a couple of weeks ago. Three painfully dismal lessons had ensued, resulting in Professor Kaiser giving him two days off to 'get some rest'. Ironic, really, when at the time he had been sleeping twelve and thirteen hours a night. Perhaps if he played badly enough today, Professor Kaiser might do the same again.

As it was, he didn't even have to try.

'Put some effort into it, Flynn!' Professor Kaiser was pacing the room, running a hand over his balding head. Never a good sign.

Flynn stopped, mid-bar. 'What, again?' he asked testily.

'*Ja, ja*, again! Again from the beginning. You play as if you are in a – how do you say? – a *coma*! Where is the melody? It, I cannot hear. You need to make it sing. Sing! Rise above the chords—' He hummed a few bars. 'Yes?'

Flynn nodded wearily. His fingers felt like lead against the keys and his whole body ached with tired-ness. The clock on the piano read quarter past two. He couldn't believe that only fifteen minutes had passed. Gritting his teeth, he returned to the first bar.

'*Nein, nein!*' Professor Kaiser cried. And so the torture went on.

He was not in the mood for Jennah when she caught up with him in the hall. Bouncy, sparky Jennah who always had a smile for everyone and a lot to say.

'Are you coming to the pub after class?' she asked.

'No, I'm going home. Anyway, you know I'm broke.'

'Me too. So? Harry will buy us drinks. Oh, please come with us, Flynn. It'll be fun.'

'I'm going home,' Flynn repeated between clenched teeth.

'Are you OK?' She put her hand on his arm.

'I'm fine.' He had pushed her hand away without even realizing it.

Jennah stepped back quickly, her face registering hurt and embarrassment. 'OK, well if – if you change your mind—'

Flynn turned away before she had the chance to say anything else. He couldn't even trust himself to be civil.

There was a four-pack in the fridge. Harry must have been shopping. Flynn took it to his room and turned his stereo up loud. *Don Giovanni* on full volume. Tough luck, Boney downstairs – if you don't like it you can go to hell. He drank the beers quickly, staring out of the window at the late-afternoon sun. The branches on the trees looked like claws.

He awoke with a pounding head. The luminous numbers on his alarm read 10:13. Gritting his teeth against the pain, he stumbled out of bed and headed for the bathroom. No pills in the bathroom cabinet. He had climbed up on a stool and knocked half the contents of the kitchen cupboard onto the counter when Harry came in and switched on the light.

'Bloody hell.' Flynn sat down heavily on the edge of the sink, squinting against the painful light.

'What are you doing?' Harry looked at him in disbelief.

Flynn groggily rubbed the back of his hand over his eyes. 'Painkillers,' he mumbled.

Harry started collecting up the strewn contents of the cupboard. 'Aspirin?'

'Yeah.'

He handed Flynn two tablets. 'God, you stink! Have you been drinking?'

'Bit.' Flynn downed the tablets with a mouthful of tap water.

'You should have come to the pub with us!'

Flynn groaned, splashed his face with water and sank heavily to the floor, leaning against the fridge. He looked up dizzily as his eyes grew accustomed to the light.

'Coffee?' Harry offered, putting the kettle on.

Flynn nodded gratefully. There was an interminable silence as Harry waited for the water to boil, stretching further still as he proceeded to methodically fill the mugs. Flynn rubbed his face. His eyes throbbed with an aching pulse.

Harry handed Flynn his coffee and sat on a stool on the other side of the room. 'You know, I'm beginning to worry about you.' His voice was even.

Flynn couldn't tell if he was serious or not. So he said nothing.

'Hardly talking, sleeping all the time. It's not healthy, you know!' Harry gave a brief smile.

'So?'

'Jennah was wondering whether it was André's concert that upset you.'

'Don't be absurd.'

'Well, I could see her point. Last month you went underground for about a week when someone mentioned his name at lunch.'

'It had nothing to do with that.'

'Well then, what is it?' The intensity of his own voice seemed to surprise Harry a little, and he gave a quick, false laugh. 'Why aren't you speaking to anyone? Why are you getting drunk on your own?' Another strained laugh.

'Who cares?' Flynn put his hands over his face, wishing he could yell at the top of his voice to drown out the sound of Harry's infuriating voice. Why did that guy have to talk and talk?

'Have you thought of going to see one of those counsellors at the university?' Harry suddenly suggested.

'Please tell me you're joking.'

'Shall I give Rami a call then?'

Flynn lowered his hands from his face and looked up in horror.

'Well, I just thought—' Harry began quickly, then stopped.

'This has got nothing to do with my brother!'

'OK, sure. I just thought . . . since he's a doctor . . . he might have been able to . . .' Harry tailed off awkwardly.

Flynn shook his head slowly in disbelief. Harry and Rami had sort of hit it off when Rami had been helping Flynn move in. But God forbid that Harry should actually call him. There was a long silence.

'Well at least it's the weekend tomorrow,' Harry said with false cheer.

There was nothing to be said to that.

Flynn woke the next day at two in the afternoon. Harry was in orchestra rehearsals, thank goodness. He ate some dry cereal from the packet and drank Coke from the bottle and tried to go back to sleep. It didn't happen. He tried to read. Tried to watch TV. Even tried to practise. No activity was tolerable for more than a couple of minutes. After going through each of them repeatedly in a sort of crazy triangle, he collapsed on his bed, exhausted and suddenly close to tears.

He tried to think back to the first part of that week. The part when he had been full of energy and was continuously looking for ways to burn it off, when no task had seemed too arduous and no mountain too hard to climb. It will come back, he kept telling himself. It will, it will. You're just feeling shitty because, because . . . It was impossible to find a logical explanation. Because the world is crap, was all he wanted to say. But the world hadn't been crap a few days ago. So what had changed? He thought of André, thought of Harry and Jennah's playful flirting on the bridge and wanted to cry. So maybe Harry had been right. Maybe the concert had upset him after all. How pathetic.

'Do you have to keep humming that godforsaken tune?'
Several days had passed and the greyness of the

previous week was just a distant memory. Flynn's eyes were on fast-forward, his body radiated energy and this morning even the college canteen seemed to glow.

Flynn gave the ketchup bottle a violent shake and raised his eyebrows at Harry. 'The Rach Three? A god-forsaken tune?'

'It wasn't meant to be hummed! And how can you eat a hot dog first thing in the morning?' Harry was tired and essay-grumpy.

Jennah glanced up from under her curtain of hair and gave Flynn a sympathetic grin. The three of them were sitting at a table in the empty canteen, amidst piles of papers and books, finishing off some last-minute coursework.

Flynn returned to the ketchup bottle and started humming again. First movement of Rachmaninov's Third Piano Concerto. Such an innocuous start – a series of slow, simple notes. A deceptive, pragmatic beginning to a piece so fraught with madness that by the end it left pianist and listener alike in a state of drained mental exhaustion.

He had started running again. Rachmaninov playing on his iPod. The dew still fresh on the grass, the pink orb of the dawn sun just visible over the trees. At that deserted hour, the park had seemed to hold secrets and promises that made him fizz with excitement. At such a time, anything was possible.

Harry put down his pen and glared at Flynn. 'Would you *stop*?'

Flynn ignored him and bit into his hot dog.

'OK, I'm done,' Jennah said. 'If I have to read through this drivel one more time, I think I'm going to scream.'

'Oh God,' Harry moaned. 'I haven't nearly finished. I don't even understand the last question. What the hell is ars antiqua, anyway?'

'Who cares?' Flynn replied.

'I think it's a type of thirteenth-century French music, but I'm not sure,' Jennah said.

Harry reached for the heavy tome of *Grove's Dictionary of Music* and began flicking crossly through the pages. 'I bet it's not even in here—'

'Come on, come on, give it to me.' Impatiently, Flynn grabbed the dictionary from Harry and ran his finger down the page. 'Here we go – *ars antiqua*: when rehearsals go on for so long, your arse goes numb and feels like it has turned to stone.'

Jennah snorted and, when Harry scowled, quickly covered her mouth with her hand.

'Very funny,' Harry snapped, holding out his hand for the dictionary. 'Give it back.'

Flynn leaped out of the way. 'Hold on, hold on, what else have we got in A? *Accidentals*: when a music student is so drunk he can no longer control his bodily functions. Or how about *arco*: a musical term employed when one uses the bow in a sweeping motion to knock off the head of the person in front? Or what about *attacca*?' Flynn went on. 'When a cellist decides he can take no more and gores the conductor with his spike!'

Jennah made a choking noise and brought her other hand to her mouth.

'Oh, for God's sake don't encourage him!' Harry turned on her.

'Sorry, Harry, sorry,' Jennah said, bursting into laughter. 'We will help you, we will. Where are you up to?'

'Next word!' Flynn announced. '*D.C.* What does *D.C.* stand for, Harry? And no, it's not the capital of America.'

'Do I look like I want to play this stupid game?'

'Bzz. I'm afraid that answer is incorrect, Mr Jenkins. Miss Dawson, question to you. What is the definition of the musical term *D.C.*?'

'Um . . .' Jennah glanced nervously at Harry, her shoulders still shaking with suppressed laughter. '*D.C.* stands for *da capo*, which means "return to the beginning".'

'Yes – point to Miss Dawson. *Da capo* is when all the musicians – usually cellists – have lost their place in the music so they have to start from the beginning again.'

Jennah was biting her thumb, laughing soundlessly.

'Are you going to give me that dictionary or not?' Harry demanded, his face reddening.

'*Discord*,' Flynn went on, ignoring him.

'An unpleasant clashing combination of sounds?' Jennah suggested, wiping the tears from her eyes.

'Correct! Harry Jenkins holding the world record,

playing a hundred and seventy-nine discords when not meant to in one rehearsal.'

'Ha bloody ha,' Harry said.

'*Castanets*,' Flynn continued. 'A percussion instrument generally used for pinching each other in the groin area during rests.'

'You're both nuts,' Harry said.

'*Impromptu*,' Flynn said. 'When, in the middle of a concert, the musician gets so bored he feels it is necessary to lighten the mood by improvising without telling the other musicians and the piece takes a turn for the worse.'

'You two are driving me mad!' Harry dropped his head to the table with a clunk.

'Sorry, Harry!' Jennah said, still laughing. 'We will help you, we will! I think Flynn should write a revised musical dictionary and present it as his final-year dissertation to Myers. Can you imagine the look on his face?'

'Hey, excellent idea!' Flynn suddenly exclaimed. 'I'll write a dictionary. *The Flynn Laukonen Revised Dictionary of Music!* Jennah, you're a genius!'

'Jesus Christ,' Harry said.

The piece was made up of drops of icy water melting from an overhanging tree. Each simple note caused a stab of bittersweet pain as it fell against his skin like a pebble into still water, sending shivers down his spine. Flynn felt as if he could taste each note, feel it inside him, and as the late-afternoon sunlight slanted over Professor Kaiser's dusty study, it was almost too much to bear. He came to the end of the piece and immediately wanted to play it again, to experience again the intense sensations created by nothing more than a simple arrangement of notes, longing for the piece once more like fresh juice on a hot summer's day. Each note was more poignant than the last, more exquisite, until you didn't feel as if another could surpass it and then one did and it was utterly overwhelming, so much so that your chest ached and your eyes stung and your whole body felt as if it would burst.

The door crashed open. 'Blimey, Flynn, the canteen will be closing soon. Isn't Kaiser letting you have lunch any more?' Harry stood in the doorway, impatient and uncomprehending, rubbing his nose.

Flynn stopped, breathing hard, wiping sweaty palms against his thighs. For a moment he wanted to hit Harry for coming in like that, for breaking the spell, for cutting the piece at its most poignant, for bringing him back to reality. Then his anger turned to excitement.

'This has nothing to do with Kaiser. I've found this fantastic piece – it's so simple but incredibly beautiful, by some obscure Russian. We could adapt it for the cello – it's practically all melody.' He jumped up and a pile of books toppled to the floor as he tried to gather the loose sheets of music from the top of the piano. 'I think it could work as a duet with a little variation. It's like two melodies, actually, not one, running together, entwining and then separating—'

'Flynn, not now! I'm sure it's great and wonderful but can we please go and get some lunch? We've got Musicianship in less than twenty minutes and I haven't had a break all morning.' Harry's voice sounded heavy and fed up. He didn't understand.

Flynn tossed a couple of books to the floor. 'Forget Musicianship! This is much better! Professor Kaiser's out all afternoon – if I could just find the last page . . . Go and get your cello, Harry!'

'You're not listening to me. I need to have lunch! Unlike you I need food in order to survive. I've been playing all morning, my fingers are sore. I am not going to play through my lunch break as well, however amazing your Russian piece is . . .'

Harry's voice tailed off as Flynn felt sparks of uncontainable laughter igniting within him. 'Go and get your cello now!'

'Stop laughing – it's not funny. I'm not going to do this!'

'Where has the last page gone? Go and get your cello, will you? D'you understand the importance of this piece?'

'I *understand* that you're trying to give me a nervous breakdown. I *understand* that you're trying to starve me into submission.'

Flynn tipped a pile of books onto the floor. 'This is a million times better than food! It's a million times better than sex!'

Harry shot him a meaningful look. 'Oh, and you would know!'

'It's a million times better than anything you've ever heard in your life! God, where is that bloody page?' He upended another pile of manuscript paper.

'Doesn't Kaiser say anything when you trash his room like this?'

Flynn tore a sheet of manuscript paper from his pad. 'I've lost the last page. Never mind, I'll write it out again. Go and get your cello. Bet you I'll be done by the time you get back!' Kneeling on the floor, the paper on the piano stool, he began scribbling away.

'I'm sure you're right,' Harry said drily. 'Take your time because I'm going to go and eat.'

He would come back. Flynn knew he would. Harry might be a bit sluggish and droll at times but even he had to be intrigued by this. Chewing his lower lip hard, Flynn wrote down the music as fast as his hand would allow, excitement brewing up inside him. He could write out whole sonatas from memory in minutes. Harry would be astounded. He couldn't get the notes down fast enough – only the limitations of his hand slowed him. His brain was on fire.

After a while, Harry returned, cello in one hand, sandwich in the other. Flynn brandished the sheet of manuscript, panting a little.

'Aha!'

Harry snatched it from him. 'What's this?'

'The last page. I wrote it out.'

'Very funny. You found it.'

'No! Look, it's in pencil. Written out by my own fair hand, for you, my best friend!'

Harry gave him a quizzical look. 'Have you been drinking?'

'No, I'm high on Liadov! Come on, let's get started. We haven't got much time. Get your cello out. Come *on*!' Flynn got up and went over to grab Harry's cello, knocking it over and rescuing it by its neck in the nick of time. He started unzipping its case.

But Harry hadn't moved from the piano stool, frowning over the music.

'I told you,' Flynn said. 'It's so simple, it's incredible! You have to hear it first so tune up and move.'

But Harry was still frowning. 'You actually wrote all this out? Just now?'

'Yes. It's all there. Come on!'

Shaking his head, Harry slowly put the music down and reluctantly accepted his cello. Flynn impatiently thumped on an A. Harry began tuning up, painfully slowly.

Flynn thumped the A and D-minor chords a couple more times for good measure. 'OK, got it? Good, let's start.'

'Oh my God,' Harry said flatly to no one in particular. 'He won't even let me tune up properly.'

'Stop moaning. Are you ready?'

Harry gave him a look. 'Can I just ask you something?'

'What?'

'If we're skipping Musicianship and Kaiser is out all afternoon, then what exactly is the rush?'

'We've got to adapt it for the cello. We've got to compose some variations. There's not much time!'

'Oh, sweet Jesus,' Harry moaned.

'Hi. I brought some beers to get us in the mood!' That evening, Jennah stood on the doorstep brandishing a four-pack, hair whipping over her face in the chill evening wind.

Flynn was in a T-shirt and jeans, towel round his neck, midway through drying his hair.

'So whose idea was it to resurrect our trio?' Jennah asked, stepping into the living room and taking off her jacket. She was wearing a wine-coloured shirt and faded jeans and smelled of soap.

'Mine, I suppose.' Flynn looked at her uncertainly. Perhaps she thought it ridiculous. Free of coursework for one evening, he had managed to persuade Harry to call Jennah and arrange a rare rehearsal.

Jennah smiled disarmingly. 'Good thinking. Are we going to go busking again soon? Maybe if we're good enough I could give up my job at the music shop!' The silver hoops in her ears caught the light as she laughed.

Harry came in from the kitchen. 'Hi, Jen! Hey, beer, just what I need.' He leaned forwards to kiss her cheek with his usual unaffected ease, grabbed a can and sat down. 'Here's to our trio!'

Jennah laughed.

Flynn took another deep swig and crammed a couple of Pringles into his mouth. 'Shall we get started?'

Harry and Jennah exchanged glances.

'No rest for the wicked,' Harry said.

'By the way, why weren't either of you in Musicianship this afternoon?' Jennah asked as she began assembling her flute.

Harry rolled his eyes. 'Ask Flynn.'

Flynn, pretending he hadn't heard, sat down at the piano and played an A.

'Flynn?'

He half turned on the piano stool. 'We were busy,' he replied, suddenly shy.

'Busy doing what?'

'Having a *ball*,' Harry said sarcastically. 'Flynn made me skip Musicianship just so that we could do ten times more work on some bloody piano sonata by some bloody unknown Russian and insisted that we not only transpose it but also write in a cello part and compose a bloody variation!'

Jennah looked across at Flynn, trying not to laugh. 'Seriously?'

'Mm.'

The laughter escaped her. 'Oh, dear God, why?'

'That's what I said!' Harry exclaimed.

Flynn shrugged, embarrassed.

41

Jennah stopped laughing. 'Must have been quite something,' she said. 'Can I hear it?'

'God, no, I never want to hear that piece again!'

But she was looking at Flynn. 'Please?'

He made a casual gesture with his hand and shoulder as if to say 'Why not? and looked over at Harry.

'Fine!' Harry exclaimed, pretending to be more irritated than he actually was.

Flynn went to dig out the music from his bag for Harry, who was still tuning. When he returned to the piano stool his palms were suddenly damp. He wiped them on his jeans and glanced at Harry.

Harry nodded, raised his bow and then stopped. 'Are you playing without music?' he asked in surprise.

Flynn shrugged and turned back to the piano. A sharply inhaled upbeat and they were away.

The first few bars were tentative, fearful almost. Harry's notes blended in with Flynn's, then pulled away. They kept it slow, teasing the melody out gently, the notes climbing then receding again. Harry only faltered once, twice, briefly losing tempo but quickly recovering. The piece soared to its delicate crescendo before ebbing away, and Flynn lost himself in the last few bars, the poignancy of the piece threatening to overwhelm him yet again. He opened his eyes reluctantly to Jennah's clapping and turned round with a half-smile.

Jennah's eyes were bright. 'Oh, wow,' she breathed.

Flynn turned to Harry. 'See?' he said with feeling.

'That's beautiful. You put in the cello part yourselves?'

42

'Well, Flynn did,' Harry admitted.

'Where did you find it?' Jennah asked.

'On an old LP from a second-hand music shop. Took me for ever to track down the score. It's good, isn't it?' Flynn couldn't keep the grin from his face.

'It's beautiful.'

Flynn felt the flush of pleasure in his cheeks and raised his eyebrows at Harry.

'It's beginning to grow on me, I suppose,' Harry said defensively. 'So are we going to have a bash at the old Mendelssohn or what?'

'Yeah, let's go.' Jennah propped her book against the table lamp.

'Do you want my stand?' Harry offered.

'No, I'm good.'

It took Flynn a moment to find the music on the top of the piano, buried under a pile of Rachmaninov sonatas. It had been quite a while.

'Ooh. You know, that last arpeggio sounds a little odd to me.' Jennah stopped at bar eleven.

'Be more specific, Jen,' Harry said.

'It's just not quite, um, I dunno.'

'It's too disjointed,' Flynn chipped in.

'Yes, that's it, disjointed.'

'Try holding your notes a little longer,' Flynn suggested. 'And, Harry, lighten your bowing on the lower part. And I'm not keeping tempo, sorry.'

'Let's try it again,' Jennah suggested.

They did. It sounded only fractionally better.

'Keep going,' Harry said between gritted teeth.

But on bar fifteen, Flynn had to stop. 'You know, I've just had a really good idea.'

Harry let out a heavy sigh. 'Can we play it through just once without stopping?'

'Hold on, let's hear Flynn's idea,' Jennah said.

'Well, these two sections are just an echo of the first one. Three sections altogether, for three instruments. We each need to dominate in one.'

'I've never heard it played like that,' Harry objected.

'Yes, but don't you think it would sound brilliant?' Flynn drummed his fingers against the edge of the piano stool with impatience. 'Come on, let's try. From the E flat.'

'Hold on,' Jennah interjected. 'Who's dominating which bit?'

Flynn thought for a moment. 'Flute, piano, cello?'

'Why do I have to go last?' Harry protested annoyingly.

'It doesn't really matter,' Flynn said. 'But shouldn't it go from light to heavy?'

'Are you calling me heavy?'

'No, he's right, Harry,' Jennah said. 'It makes more sense that way.'

'Why not heavy to light?'

'Harry!' they both shouted simultaneously.

'OK, OK.'

* * *

44

'I don't think that was bad at all,' Harry announced when they had finished.

'I think that middle section needs working on,' Jennah countered.

They both looked enquiringly at Flynn. He breathed in deeply, trying to quell a rising knot of energy threatening to burst from within him. 'It was so-so. The middle section's still dragging. We need more clarity on the arpeggios. But you know what? We could make a really good variation on this!'

Jennah's eyes lit up. Harry groaned in dismay. But his reluctance only fuelled Flynn further.

'Listen!' He raised his voice, half laughing, and played a few notes on the piano. 'This . . . Or this . . . Or even this! Yeah, why not this?'

Harry leaned back in his chair and arched his back. 'I need a break,' he said. 'Coffee, Jen?'

'No thanks.' Her eyes were on Flynn. 'That sounded great!'

'Yes, yes.' Flynn played it again. 'See? It could go up like that . . . And then your bit would go like that . . . And Harry's like this – no, like this . . . You see, super-imposed it would sound something like this . . .' He brought his left hand back to the keys.

'Ooh!' Jennah said.

Flynn jumped up and went scrabbling around for his manuscript pad.

'What the—?' Harry began, returning with the coffee as Flynn thrust a sheet in his face.

'Write it down before I forget it!' Flynn ordered.

Harry took the sheet reluctantly. 'As long as I can give this in for my next Musicianship assignment.'

'You can do what you like with it!' Flynn played the first couple of bars through quickly. 'OK, Harry, that bit's yours. Jennah—'

'Hold on, hold on,' Harry protested. 'Do I look like a speed-writer to you? Play it again, slowly for goodness' sake.'

'A, C, B, D, E, F sharp, D sharp, B, E,' Flynn called out impatiently, thumping out the notes on the piano. 'Then repeat a third higher.' He turned to Jennah. 'And your bit goes . . . like this, yes? Or like this?'

Jennah was laughing. 'Flynn, slow *down*!'

Flynn laughed with her in excitement. 'But don't you think it's good?' he urged, all modesty gone to the wind. 'And then the next bit—' He returned to the piano. 'See? See?'

Jennah was nodding slowly and smiling.

'Write it down!' Flynn yelled, laughing. 'Write it down. I promise you, it's going to be brilliant!' Turning back to the piano, he began scribbling down the first few bars of his part, but not before he caught Harry peering into his empty can of beer. Let them think he was drunk, he told himself wildly. What did he care? The utter head-rush from composing was a million times better. His hand shook with suppressed excitement. He swung back wildly to face them again, knocking over Harry's music stand in the process and sending music books sprawling.

46

'You know what? This could be the overture for an opera!'

Harry was the first to laugh and even Jennah was having trouble keeping a straight face. 'An opera with just a trio and no singers. That'll be the day,' Harry chortled. 'You really are pissed.'

'No, stupid! We can put the other parts in. I'm talking about the overture, we don't need voices yet.'

Jennah leaned forwards. 'Come to think of it, this does sound a little *Don Giovanni*-esque.'

'Oh,' Harry begged, 'please don't encourage him.'

'Come on!' Flynn urged them, and watched with increasing frustration as Jennah slowly began to write down her part, pausing, then humming, then pausing again. 'How does it go after that?'

Flynn quickly thumped out the notes on the piano and then turned to Harry. 'Have you got your bit yet?'

Harry let out an exaggerated sigh. 'Really, Flynn, do we have to do this now? I thought we were going to practise the Mendelssohn. I don't think I can cope with any more composing.'

'This is heaps better! This is going to sound great. This is going to sound fantastic!' Flynn grabbed Harry's sheet and started writing the notes down for him.

Harry leaned forwards. 'How can you just write it out like that? What's that – oh no, why so many sharps?'

'That's the first bit.' Flynn thrust the sheet back at him. 'OK? Jennah, are you ready?'

'Yes, yes, I think so,' she said eagerly.

They started playing. Fabulous until the ninth bar.

'No, no, no!' Flynn hit the side of the piano in frustration. 'It goes from A minor to E major. And, Jennah, you go down a third.'

Harry squinted at his manuscript sheet. 'I don't get this. I thought that this bit was in A minor.'

'Yes and on bar four it goes into E major!'

Harry emitted a loud groan. And so it went on.

An hour later, it was beginning to come together and Flynn could feel his heart thudding in excitement. This was something, this was really something. In fact, it was more than something. It was amazing! Not really a variation because it was moving further and further away from the original, but this was something new, something dramatic. Jennah had come to sit beside him on the piano stool and was scribbling down the music as he played.

She kept laughing. 'Slow down, slow down.'

Flynn turned to Harry. 'OK, OK, your next bit—'

'Listen, Flynn, I agree that this is sounding great but I don't think I've got the energy for any more,' Harry said suddenly, putting down his bow. 'Would you mind if I left it for another time? My back is killing me and I'm really knackered.'

Jennah turned to him, her eyes bright. 'But, Harry, don't you think this is brilliant?'

'I do, I do, but I can't keep up any more.' Harry slumped over on the sofa.

Jennah turned back to Flynn. 'Shall I write out his part?'

Flynn handed her the manuscript pad. 'OK, here we go . . .' He began to play Harry's part.

Jennah wrote fast, her hair falling in her eyes, her lower lip caught between her teeth.

By one o'clock in the morning, only Flynn was left writing. Jennah was curled up in the armchair playing with her hair and Harry was passed out on the couch. Still the music rang loud and clear in Flynn's head, and his hand ached from the effort of trying to keep up with the notes as they poured out of him. It was difficult to sit still; he wanted to leap, spin and dance to the sound of the music bursting inside him.

Christ, he thought, Harry and Jennah don't know what they are missing. They don't know how fabulous this is going to be. They don't realize . . . Perhaps this is what Mozart had felt like? A step ahead of everyone else. Able to produce effortless music that would be played for centuries to come. Unappreciated in his time yet labelled a genius after his death.

Chorus, he had to have a chorus! Ripping off one sheet, he started on another, humming to himself . . . Basses, tenors, altos, sopranos. The music rose and rose inside his head, reaching a crescendo so powerful, so pure, it was uncontainable. He could barely make out the separate notes, could hardly break the music down into bars, could no longer get his hand to keep up with his head. He felt something brush his cheek.

'I'm off, Flynnie. Don't wear yourself out.'

Jennah, her hair bedraggled, smiling, leaving.

'No!' He jumped up. 'No, don't go. You've got to help me with this, you've got to help me find a story, you've got to help me write this. I can't – I can't keep up.'

Harry was yawning on the sofa. 'How can you compose? You're completely plastered!'

'Seriously, don't go,' Flynn begged her. 'I need you to help me with this.'

'I'll help you tomorrow, I promise. It's superb, Flynn, but I'm *so tired*!'

'Come running then.'

'What?'

Yes! He was suddenly overcome by a terrific urge to run through the empty park, over the damp grass, cloaked in a blanket of stars, the ground brushed silver by the moon.

He crashed into the hall for his trainers. 'Come on! Come on!' he urged their blank faces. 'The park is magical at night. You'll feel as if you can fly!'

'Flynn, it's one o'clock in the morning and the park's closed,' Harry interjected. 'I'm walking Jen to the night bus. You can't go jogging at this time, you nutter.'

'I can, I can, and you're coming with me!' He grabbed Harry's sleeve and half dragged him into the hall. Harry tried to shake him off. 'Get off, Flynn, stop being daft.' But there was a serious edge to his voice.

'Perhaps you should lock the door and take his keys,' Jennah was saying. 'He'll fall flat on his face if he tries running now.'

Flynn ignored them both and tied his trainers, grabbed his keys and stood up. 'I'm off. Come on!' He grabbed Jennah's hand but she pulled him back.

'Flynn, you're drunk, silly. Bed's a much better option, believe me.'

He laughed at them both, pushed Harry off balance in order to reach the door and raced out into the street.

The air was sharp and cold, the pavement glistening from the earlier rain. The faint swish of cars drifted over from Bayswater Road as he jogged towards it, pacing himself now, in the mood for a really long run. He would continue the opera when he got back. There was no need for him to sleep tonight. His mind was on fire and his body needed no rest. Energy filled him like a sharp, white light. He scaled the railings with ease and dropped down into the park with a gentle thud, the traffic behind him fading, replaced gradually by the steady thump of his trainers against the path. The grass was gleaming, wet and magical and shrouded in shadows. His heart soared with joy.

'Flynn, stop!'

'Flynn, wait up!'

The voices drifted from a distance behind him and he slowed his pace a touch. Then he turned round to face them and jogged backwards, watching them emerge from the shadowy path. Harry was heaving, Jennah's cheeks were flushed red.

'Come on, slowcoaches!' he yelled at them, and turned round again. But this time their footsteps did not follow him and so he turned and ran back to find them collapsed on a bench. 'Come on!' he urged, jogging around them in a wide arc.

'Flynn, this is mad!' Harry got up and tried to block his way but he dodged him easily, laughing. 'You're going to fall down in a minute and then you'll feel sorry!'

Jennah and Harry got up, hands dug deep into their pockets, looking cold and miserable, their eyes following him as he completed another lap of his circuit. Then their heads leaned together and they appeared to be in deep discussion. Snippets floated across to him over the grass.

'I'll walk you back to the main road and get you a cab,' Harry was saying.

'No! I don't care about that. I just want to make sure you get him home OK.'

'I will. He'll run out of steam eventually. He'll have to.' Harry's voice did not sound too certain.

'I'm surprised he hasn't fallen over yet.'

A long silence. Then, 'I'm not sure that he's drunk,' Harry said.

'What?'

'I only ever saw him drink one beer.'

'He must have drunk more!'

'No, seriously. There were three cans left in the fridge and we drank the other two.'

'He must have been drinking something else.'

'There's no other booze in the flat.'

Jennah's voice sounded odd. 'What does that mean?'

'I don't know. All I can say is that when Flynn's pissed, he slurs his words and goes all sleepy.'

'So what's wrong with him?' A pause. Then Jennah's voice again, aghast. 'Do you think he's on drugs?'

'Doubt it, he's always broke. He gave up smoking because he couldn't afford to buy cigarettes! Anyway, he's totally anti-drugs. Remember what he said at Kate's party when Clive was passing around that joint?'

'Oh, yeah . . .' Jennah's voice shook. 'Get him to stop, Harry. He's beginning to scare me.'

Flynn continued running around them, amused by their conversation and sorry at their own apparent lack of excitement. They looked tired and anxious and he only wished he could get them to join in the fun.

'Come on!' he shouted at them again, jumping up and down in frustration. 'Look at the park – isn't it beautiful? The sky's full of stars. Look, look!'

They wouldn't even look. What were they like? Harry suddenly strode out towards him, and Flynn moved away from the path.

'Come on, race you!' Flynn shouted at him, making for the trees. But the anguish in Jennah's voice stopped him short.

'Harry, don't chase him!' she shrieked.

Flynn slowed to a fast walk and heard their footsteps on the path behind him. He felt Harry's hand on his shoulder.

'Come on, stop messing around. Let's go back now.'

Flynn spun round and walked backwards, facing them. 'If you think the park is beautiful now, wait until dawn,' he said breathlessly. 'The sky is streaked by a million shades of pink and orange, and the sun rises like a golden globe of fire, hanging just above the horizon.'

Harry looked odd. 'I'm sure it does,' he said shortly.

'I'll show you.'

'Flynn, we're all knackered. Dawn is in six hours. Let's go home now, OK?'

'Let's run!'

'No!' they chorused in unison, but Flynn felt the laughter bubble up inside him.

'What's so funny?' Harry demanded.

Flynn stopped and leaned forwards, hands on knees, laughter cascading out of him. 'The anti-running campaign!'

'What?'

'You two. Should be the anti-running campaign.'

'Yeah, OK. Ha ha. Let's go now.'

'Only if you help me write the opera.'

'Yes,' Jennah said suddenly. 'We will, Flynn. OK? Maybe not right away because we're all pretty tired, but we will. Let's just go home now, OK?'

He nodded. He would. Anything to please Jennah.

She wasn't like Harry. For a start she was pretty. Very pretty. The anti-running campaign. He laughed again. And continued laughing all the way home.

Dawn rose without Flynn even realizing it. Suddenly the black windows were filled with a pink hue and, when he next looked up, sunlight was streaming through the panes. He stretched out his legs on the carpet and pulled back the fingers of his right hand. His wrist was sore. He surveyed his bedroom carpet, covered with sheets of music, and smiled to himself. His opera was well underway. Shivering from sitting motionless for so long, he got up and padded into the kitchen to make himself some coffee. He felt a little strange, but not in the slightest bit tired. He didn't really need sleep. There was too much to do and, anyway, he wasn't like others. Nearly all the greats had needed little sleep. Went with having a brilliant mind.

The kettle took for ever to boil. He hoisted himself onto the counter. The oven clock read 8:15. He looked over at the kettle again. Come on, come *on.*

The door opened, making him start. Christ, it was Jennah! She had spent the night on the sofa bed. He had forgotten.

'Morning, you.' Her tousled hair hung in her face and she wore an oversized sweatshirt – one of Harry's, presumably – that skimmed her bare thighs. Flynn stared at her.

She gave a little yawn and blinked sleepily. 'Ooh

good, you've got the kettle on. Can you make me some coffee?'

'OK.' He felt his pulse quicken. 'Did I wake you?'

She gave a little smile and looked pointedly at his feet. He realized that he was drumming his heels against the cupboard doors again and stopped. 'Sorry.'

'Doesn't matter. Got to get up anyway – rehearsal at ten.' She brushed the hair ineffectively out of her eyes. 'Have you recovered from your midnight run?'

He bit his lip to hold back a grin. 'I've almost finished the overture.'

Her face registered mild shock. 'What?'

'You know, the opera!'

She frowned in disbelief. 'Have you been writing all night?'

He nodded triumphantly.

'And you're going to lectures today?'

'No! Well I'll have to see Professor Kaiser after lunch but I'll keep going until then.'

Jennah sat down on a stool, drawing her knees up under her jumper. 'Flynn, why?'

'Because it's great! Because I've got all these ideas and they keep coming! Because I love composing!'

Jennah regarded him silently for a moment. She looked pale in the morning light. 'Why not save it till the next Musicianship assignment?' she asked quietly. 'Why are you wearing yourself out like this?'

'I'm not wearing myself out!' he exclaimed. 'I couldn't sleep if I tried. I don't need to sleep.'

56

'Flynn, everybody needs to sleep.'

'Yes, but not all the time.'

Another long silence. Jennah looked keenly at her toes. The kettle clicked and Flynn jumped off the counter.

'I know it's really none of my business,' Jennah began softly, 'but you're one of my closest friends and I don't – I don't want anything bad to happen to you.'

'Nothing's going to happen to me!'

'I'm just scared that if you carry on having no sleep and working so hard, you'll go all funny again like before.'

'What d'you mean?' He looked at her, stung.

She glanced away awkwardly. 'Come on, you know – last week, for example. You nearly bit my head off when I suggested you came to the pub and then you went underground for about three days. Harry said you wouldn't even get out of bed.'

'I was feeling ill.'

'I know.'

'I said I was sorry.'

'It's not that, Flynn. I'm just afraid that you're going to – I don't know – burn yourself out again.'

'No I won't! This is great – I feel brilliant!' He finished pouring the coffee and handed her a cup.

Jennah didn't smile. 'You were acting so weird last night.'

'I was just feeling energetic!'

'We thought you were drunk.'

'I wasn't – I just felt like going for a run!'

'OK. But, Flynn, you know this whole Royal College thing? It's really high pressure for all of us this year and especially for you, with that mad professor. Just – just try and take things easy, OK?'

He smiled and shrugged. 'I will. I am.'

'OK.' Jennah looked down, her eyes troubled. She drank her coffee in silence.

CHAPTER THREE

'No, no, no, no, no.' Flynn rolled over, head hanging off the side of his bed, and scrunched up his eyes. There was no pain this time, no headache, and yet he knew – as sure as he knew from the late-morning sunlight streaming through the curtains that it was a fine day – that it was back, and back with a vengeance.

Getting out of bed was unimaginable, going back to sleep impossible. There was a familiar weight on his chest – a crushing weight of interminable sadness from which there was no escape. After ten minutes or more of lying absolutely still, wishing the day away with all his might, he sat up and blearily surveyed the room around him. Manuscript sheets scattered the floor amidst empty beer cans, dirty plates and scraps of paper covered with his own familiar scrawl – lines from a poem, verses. God, what was this? Memories of the last few days began to jar together like pieces of a poorly edited film. An opera? He had been writing an opera? Jesus Christ! The sight of such a ridiculous flight of fancy sent a shrill stab of agony through his head. He fell back against the pillows, closing his eyes. Who had he told? What had he said?

Oh no, Jennah! She must think he was a complete idiot! What had he been thinking? There was the HS essay for Monday. Why couldn't he have done that while he had the energy instead of trying to write a stupid opera?

He rolled over on his side and squinted down again at the music lying on the floor. He couldn't even read it properly – his eyes wouldn't focus. He couldn't hear the notes in his head, couldn't imagine that they made any sense, couldn't comprehend how he could have possibly imagined that he was in any way capable of composing anything – anything at all. He wished he could burn it all, set fire to the damn floor, but he didn't even have the energy to stuff the papers in the bin. He didn't need to look at his alarm, he could tell by the sunlight that it was gone eleven and he knew he had been asleep for more than thirteen hours, although he felt as if he hadn't slept at all.

It was Wednesday. He had already missed Aural and Musicianship. He went into the kitchen to find a scrawled note from Harry explaining that he hadn't been able to wake him. With a jolt, he remembered that he had a piano lesson at twelve and lectures all after-noon. The last time he had missed a lesson with Professor Kaiser when he had been holed up with flu, the professor had come round in person to check he was all right – or rather to check that he wasn't lying. The idea of him coming round again was intolerable.

A shower was far too much effort. Cold water splashed over his face would have to do. A feeble attempt with the toothbrush – the taste made him want to retch. Puffy white face, purple smudges under his eyes. Two angry red lumps appearing on his forehead. God, he was hideous with his acne spots and crazy blond hair sticking out at all angles. He tried to flatten it with water, but it made no difference. He tried again. His fist hit the mirror with such force that it cracked down the middle. He bit his lip to hold back furious tears.

'Jesus, there you are! You were sleeping like the dead this morning. I banged on your door but couldn't wake you up.' Harry fell into step with Flynn as he headed down the second-floor corridor. 'I picked up some handouts from Aural and Musicianship for you. We just—'

Jaw clenched so that it ached. 'Harry, not now, OK?'

'Yes, sure. Are you – do you want to get some lunch?'

'I've got a lesson.'

'All right, but hold on a minute. Are you OK?'

'I'm fine!' The tone was more aggressive than he had meant it to be, but losing Harry at this point was imperative before he exploded. He burst through the fire door and let it slam behind him.

The final movement of the Rach Three had too many notes, Flynn decided. Too many notes with too little time to play them in. It was killing him, having to play this particular bit over and over again until his shoulders ached and his fingers felt numb.

'*Ach nein*, that is not right,' Professor Kaiser said coolly for the third time that morning.

Flynn could have hit him. Instead he dropped his arms to his sides and let out a long, deliberate sigh of exasperation.

'Let's take it from the start again,' Professor Kaiser said evenly.

No. The start was too far back. The start was nothing but fragments of music he could barely remember. The whole piece was completely alien to him today. Flynn stared at the blurred page numbly, unmoving.

Professor Kaiser flicked back a few pages. 'From the start,' he commanded, tapping the page. 'Come on, try and put a little more emotion into it this time. I can see that you are tired, Flynn, but you are not trying as hard as you could be today.'

Hands clenched so as not to punch the bloody piano. Jaw clenched so as not to shout at the bloody professor. Staring at the page through a thick fog, trying to make sense of the masses of tiny notes, trying to translate them into some sort of sound in his head, some sort of feel in his fingers. Deep breath. Forget the notes, just feel the music. The music. Concentrate on the music. But where had it gone? Forgotten in some rotting cavity of his decaying mind, buried under a thousand thoughts of death and despair. The loud ticking of an irritating clock he had never noticed before. Professor Kaiser's small impatient sigh. He held his breath. Played the first three chords. Then a blank wall came up and hit him in the face. He stared down at his fingers, still holding down the notes from the last chord. They had to move somewhere, but where, he had no idea. It was a cruel joke. All those glossy black and white notes to choose from and not an idea where to go.

'Are you not well?'

The words cut through him like a knife, making him jump. Professor Kaiser's tone was heavy with concern – or was it irritation? Flynn was too tired to tell.

He looked up, his jaw set. 'I can't play this piece.'

'*Ja*, I can see that you are having some difficulty, which make me surprised because of how well you played it last Monday. There is for sure something not right today.'

'I'm fine. I just can't play it. I've forgotten the notes.' He was surprised by the flatness of his own tone as he raised his gaze to meet Professor Kaiser's.

Professor Kaiser smiled. 'You have not forgotten anything, Flynn, you are just tired. Burning the candle at both ends, as the English call it. You must be more careful – you have much to do this year. Go home to bed, have some sleep and take some vitamins. I know you have been practising very hard recently and that is maybe some reason too. I will see you on Friday if you are feeling better. If you are not, then next week.'

Flynn was being dismissed and that was it. Obviously he was tired or coming down with something, there was no other logical explanation. It was simply not possible that he had just forgotten the notes. It was simply not possible that he should not be able to play a piece that he had been practising every day for the last six months. He was at the Royal College of Music, for Christ's sake – it was only meant for talented people. He had to have talent, or else he wouldn't have been accepted here. And yet that was the greatest joke of all. That somehow he had fooled them. Somehow he had duped them all into believing that he was this great musical talent when really – really he was just a nobody.

When competing against André for the scholarship he'd just ended up looking like a fool. When the chips were down he couldn't play a note. His brain had shrivelled up and died and all that practice on the Rach Three had gone to waste. The music had disappeared into some kind of abyss and he was unable to retrieve it. He was a fraud, he was an idiot and, worst of all, he couldn't play the piano to save his life.

There was a scrawled note on the kitchen counter. *Staying over at Kate's. See you tomorrow.* Flynn crumpled the note as soon as he had read it, and tossed it onto the floor. At least that meant he wouldn't have Harry breathing down his neck tonight, acting all brotherly and concerned. At least he wouldn't have to make an effort to be civil. At least he could just be left alone.

He stood in the middle of the living room, the late-afternoon sunlight streaming through the windows, and looked around him. It wasn't even five o'clock. What on earth was he going to do? His eyes rested in turn on the piano, the TV, the pile of library books for his Musical Analysis essay. Of course there were things to do, there were always things to do. But the thought of doing anything filled him with unbearable apathy. Even turning on the television for the usual evening menu of soaps and quiz shows didn't seem worth it.

The weather had been glorious all day and the golden light outside promised a magical sunset. He thought of the couples and families strolling in the park, enjoying the late-afternoon sunshine, and was filled with an inexplicable sadness. The light would be shimmering on the Serpentine, the raised voices of children echoing from a distance. The leaves on the trees would be stirring in the breeze, the sunlight flooding the grass with golden confetti, the sky a deep, painful blue. The thought of going to the park was inconceivable – the sight of such aching beauty would infuse his soul with pain.

Sinking down against the living-room wall, Flynn thought back to Jennah's comment that other morning. *You went underground for three days.* Was it happening again? Was he going underground? He couldn't play a note, couldn't tolerate the presence of others, couldn't tolerate his own presence, for that matter. Why is this happening to me? he asked himself desperately. What is wrong with me? He pressed his fingers over his eyelids and took some rapid, shallow breaths. I can't bear this, he thought. I can't bear feeling like this. I can't bear living like this. I can't bear being me. I want to be Harry,

65

or Jennah, or anyone else who seems happy most of the time, or at least not miserable. I feel as if someone close to me has died, or as if I've suffered some terrible loss. Yet nothing bad has happened and there is no reason for me to feel this way. A few days ago I believed I could write an opera, I was a musical genius and playing was effortless fun. I loved my friends, I loved my life. But now, just existing is pure agony and all I want is escape. Escape from this world, escape from this life, escape from myself. And the only way to achieve that is through death. His breathing had grown ragged and he was aware of a hot wetness beneath his fingers. What is wrong with me? he screamed silently to himself. Oh God, what is wrong with me? Why can I feel nothing but pain?

Sleep, he thought to himself suddenly. Sleep might be the answer. This was a transitory experience, he would get through it. Three days it had been last time, Jennah had said. Three days was not so long. If he slept then at least he wouldn't be able to think and his senses would cease to be barraged with stimuli that he couldn't bear. Yes, he would sleep until this intolerable feeling passed.

Flynn double-locked the front door, turned the ringer off the phone and pinned his curtains to the wall to block out as much daylight as possible. He undressed and rolled into bed, pulling the duvet over his head and breathing in the hot, stuffy darkness, his eyes tightly closed. Don't think, he told himself. Don't think, don't feel – just sleep and forget.

66

He lay motionless for what seemed like an eternity, determined not to toss and turn. Finally he felt just too uncomfortable and rolled onto his back, his arm across his eyes. The bed was too hot. The dusk sun reached him through the curtains, drenching the room and filling his closed eyes with a bright pink luminance. He felt restless and thirsty, his leg itched and he needed to pee. Jesus Christ! He sat up, kicking off the duvet, and saw from his clock that he had been lying there for nearly two hours.

Sleep felt a million light years away. The sun was setting now and his bedroom was filled with a gentle warm glow. His heart began to thud painfully. If I don't go to sleep now, I'll go crazy, he thought. Why won't you let me sleep, God, why? You allow me to suffer like this and yet you refuse to let me sleep! What are you trying to do to me? Biting his lip, he got up and furiously pulled on his clothes again. He would get himself to sleep, damn it, he would. He would knock himself out if he had to.

He grabbed his wallet and rushed out of the flat. He strode down the street towards the off-licence, resisting an urge to run, hating the last of the evening sunlight, warm against his face. He bought a bottle of whisky with the last of his change and returned home, heart still thudding, the glass chinking irritatingly against the loose coins at the bottom of the plastic bag.

There was a bottle of aspirin in the kitchen cupboard. He thought of taking them all before remembering it was a slow and painful way to die. Downing four with a swig from the bottle, he felt a certain flash of self-destructive satisfaction. The whisky burned his throat. He felt as if he were giving God the finger. I can beat you on this, he told him. If you make me suffer, then this is what I'll do.

He returned to his bedroom with the bottle. He felt too hot. He threw open the windows and cranked up his stereo. *Don Giovanni* was still in the machine. Perfect. Always *Don Giovanni* when he was down. He threw off his jeans and collapsed against the pillows, bottle in hand. How much till I pass out? he wondered. He would get there eventually. He had all the time in the world . . .

As it was, he never found out. Time ceased to exist, although suddenly the window had filled with darkness and the air wafting through was chilled. Every time he went to the loo, the room spun a little bit more. It was strangely satisfying. The last time he tripped and banged his elbow against the door jamb. It didn't even hurt. He could no longer feel pain. This is what I want, he thought. This is what I want all of the time.

Ow, stop! Ow, ow, stop! He realized after a while that he was only thinking these words, not speaking them. Speak! he told himself angrily. Tell them to stop shaking me like that!

'Wake up! Flynn, for Christ's sake, wake up!'

Stop shouting, he tried to say. Stop shouting. Get off!

'Open your eyes! Would you just open your eyes?'

68

He took a deep breath to reply and found himself blinking at the strangely patterned blue carpet. It looked vaguely familiar but was at an odd angle, stretching out from beneath his nose. The shaking stopped. His arm felt sore from where it had been gripped. He lifted his head and closed his eyes as the carpet began to whirl. There was a hand on his chest, pushing him backwards. He felt a hard wall behind him and sat leaning against it, his head falling back with a dull thud. Harry's face swam into view.

'What?' he demanded irritably. What was wrong with the guy? Why did he have to wake him up like that?

Harry swore. Flynn blinked hard, trying to keep his eyes open and his head up. Harry hardly ever swore.

'What the hell have you been doing?' Harry's voice was breathless as he sank down to a squatting position against the opposite wall. They seemed to be in the hallway, outside the kitchen.

The bottle of aspirin was now in Harry's hand. 'Whisky and aspirin? Are you trying to kill yourself?'

Sluggishly, Flynn's mind returned to the alcohol and the pills, the golden sunlight and the unbearable pain of being. 'What time is it?' he slurred.

'Just gone one,' Harry retorted. 'In the *afternoon*. What's *wrong* with you?' His voice was high-pitched in disbelief, or perhaps it was disgust. He looked odd and flushed.

'I had a headache,' Flynn lied easily.

'So you drank half a bottle of whisky?'

Flynn groaned. 'I don't remember. I'm going to bed.'

He moved to get up but Harry stopped him. 'Wait!' There was a look of sudden concern in his eyes. 'I thought for a minute you were dead!'

'Well I'm not.'

'But you could have killed yourself. Are you crazy?'

'Yes,' Flynn snapped. 'I'm crazy, Harry, OK? Just leave me alone.' His head throbbed so badly it hurt to speak.

'Listen.' Harry sounded faintly desperate. 'We're mates, aren't we? Just tell me what's going on.'

'There's nothing you can do.'

'I'm sure I can think of something! Come on, Flynn, help me out here. I've got to go back to class but I can't just leave you like this!'

'You can! Just go!'

Harry stared at him, shocked and hurt, and for a minute Flynn felt almost sorry for him. Then his pity turned to anger. Harry had woken him up. Now he was back to reality, with a crashing headache to boot. God knows how long it would take to get back to sleep again. He reached out his hand for the bottle of aspirin but Harry jerked it away.

'Just give it back, Harry.' Clenched teeth.

'You've got to be kidding.'

His jaw ached. 'Just give it to me! I've got a splitting headache, OK?'

'You prefer a headache or having your stomach pumped?'

70

Flynn lunged but Harry was quicker. He jumped up and strode into the kitchen.

Stumbling to his feet, Flynn followed him, cursing. He had to lean his hands against the walls to keep them from rocking.

'Fuck you, Harry!' He reached the kitchen doorway to find Harry washing the aspirin down the sink. As Flynn staggered inside, he saw Harry reach for the bottle of whisky, left on the counter.

'Don't you dare!' Flynn threw himself across the length of the small room and caught Harry just as he was lifting the neck of the bottle. It smashed against the lino, glass chips flying, and Harry fell heavily against the edge of the sink. Flynn crashed to the floor.

Neither of them moved for a moment, transfixed by the steadily growing pool of liquid. The smell in itself was intoxicating and Flynn felt wildly sick. He pulled himself to a sitting position against one of the cupboards and looked up. Harry sank heavily onto a stool, holding his side.

'Sorry,' Flynn said. His voice shook.

Harry looked at him, breathing hard. 'Christ . . . I think you're becoming an alcoholic.'

'I'm not. I just wanted to sleep.'

Eyes wide and uncomprehending. 'Why?'

'Because I'm shattered, OK?'

'All you ever do these days is sleep!' Harry exclaimed. 'I don't understand. The other week you were so hyper you were writing operas all night!'

'Well I've decided sleeping beats being awake, OK?'

Harry sagged back against the wall, lost for words. Then he gave a small smile. 'Your cheek's bleeding, by the way.'

Flynn felt a sore patch under his left eye. His fingertips came away with a red smear.

Harry managed a laugh. 'This is all a bit dramatic, isn't it?'

Flynn nodded, suddenly drained. 'I'm going to go to bed, Harry.'

'It's the middle of the day!'

Exhaustion pressed down on him, dull and aching. The pain in his head was nearing intolerable. He needed to get away from the stench of whisky before he threw up. 'Just let me sleep this off.'

Harry bounced up. 'Coffee!' he declared. 'Coffee's what you need!'

But Flynn got unsteadily to his feet. 'I'm going to bed,' he repeated, his voice barely audible even to his own ears, and left.

There were lots of different types of headaches, Flynn thought to himself. Apart from the severity and the different locations and types of pain, some headaches had a shape, a smell, a taste, even a colour all of their own. By the third day in bed, Flynn could only think about the throb in his head, and the pain that seemed to reverberate throughout his body. A single shaft of metallic silver piercing him between the eyes. Night and day existed only within the demarcations of the luminous digits of his alarm and the rising and fading glow behind the closed curtains. He dozed in fleeting snatches, waking at excruciatingly regular intervals as Harry crashed around in the mornings, at lunch time, then again in the evenings, banging incessantly on his door with offers of food or coffee and trying to engage him in pointless conversation whenever he made a dive for the bathroom.

Cello practice from the next room was the worst thing he had to endure. He didn't want to hear music of any description. Didn't want to think about music, nor hear it in his tortured dreams; wished he could forget about its very existence.

Then, late one night, he was roughly pulled from his hazy state by a painful ring at the door, forcing him to acknowledge consciousness. He fought hard to stay asleep, panicking as he felt the cloak of drowsiness begin to lift, but then found himself straining to hear who it was. A man's voice greeted Harry indistinctly. Not Jennah then. Harry's dad over on business? Professor Kaiser? Dear God, not Professor Kaiser! But there was no clipped accent and he heard the door close and the voices move into the living room. Glancing at the chair wedged firmly beneath the door handle, Flynn crossed to the wall opposite his bed and sat down with his ear against it. He was going to figure out who this was.

'I'm sorry to have dragged you out like this,' Harry was saying.

'Not at all – I'm glad you rang,' the voice replied, strangely familiar.

'Would you like a coffee or something?'

'No, no thanks.' The voice was earnest and low. 'Is he asleep?'

'I suppose so. Every time I knock on the door he claims that I've woken him up, although how someone can sleep round the clock for three days—'

Jesus, they were talking about him!

'Is that how long it's been?'

'Yes.'

'And it's happened before?'

'Well yes, though never as bad as this,' Harry said. 'But last month after we'd been to this concert he shut himself away for a few days and there were several other times before that . . . I just never thought it was anything serious, until this time.'

'Did something happen at uni? Have you got exams or a recital coming up?'

'No, our exams aren't until the summer. We have a lot of coursework to hand in at the moment, which *is* kind of stressful, but Flynn seems to get good marks without much effort at all.'

'Has something happened with his practice then? That professor can be a bit of a slave-driver, I gather.'

'I don't think so. Flynn was really into his composing just before this happened and he was trying to write an opera.'

A short laugh. 'Yes, that sounds familiar.'

Flynn recoiled violently from the wall, heart hammering. Rami! He stared into the darkness, breathing hard. How dare Harry? How dare he? He didn't want his brother here! Rami would never understand! Calm, sensible Rami, living in suburbia with his equally calm, sensible wife, Sophie. Both of them doctors, both of them successful, both of them very much in love and trying for a baby. Blood rushing to his face with fury, he pressed his ear back to the wall.

'Has he stopped practising?'

'Completely,' Harry said. 'He's stopped doing everything. He doesn't leave his room unless it's to go to the bathroom.'

'Has he been drinking?'

Flynn drew back from the wall again, his heart pounding. He breathed deeply, trying to suppress the tears of fury rising behind his eyes. You traitor, Harry! It was none of your damn business – you had no right! How could you do this behind my back? I thought you were my friend! Why, why?

He looked wildly around his chaotic room. For the first time he noticed the clothes strewn haphazardly around, torn-up shreds of manuscript paper littering the floor, empty bottles, dirty plates and coffee mugs, collapsed piles of CDs, books thrown in rage lying next to the wall. All at once he was acutely aware of himself, smelly and unwashed, greasy hair standing on end. The thought of pulling on some clothes and making a run for it flitted briefly across his mind but he didn't feel he would get very far. There was nowhere to go. Gnawing his thumbnail in despair, he pressed his ear back to the wall.

'Is there something else that could have rocked the boat?' Rami was asking. 'A girl, for instance?'

A long silence. 'I don't think so. He hasn't really been seeing anyone . . .' Harry tailed off awkwardly.

Flynn held his breath, feeling his face burn. Then Jennah's name made him start.

'. . . a good friend of ours at the Royal College . . .' They had moved into the kitchen – damn!

'. . . often speaks about her . . .' Rami's voice now.

'. . . nothing going on, but she . . .' Infuriatingly, the end of the sentence was lost.

'. . . have a boyfriend?' Rami again.

'. . . not working out . . . she's been . . . since they first met.'

'. . . what about him?'

'. . . not sure . . . kind of shy . . .'

'Maybe . . .'

Transfixed, Flynn flinched violently on hearing the living-room door open. He climbed back into bed, his heart thudding painfully in his chest from what he had overheard. Then came the inevitable knock on the door. He scrunched up his eyes.

'Flynn, it's Rami.'

I know it's you, you idiot. Just go away.

'Flynn, come on. Open the door.' His voice, deep and calm as usual. 'I'm not going to go away, so you may

76

as well let me in. Stop being a baby – I only want to talk to you.'

Stop being a baby. How many times had he said that before? When was he going to realize that a twelve-year age gap meant nothing any more?

'I'm getting concerned, Flynn. If you don't open the door, I'll have to force it.'

He would too. Furiously, Flynn jumped up, kicked the chair out of the way and fell face down back into bed. He heard the door open, then close.

His desk light clicked on and the swivel chair creaked. 'Blimey, what's been going on in here?'

Flynn breathed heavily into his pillow, his lungs crying out for air.

A hand on the back of his head. 'Hey, you.'

He screwed up his eyes. Go away!

Another creak as Rami sat down again. 'What's going on, Flynnie?'

Irritation sparked at the stupid childhood nickname.

Flynn turned his head towards the wall a fraction to allow himself to speak. 'I'm just tired. Leave me alone.'

' 'Fraid not. I've driven all the way down from Watford and I haven't seen you in nearly two months, so I'm going to expect a bit more than this.'

Flynn fought to keep his voice steady. 'I'm tired, Rami. I didn't ask you to come, so just leave me alone, OK?'

There was a long silence. 'I'm concerned, Flynn.

Your friends are concerned. Professor Kaiser's concerned. We're just trying to help.'

'I don't want your help!'

'You're being childish.'

'Oh, shut up!'

'Listen.' Flynn could tell by Rami's tone that he was struggling to stay calm. 'I'm not going to ignore you while you're like this, however unpleasant you decide to be. But if you refuse to talk to me then I'll have to find someone else who can. Do you want me to call Mum and Dad?'

Before he knew what he was doing, Flynn sat bolt upright. 'Don't you dare! This is none of your business! You know how much Dad's having to fork out for me to be here! You know how Mum worries about the slightest little thing!'

'Flynn, OK, you're talking to me now. I won't—'

'You have no right to blackmail me into speaking to you! You can't just come in and demand that I do what you want! This is none of your business! Harry had no right to call you!'

'Hey, hey, easy, Flynn! Calm down. I'm sorry I said that.'

But the suppressed fury continued to erupt within Flynn until all he wanted to do was throw things and punch Rami's stupid face. All he felt was anger, pure and undiluted and of such power it was as if he would burst with the force of it. He hated himself for actually wanting to hurt his brother, while at the same time knowing nothing could bring him more satisfaction.

'I just want to be left alone! Get that through your thick skull! This has nothing to do with you. Go back to Watford! Go and live your life and let me live mine! I don't want you here! I don't want you to come and – and – I don't – I don't want—' Suppressed sobs were building up in his throat. He gulped for breath and pressed his hands to his face, horrified to feel hot tears against his cheeks.

'Hey – hey—' Rami was on the edge of the bed now, gripping the back of his neck.

'I don't w-want you to – to—'

'You don't want me to be here? But I am, Flynn, and it's not the end of the world. Harry rang because he was worried. I know you just want to be left alone. If I'm feeling crap I usually want to be left alone too. But sometimes what we want is not always what's best. Sometimes when things get in a mess it's too much to manage alone. Remember when Sophie and I broke up for a while? I didn't leave the house for a week. And you came over and forced me out for a game of tennis. Getting out of the house did make me feel fractionally better!'

Flynn pressed the heels of his hands against his eyes, sniffing hard. 'I'm not going out!'

'OK, I can't make you. But you *are* going to try and tell me what's going on.'

'Nothing!'

A small sigh. 'Flynn, something's not right, that much

is obvious. You're in bed all the time, you're drinking yourself silly, you've stopped going to lectures, you won't talk to anyone. You've even stopped *practising*!' A smile in his voice. 'What on earth could be bad enough to cause that?'

'I don't know!'

'Something must have happened.'

'Nothing happened! I just feel crap all the time!'

'Crap as in ill?'

'Yes! I don't know – just crap!'

'Are you in pain?'

'Yes, no, I dunno.'

'You must know, Flynn.'

'Well I don't! Stop playing fucking doctors with me!'

There was silence for a few moments. Rami was looking at him carefully.

'I think you're depressed, Flynn,' he said suddenly. 'It's not that unusual – a lot of people suffer from depression. It can be biological, or there can be a psychological reason. Either way, there are lots of different kinds of treatment available.'

'There's nothing you can do. There's nothing any-one can do!'

'That's nonsense, Flynn. People get treated for depression all the time. Listen, I've got a colleague at Watford General who is very successful in treating patients with depression.'

'I'm not going to see a psychiatrist!'

'Flynn, a psychiatrist is just a doctor who specializes

in a certain part of the human anatomy. You're not well and so you see a doctor. That's what we're for, mate.'

'What the hell is a psychiatrist going to do about it?'

'Talk to you first, better than I can, and hopefully you won't swear at him as much. Then most likely prescribe you anti-depressants.'

'How are pills supposed to help?'

'Clinical depression is due to an imbalance of the chemicals in the brain. Anti-depressants just correct that imbalance.'

'Why can't *you* prescribe them to me?'

'Because it would be better for you to see this guy first. I'm not a psych. Don't let's argue about this, Flynn. I'll take you to see him tomorrow and if he's of no help I'll prescribe you a short course of anti-depressants until I can find someone else.'

'I don't want to take fucking pills! They're not going to work!'

'Look, just try them and then we'll have this discussion. But you have got to stop drinking. Alcohol might make you feel better temporarily, but it's a depressant. It leaves you feeling ten times worse.'

'So Harry told you I'm an alcoholic?'

'At this rate you will be. You shouldn't drink with anti-depressants anyway.'

'I never said I was going to take anti-depressants.'

Rami gave a short, exasperated sigh. 'You're going to give them a try, Flynn, because you're not stupid and you don't want to feel like this all the time.'

The faint glimmer of hope that had started to grow within him was suddenly replaced by a knot of fear. 'What if they don't work?'

'Then you'll try a different type, or other treatments such as talking remedies.'

'Therapy? I don't think so!' Flynn exclaimed.

'Let's cross that bridge when we come to it.'

Suddenly drained of all arguments, Flynn fell silent. His mind was reeling. Was this what they called depression: wanting to cry all the time, unable to tolerate doing anything or speaking to anyone? But, as a doctor, Rami was bound to try to find something medically wrong. That was just the way he was. But this wasn't just a sore throat – how could pills possibly take the pain away? And yet if alcohol managed to close down his senses and stop him from feeling so keenly, then perhaps there were pills that would do the same thing. But a psychiatrist? Was he really losing his mind?

'How's the old plink-plonk?' Rami asked, breaking the sudden silence.

Flynn rubbed his eyes and managed a wry smile. 'Doing my head in.'

'Professor Kaiser still as intense?'

'He's all right. Goes crazy when I'm like this, though.'

'We all have our off days. Working on anything special?'

'The Rach Three and "La Camp", still.'

Rami grinned. 'No longer punching the piano over it, I hope.'

Flynn smiled slightly in reply. He remembered the endless practising of 'La Campanella' in his early teens. One day he had got so frustrated with the piece that he had punched the piano, fracturing his little finger. Their mother had come back from the shops to find his hand swollen huge. There had been a big concert coming up the following week and she was aghast. So instead of admitting what he had done, Flynn had told her that the piano lid had fallen on his hand while he was playing. It was only when she had finished dismantling the lid that he finally admitted the truth.

Rami elbowed him in the side. 'Come on, let's go and order pizza.'

'I'm not hungry.'

'Well I am!'

CHAPTER FOUR

The waiting room of the Watford General Mental Health Unit was about as appealing as a cold shower on a winter's day. It consisted simply of the end section of a badly lit hallway, with a few plastic chairs and a coffee machine. Flynn sat on one of the chairs, elbows on knees, trying not to catch anyone's eye. There was a Gothic-looking woman on one side of the room and an unshaven old man on the other. People drifted in and out. He glanced up occasionally to try to guess whether they were staff or patients and struggled hard against the urge to flee. He entwined his fingers, squeezing them until they hurt, battling the urge to gnaw at his nails. He desperately wished he hadn't let Rami talk him into this.

Hospitals were awful. Although Ear, Nose and Throat was slightly more cheerful than this, he didn't know how Rami could bear to work there every day. He remembered how miserable he had been the time he had broken his collarbone after falling off his bike and had been kept in for observation. The nights were the worst – the strange smells, the moans and groans, the endless sound of footsteps and the exhausting lights that never went out. He would have escaped this if Rami hadn't gone and stayed the night, at Harry's suggestion. Rami had slept on the sofa bed and was up cooking Harry bacon and eggs by the time Flynn headed for the bathroom. He had refused to let Flynn go back to bed.

'I spoke to Dario last night and made you an appointment for first thing this morning,' Rami had said. 'Don't start arguing – he's a friend and has put himself out to make time to see you.'

Flynn hadn't said a word to him in the car, despite Rami's attempts at idle chit-chat. It was drizzling and the steady swish of the wipers made him want to scream. They sat head-to-tail in traffic all the way up Watford Road and then Rami had brought him here.

'I'll wait with you,' he said.

'Don't wait with me,' Flynn had whispered between clenched teeth. 'I'm not a child!'

'OK then. Come and find me when you're done?'

Flynn had nodded, desperate to get rid of him, and had now spent the last fifteen minutes anguishing about whether to stay or go. If he left, Rami would probably never speak to him again, which wasn't necessarily a bad thing, yet a certain kind of loyalty entrapped him and, with a mounting sense of dread, he found himself watching the minutes tick by. I can't believe I'm here. A psychiatrist? Christ. This is a complete joke.

He started when a voice called his name. A dark-haired man in a stiff blue suit with a non-descript face hovered nearby. Flynn got up, feeling as if he were moving in slow motion, and followed the man down a long corridor and then another, through several fire doors and finally into a messy office. Once inside, the man turned and shook Flynn's hand, shooting him a brief smile.

'I'm Dario Ludic. You must be Rami's brother.'

Flynn nodded wordlessly, unable to articulate the slightest sound. He could not believe this was happening. At the doctor's without so much as a cold. What on earth was he going to say – oh, I'm here because I sometimes feel a bit fed up?

Dr Ludic indicated a seat opposite his desk and Flynn sat, too close for comfort, staring at the piles of folders strewn across his desk. Dr Ludic took out some paper, spent several seconds hunting around his desk for a pen and then asked for Flynn's details – name, date of birth, nationality, family background, schooling . . . The list went on. Flynn answered robotically, chewing his thumbnail and staring at the stained, beige carpet.

Dr Ludic didn't look up as he wrote. Minutes passed. The doctor continued to write into the silence. Then he looked up and started talking about data protection acts and patient confidentiality, and Flynn continued to nod and wondered how soon he could politely leave. But, unlike the GPs, Dr Ludic seemed in no particular hurry. And there was a box of tissues on the coffee table that separated the two chairs. For some reason that box of tissues was asking to be picked up and hurled out of the window.

'So tell me a bit about what's brought you here,' Dr Ludic asked eventually.

Flynn looked across at the doctor. He looked straight back. Flynn averted his gaze and pulled a face. There was a long silence. He could feel his cheeks reddening. There was only so long he could keep examining the carpet for.

'Rami mentioned you seemed depressed. Would you agree with that?'

Flynn chewed the corner of his lip. 'I don't know,' he mumbled finally.

Dr Ludic wrote something down. Was he going to take down his every word? Uncommunicative, he would hazard. Monosyllabic.

'Can you try to describe how you've been feeling recently?'

Flynn opened his mouth to say 'crap' and stopped. 'Down,' he substituted.

'Describe what feeling "down" consists of.'

They were going around in circles. Flynn fleetingly thought back to the agony of the past few days and knew there was no way of putting it into words. He couldn't describe his innermost feelings to a perfect stranger, especially when those feelings revolved around fear and torment and morbidity.

Finally, Dr Ludic asked him a series of one-word-answer questions relating mainly to his sleeping habits, daily routine and social interaction. As Flynn replied, he started scribbling again.

'So when did this all start?'

'A few days ago.'

He looked surprised. 'Have you felt like this before?'

A shrug. 'I suppose so.'

'When was the last time?'

'Mm – maybe a couple of weeks ago.'

'And is there ever any trigger?'

He shook his head.

'You said you were at the Royal College of Music.'

'Mm.'

'That's a competitive place. I imagine it's quite a high-pressured environment.'

Another shrug.

'What do you play?'

'Piano.'

'You must be very talented.'

He managed a polite smile. Silence.

'Would you say you were talented, Flynn?'

The question startled him and for a moment his eyes met the doctor's, caught in surprise. He felt the heat rise to his face. Surely Dr Ludic couldn't expect him to answer that? But his prolonged silence and unwavering gaze strongly suggested that he did. Searching for an answer just led Flynn to a series of blanks.

'I suppose other people do,' he mumbled eventually, looking away.

'And do you agree with them?'

Flynn thought about it. If I say yes I sound boastful, if I say no I sound as if I'm lying. And the truth? Maybe it's worth focusing on that. Seconds ticked by, the blood was hot in his cheeks, but Dr Ludic seemed prepared to wait this one out.

'Sorry,' Flynn managed at last.

'It's OK, some questions are more difficult than others. Take your time.'

He took a sharp breath. But the answer had been there all the time. 'Not really,' he mumbled.

Dr Ludic raised his eyebrows. 'Not really?' he echoed. 'What makes you think that?'

Flynn shrugged again and pulled a face in embarrassment. 'Anyone can play the piano if they practise hard enough,' he began to explain. 'I've been practising like crazy since I was four. So people think I'm talented. But talent is something solid and permanent, it – it doesn't vary depending on your mood. I – I can hardly play a thing when the chips are down.' He stopped and bit down on his tongue. Hearing it said aloud was faintly horrifying. Worse still was finding himself struggling against the urge to cry. He held his breath. Don't, Flynn, you stupid fool . . .

'Because you find it difficult to play when you're feeling down, you think you have no talent?'

He shook his head quickly, frantic with embarrassment, and managed a painful smile. 'No, you don't understand,' he said, all of a sudden inexplicably desperate that he should. 'I can barely play at all. I don't

89

practise because I can't. I can't read the notes and I can't remember the music. It's all just a con. And the crazy thing is that I haven't been found out yet.'

'Bye, thanks, I'm off.' Flynn turned on his heel from the patient's bed where Rami stood, white-coated and stethoscoped, clipboard in hand.

'Wait!' He heard Rami's hurried footsteps in the hallway behind him, trying to catch up. Flynn did not slow down and Rami reached him on the stairs, grabbing his shoulder. 'Hey, hey, hold on. What's up? What happened? What went wrong?'

Flynn half turned, forcing a smile. 'Nothing, OK? It was fine, he was fine. Turns out you were right. I'm depressed or whatever. I've got to take these pills and go back and see him in a fortnight.' He thrust the prescription towards him.

Rami looked from the paper to his face. 'What's the matter? Why are you upset?'

'I'm not upset!'

'OK, then let's go to lunch.'

'It's not even twelve. I've got lectures this afternoon.'

'You can miss lectures for another day. I know this great place round the corner. Come on, I know you never eat lunch because you're always broke. Let's go and stuff ourselves.'

Flynn didn't have the strength to resist and ended up having lunch with Rami, who promptly dived into a medical book, looking up the pills that Flynn had been prescribed. Flynn felt drained and wrung out. A sense of unreality had set in. He had told that damn psych what the problem was and the psych had started insisting that he was suffering from clinical depression. But he wasn't ill! He was depressed for a very good reason! Previously, he had not even been able to articulate it properly to himself and then suddenly it was out in the open, but instead of the light bulb going on and everything falling into place, it was this silly diagnosis.

Then again, perhaps the psych had failed to grasp the full significance of what he had said. Thirteen years of practice, for what? For tricking people into believing he was something he was not? Professor Kaiser, Harry, Jennah, his parents, his brother. All brilliantly fooled. And he was supposed to feel fine. Given pills because if he wasn't feeling fine then there *had* to be something wrong with the chemicals in his brain. How absurd.

CHAPTER FIVE

Flynn thought it was possible, it was just possible, that he had somehow, somewhere, sensed a chink in the solid black armour of despair. The urge was to chase after that chink, to rush after it as desperately as he could in order to tear it open so that the chink became a great gaping hole for him to step through, back into the land of the living. But it was such a small chink, so subtle, in fact, that he wondered if he might not have imagined it. Terror flooded through him that if he chased it, or even sought it out in any way, then it would disappear or reveal itself to have been nothing but an illusion and he would be left, encased in this black armour of steel, without hope that any glimmer of escape would ever appear in it again. Sometimes the chink would appear in the form of a moment of instinctive laughter at something on TV. Sometimes it would be nothing more than a brief moment of respite caused by the swaying branches of a tree outside a window. Sometimes it would be a sudden thought – lucid and remarkable by its lack of pain – flitting into his mind. But whichever form it took it brought with it, in those moments of bitter anguish, such a desperate surge of hope that it was almost untouchable, and flitted away like a golden butterfly into the bright blue sky – beautiful, unreachable and completely transient.

He decided not to go back and see Dr Ludic again. There was really no point. He wasn't down any more. He was fine. Everything was back to normal. There was absolutely nothing wrong. When Rami called him to bend his ear about the cancelled appointment, Flynn told him that he was feeling fine, that they had all made a mistake, that he wasn't suffering from depression after all. On several occasions he was tempted to stop taking the pills, but something – perhaps a small knot of fear that the nightmare might return – prevented him.

Neither he nor Harry mentioned what had happened – it was easier not to. It was easier to blot out his hungover conversation with Harry, Harry's phone call to Rami, the two of them behaving like concerned parents of a wayward child. It was far, far easier to pretend it had never happened, to go back to what they had been, and so life returned to relative normality.

As usual there was no shortage of work to be handed in; together he and Harry polished their duo for piano and cello and handed it in as a joint Musicianship assignment. Spring continued to blossom and the park began to smell of early summer. Jennah played in a chamber-music recital at St John Smith's Square. Charles was conspicuous by his absence. The vast oak trees in Hyde Park were heavy with green. Daisies speckled the long grass. Flynn started running again. *Don Giovanni* was slowly buried under a mounting pile of CDs, to be replaced by Rossini and Puccini. They continued rehearsing the trio. He conducted 'The Montagues and the Capulets' at the Royal College's charity concert. Life was tolerable rather than sweet, but he could manage, he could manage.

Professor Kaiser began to smile again. There was a show-case of young musicians coming up at the Royal Albert Hall next month. 'I would like you to take part, Flynn,' he said.

It was at the end of a particularly gruelling two-hour session. Flynn looked down at his hands, splayed over his knees, the fingernails bitten down to the quick. 'That's soon.'

'It is a big event. We have been asked to enter just one student for the keyboard category.'

'What about André?'

'We are not talking about André. I am asking you.'

'But why?'

'Do you think you could do it?'

'I don't know.'

This clearly wasn't the reaction Professor Kaiser had expected. '*Ach*, where is your enthusiasm? This is a huge opportunity! You will have exposure to many important people in the world of music!'

Flynn gave him a look. 'The Rach Three?'

'*Jawohl!* Of course!'

'Next month?'

'It's there, it's there,' Professor Kaiser insisted. 'It only needs now a bit of polishing. Keep up the hard work and you will be ready.'

'That's huge,' Harry said when he told him. 'Rose King did it last year and she started getting concert bookings after that.'

'Maybe I should say no,' Flynn suggested.

Harry looked at him in disbelief. 'Are you joking? This is the opportunity of a lifetime! You can't just say no. Professor Kaiser would never let you, anyway.'

'Well, after Rose King I'm bound to be a huge disappointment. And André must have turned it down because he was too busy touring or something.'

'Don't be stupid. André would have jumped at the chance. They asked you because your Rach Three is far more exciting than anything André's playing at the moment.'

Flynn shot him a sceptical look. 'But it's only a month away, that's no time at all.'

'Other people would kill to play in that concert. Damn it, *I* would kill to play in that concert. Important people will be there. You'll start making a name for yourself before you've even left uni. Jesus, Flynn!'

'What if I mess it up?'

'You won't mess it up.'

'I could.'

'But you won't. You're far too good. Your Rach

Three sounds fantastic now. Everyone's talking about it.'

Flynn was touched by Harry's encouragement but still unconvinced. However, Harry had one thing right – Professor Kaiser wasn't going to give him much choice.

Thanks to Harry, the news didn't take long to spread. People he barely knew were coming up to congratulate him in the corridors. Flynn was on edge, unsure as to how genuine their congratulations were. No doubt they would all give an arm and a leg, as Harry put it, to play in the concert. They surely wondered what on earth he had done to deserve it. They must suspect that he wasn't really good enough.

His lunchtime runs were forced to cease. If Professor Kaiser was in his study then he used the baby grand in the concert hall on the ground floor. Rehearsals would start with the London Philharmonic Orchestra a week on Saturday. The Philharmonic! It was hard to believe.

He was having trouble with the heavy chords in the third movement, and Professor Kaiser continued to reiterate that they needed more weight. Those chords exhausted him. He played the section through for what felt like the hundredth time that day and stopped, hands on knees, gazing blindly at his distorted reflection in the shiny ebony in front of him.

The sound of clapping made him jump. He looked up. Jennah was sitting in the third row, feet up on the seat in front.

'It's sounding amazing, Flynn.'

Stupidly, he felt himself flush. 'Hi.'

She climbed onto the stage and perched on one of the blocks. 'I haven't seen you for over a week. Harry told me you no longer believe in lunch breaks.'

'Harry says strange things.'

Jennah cocked an eyebrow. 'Yet this is your lunch break and you're still practising.'

'I need to.'

'You also need a break.' She gave a little laugh. 'Come to the park with me?'

He opened his mouth to say no but then she added, 'I could do with some company.'

They walked down the empty path in silence. It was grey and overcast today, a chill wind brushing the tops of the trees. Flynn kicked at a pebble, hands buried deep inside his pockets.

'By the way, congratulations,' Jennah said.

'What – oh, thanks.' He pulled a face and half shrugged. 'Just means more practice.'

She elbowed him, smiling. 'No it doesn't, silly. Means a hell of a lot more than that.'

'Let's not talk about it,' he suggested.

She nodded. A few silent minutes passed. Then, 'I broke up with Charlie,' she announced.

He looked at her in surprise. 'Why?'

She gave a small shrug, face pinched and serious, chin pressed down over her burgundy scarf. 'Wasn't really working out.'

'Oh. I'm sorry.'

'We wanted different things.'

'Oh. Was it because he wasn't into music?'

Jennah laughed. 'No, no – it wasn't that. He just got too intense. Wanted to spend every single weekend with me and I didn't feel ready for that.'

'Why not?'

She gave a wry smile, crinkling up her nose. 'To be honest, he was beginning to irritate me. And, anyway, I kept feeling guilty all the time.'

'About what?'

'About the fact that I didn't love him.'

Flynn searched for something to say. Why was it that girls were so eager to talk about these things? He wished Harry were here – he would know how to respond. As it was, he felt tongue-tied and more than a little desperate not to get into a conversation about love.

'Maybe you need to give it more time,' he suggested weakly.

She shook her head and gave a faint smile. 'No, it was only getting worse.'

'Why?'

She shrugged. 'Because I'm in love with somebody else.'

He looked at her, incredulous. 'Harry?'

She burst out laughing. 'No!'

'Oh.' He looked down at the path again, surprised but not exactly disappointed. 'Oh well. Poor old Charlie then. Have to say, though, I always thought he was a bit of an idiot.'

Jennah laughed again. 'Yes, it was never really a match made in heaven.'

He looked across at her. 'So you're going out with this new guy?'

'Oh no.'

'Why not?'

'He doesn't know anything about this. I very much doubt he wants to go out with me.'

They sat down on a damp, earth-smelling bench, and Jennah smiled suddenly. 'I recognize this spot.'

'What?'

'It's where Harry and I sat when you were doing your midnight run. Don't you remember? You must have done about twenty laps around us on this path here.' She glanced at him, as if trying to gauge his reaction. 'We were worried about you that night,' she said.

Flynn just looked at her and said nothing.

'Well, not just that night . . . This year's turning out to be pretty stressful, isn't it?' She wrapped a strand of hair around her little finger.

He gave her a long look, wishing he could see into her mind. Was it possible that she knew? Was it possible that she understood?

'Sometimes I just wish I could fast-forward the next three years until we graduate,' she went on. 'It seems like we've got so much to do between now and then.'

Flynn managed a small laugh. 'Sometimes I wish I

had a double who I could send out to do all the tough stuff – you know, the exams and the socializing and the concerts . . .'

'Yes, while I stay in bed reading a good book!' Jennah laughed and nodded. Then she sobered. 'But why the socializing?' she asked suddenly.

He looked at her. 'What?'

'You said socializing was part of the tough stuff. But isn't that supposed to be fun?'

Flynn pulled a face. 'Yeah, yeah, I just meant . . .' He tailed off, unable to finish the sentence.

'But sometimes you're so social! When we were inter-railing last summer you always wanted to go out at night and practise your French on complete strangers.'

Flynn pulled an embarrassed face at the memory.

'But somehow I can't imagine you doing that now.'

There was a silence. Flynn looked down to the ground.

'Harry said you were having a tough time,' Jennah said quietly.

Flynn's head jerked upwards. 'What? What else did Harry say?'

She looked at him, slightly startled. 'Nothing. Just that.'

'Oh.' He rubbed his eyes wearily and stared back down at the damp earth. He hadn't told Harry about the trip to the psychiatrist's office. But Harry wasn't stupid. And there was three months' supply of green and white capsules on the floor by his bed.

'Sometimes I feel like there are two Flynns,' Jennah said with a small laugh. 'One who goes up and talks to strangers, who spends all night composing and goes jogging in the middle of the night. And one who's – who's really quiet and introverted and kind of, well, unhappy.' Her face was serious suddenly.

Flynn forced a laugh. 'So I guess I should just decide which one is the real me.'

Jennah didn't smile. 'Maybe neither is the real you. Maybe the real you is in hiding.'

He looked at her, surprised. 'Sometimes that's what it feels like. Sometimes, when I catch sight of myself in the mirror, for a second – for a split second – I feel like I don't know who I am. I mean, I recognize myself, but it's like it's somebody else disguised as me—' He broke off, embarrassed.

'Kind of like if you stare at your eyes in the mirror for long enough you stop recognizing yourself?'

'Yeah. Exactly like that. Except it's all the time.'

Harry pulled off Flynn's headphones just as he was getting the hang of the middle section.

'Oi!' He continued resolutely to the end of the piece, despite no longer being able to hear what he was playing.

'It's for you,' Harry said.

'Not now!' Flynn snapped. 'I'm just getting this.'

Harry shook his head and returned to his laptop, the receiver dangling expectantly from the wall.

101

Flynn gave his keyboard a thump in frustration and stood up. His concentration was all over the place this evening. Unwanted thoughts kept intruding. Jennah's smile. Jennah's green eyes flecked with gold. Jennah breaking up with Charlie. Jennah liking someone else . . .

'Hi.' It was Rami. 'How are you doing?'

'OK,' he replied guardedly.

'Harry told me you were practising like crazy. I gather you've got something big coming up.'

'Nothing big,' he replied quickly. 'Just a recital.'

'Oh.' Rami did not sound convinced. 'Am I invited?'

'I don't know!' he snapped suddenly. 'I don't even know if I'm going ahead with it!'

'OK, OK,' Rami said quickly. 'Keep your hair on. Since interrupting your practice is surprisingly similar to disturbing a mating lion, I'll be brief. I was ringing to check you hadn't forgotten Dad's birthday this weekend.'

'Of course not.'

'Liar. I'm driving down on Friday and coming back on Sunday. Sophie's on shift all weekend. Do you want a lift?'

'Do I have to?'

'Mum's expecting you. She's already complaining that you haven't called for two weeks.'

Flynn let out his breath in a painful sigh. A weekend at home was not what he needed right now. 'I'll have to take my keyboard.'

'Why? The old piano's still in good nick.'

'They go to bed at ten now! I can't practise then.'

'Flynn, it's one weekend! You can't practise the whole time – Mum's already worried about you.'

'Then I'm not coming.'

'Fine, fine. Bring your keyboard. We'll put the back seats down.'

Friday evening arrived, clear and bright. Rami came by at six. He was lowering the back seats as Flynn emerged, rucksack on shoulder and keyboard under arm. Rami pulled a long-suffering face as he helped Flynn manoeuvre it across the flattened back seats.

'Hey, you.' He slammed the boot, slinging an arm round Flynn's shoulders.

'Can I drive?' Flynn asked him.

'No, you look tired.'

'I'm fine!'

'You're on anti-depressants. Your reactions may have slowed down. You shouldn't—'

'Oh, stop being such a pain!' Flynn snatched the keys from his brother's hand.

Rami hesitated, as if wondering whether it was worth having an argument about. Flynn jumped into the driver's seat and started the engine. With a small sigh of resignation, Rami got inside.

Flynn felt himself beginning to relax as they finally left the worst of the London traffic behind them and accelerated down the motorway. He had been feeling on edge all afternoon, whether from the prospect of returning home for the weekend or just from lack of sleep, he couldn't tell, but he was grateful to Rami for letting him drive. The concentration took some of the tingling out of his muscles, some of the edginess out of his limbs. Nonetheless, Rami remarked on his finger-tapping as Flynn found himself drumming out the melody of the Rach Three against the steering wheel whenever they slowed. The bright evening sunshine bounced off the bonnet and warmed his face with its soft rays, and Puccini played at full volume on the stereo.

'Dario says you're always welcome to go back and see him, if ever you change your mind,' Rami began after a while, reaching forwards to turn down the volume.

Flynn pretended to be concentrating on the road ahead.

'It's completely up to you,' Rami went on lightly. 'If you're OK now then that's great.'

'I *am* OK,' Flynn said.

'Good.' There was a silence. 'You look pretty shattered, though,' Rami added.

'I've been busy.'

'So I gathered. I hear that practice now takes up a large portion of the night.'

Flynn let out a long-suffering sigh. Meddling Harry again.

'Are you still taking the tablets?'

'Yeah.'

'Do you need me to write you out another prescription?'

'No.'

'Let me know when you do.'

The M25 traffic dropped to below forty yet again. Irritated, Flynn swerved into the inside lane.

'You want to check your mirror before you pull across like that,' Rami said instantly.

'Don't tell me how to drive.'

'You're way too close to the car in front.'

'That's because he's too bloody slow!' Flynn snapped.

'He's in a queue of traffic,' Rami retorted.

Flynn slammed on the brakes.

'See!' Rami exclaimed triumphantly. 'You nearly went into the back of him.'

'I did not!'

'Let's not argue. You're getting tired. Why don't we swap places?'

'I'm not tired,' Flynn muttered, searching for a gap in the middle lane, which was now moving more swiftly than the left-hand one. He spotted an opening and dived into it. Several cars honked irritably.

'Pull over and swap places with me.' Rami was trying to keep his voice light.

Flynn set his jaw and pulled out again as the pace began to pick up. He floored the accelerator as they came out of the speed-restriction zone.

'You're going to get us pulled over,' Rami said after a few moments.

Flynn kept his foot down.

'This car doesn't like doing over ninety.' Rami sounded tense.

Flynn didn't let up.

'Pull over, Flynn.'

He didn't reply.

'Flynn, pull over!' Rami shouted suddenly. 'You're driving like a bloody maniac!' There was an edge of fear to his voice that gave Flynn a jolt. Rami was normally the calm one, the cool one. Rami didn't panic. Flynn cut across two lanes and braked roughly on the hard shoulder.

'Get back in the car – you're going to get yourself killed.' Rami's grip on his arm was firm, trying to force him round.

Flynn climbed over the crash barrier and headed up the grass verge. Rami followed him, still gripping him. Flynn tore with his teeth at his fingernail, struggling to hold back tears.

'Come on,' Rami urged him, his voice rising. 'Get back in the car!'

Flynn wanted to punch him. 'I'm not going.' Finger in his mouth, he tasted blood.

Rami's voice left little room for argument. 'Yes, you are. You certainly can't stay here.'

Numbly, Flynn got into the passenger seat, vision

blurring with unfallen tears as Rami started the engine, waiting an age before pulling back out. He said nothing for a while. Only a small muscle twitching in his cheek betrayed his apparent calm.

Flynn felt himself begin to shake. He had wanted to flatten all the stupid, slow cars ahead of him, had wanted to hurl the car off the road and smash his own stupid self through the windscreen. He could have killed them both. And yet the restless unease was still there. He hadn't got rid of it through driving, couldn't get rid of it whatever he did. It clung to him, an invisible cloak of agitation and self-destruction that sent acid fury shooting through his veins. He wanted to shake himself like a wet dog, run for miles until he couldn't go a step further, find an escape from this horrifyingly persistent agitation that rendered impossible even the most basic of tasks. There was fire burning through him, creating an overpowering urge to scream, kick, yell. He looked over at Rami and thought how satisfying it would be to punch his stupid, calm face. Rami, his brother. Rami, who was just trying to drive them both back home without getting them killed. Flynn clamped a hand over his eyes, breathing hard.

'Flynn, just talk to me. Tell me what's going on.' Rami's voice cut through the motorway's drone.

He couldn't talk without wanting to shout. Couldn't move without lashing out.

'Is this about going home? Do you want me to head back?' Rami's voice again, softly desperate.

Flynn fought to keep his voice steady. 'I can't sit still any longer.'

'You need a breather – we both do. I'll pull over at the next service station.'

Rami bought a packet of cigarettes when they got out. Flynn was shocked. He had not seen his brother smoke for over three years. Rami lit up, giving Flynn a little grin. 'Don't tell Sophie.'

He inhaled deeply a few times and then handed the cigarette to Flynn, who took it gratefully. They sat at a picnic table under the darkening sky, passing the cigarette between each other like a pair of teenage delinquents.

'Medicinal purposes.' Rami gave a wry grin and then caught sight of Flynn's bloodied finger. His smile faded.

Flynn dragged heavily on the cigarette, wishing his hands would stop shaking.

'Do you want me to give you some Valium?'

Flynn shook his head, stubbed out the cigarette and reached for another. Rami did not attempt to stop him.

They got back into the car a little while later. Rami did not ask him any more questions. 'If you need me to pull over again, let me know,' was all he said.

CHAPTER SIX

Rucken Cottage was beginning to show its age. It wasn't a cottage really but a two-storey house with creaky stairs, threadbare carpets and a chipped, dark-wood banister. The bare, yellowing front with its four perfectly symmetrical windows resembled a child's drawing, although the white frames and sills were cracked and peeling. Some of the glass panelling had come off the front door and the red had faded to a russet brown.

The garden that surrounded the house looked neater every time Flynn came home, though, and the clipped, bright green lawn was bordered by a row of carefully planted pansies and primroses running down each side. The old shed now housed a lawn mower instead of the bikes that they had once used to race in circles around the house, flattening everything in their wake, to the staccato accompaniment of their mother's angry knuckles on the kitchen window. The old tyre still hung from the cherry tree at the back, however. Their father had hung it so high off the ground that for ages Flynn was unable to reach it without help, but aged ten he had been able to swing upside down on it, hanging from one leg. The old picnic table was still there, the focus of many a summer birthday or barbecue, the grey wood now half rotting from the elements. As Flynn sat down, it gave a complaining creak. He remembered climbing onto it one hot summer's day in an attempt to escape Rami and the hose. One of his mother's favourite old Italian songs had been on the record player, and he had danced about as the water fell through the sunlight, showering him with gold.

The back door opened slowly with a familiar squeak. Rami was no doubt going to complain that he had left him to unload the car. But it was his mother, in her apron as usual, her grey hair pinned up in a tidy bun.

'*Hei, kulta*,' she greeted him. 'How lovely to see you!'

He grinned but, as he hugged her, felt his throat tighten. 'Hi, Mum.'

'Goodness me! You're thinner than ever and your hair has grown since Christmas! Look at those shadows under your eyes. Are you boys eating properly in that bedsit?'

'It's not a bedsit,' Flynn replied automatically. 'How are you, Mum?'

'Oh, I'm all right. The heating broke down last week and it took them five days to repair it. Can you believe it? I had to sit for hours on the end of the phone just to get somebody to talk to me. Mrs Coats lent us her blow heater and electric heater, bless her. Do you remember Mrs Coats? When you were little, she used to give you

110

lollies to cheer you up when she saw me dragging you to school.'

'I remember.'

'Well, I told you, didn't I, that she's now living in a small flat round by the green, since her husband died? Poor woman, it hit her terribly hard. So awful, to just collapse one day like that from a heart attack. Anyway, I went round to her new flat the other day and she's made it really lovely. And her daughter's come back from boarding school now, so at least she's not alone. You remember Kerrie, don't you? Pretty little thing. You used to play in her paddling pool. She's taking a gap year. I think the two of you would really get on. She's down-to-earth and very attractive in an understated sort of— Why are you looking at me like that?'

'I'm not.'

'Come on, darling, let's go inside. Dad's longing to see you. What do you want to eat?'

'I'm not really hungry.'

Rami was on the living-room couch, hunched forwards, elbows on knees, talking earnestly in a low voice. He looked briefly startled when they came in. Dad was in his usual armchair by the window.

The room looked small despite the shelves above the fireplace having now been cleared of all his old music books – candles and trinkets adorning the beech wood instead. The upright had been covered with a green tablecloth, a brass clock and more ornaments.

'Hey!' Flynn protested.

'It was looking a bit the worse for wear,' Mum said apologetically. 'It's all right – we can just pull the cloth off.'

'Is it in tune at least?' Flynn demanded, his voice coming out harsher than he had intended.

His parents exchanged glances. 'Didn't we have it tuned before you came back for Christmas?' his father wondered. 'Hello, son. Good to see you.'

'Hi, Dad.'

Flynn sat down on the sofa and Rami shot him a look.

'What does everyone want to drink?' Mum asked cheerily. 'I'm making kalakukko for dinner. It'll be ready in half an hour.'

'I'll put the kettle on.' Rami stood up. 'Tea, everyone?'

'Yes, please,' his parents answered in unison.

'Coffee,' Flynn said.

Another look. 'Decaf?'

'No.'

'Let me get it, you don't know where everything is.'

'Mum, just sit down!' Rami insisted. 'It can't be that difficult – our kitchen isn't that big.'

Mum laughed and took Rami's place on the couch next to Flynn.

'So? How's student life?' Dad asked.

Flynn chewed his thumbnail. 'OK,' he replied evasively. They had been talking about him, he had known it from the look on Rami's face when he came in.

'The old piano going OK?'

'Yeah.'

'You look tired, darling,' Mum interjected.

'I'm fine.'

A silence. The brass clock ticked loudly. Why had they covered the piano with a sodding green cloth? They might just as well have sold it for firewood if they hated it so much.

'Mum's taken up bridge,' Dad said with a wink.

'I thought that was for old people.'

'Thanks very much!'

'You're not old. That's what I'm saying!'

'OK, darling. Thank you.'

'Why bridge?'

'Mrs Coats introduced me to it. I've always liked cards. It's actually good fun.'

'So, what are you working on then, Flynn? Can you give us a concert later? We had to cover the piano – it looked so lonely there without you.'

Flynn smiled at his father. 'I'm mainly focusing on the Rach Three now.'

His father's face lit up.

'Wonderful!' Mum said.

'I-I'm going to be playing at the Albert Hall. Next month. In a concert.' He had not wanted to tell them yet but the words burst from him with a will of their own.

Silent expressions of amazement.

'It's something organized by the Young Musicians' Association. It's – it's not a competition or anything.'

'The Royal Albert Hall!' Mum exclaimed.

'That's tremendous!' Dad's face lit up with a huge grin.

'I haven't done anything yet,' Flynn said quickly. 'I've only got a few weeks left to practise. I still have to think about the notes sometimes. I've got to get the notes into my fingers so that I can forget about them. I've got to forget them first. I won't be able to play it properly until I've completely forgotten them.' He was babbling. Why had he mentioned the damn concert? Adrenaline coursed through his veins, filling him with an urge to be sick.

Mum's voice seemed to come from a distance. 'You'll be fine, darling. Professor Kaiser wouldn't have put you forward unless he thought you were completely ready. I'm sure it's coming on much better than you think it is.'

'But there's the third movement – I'm still not sure about the middle section. It's not – it's not quite—' Sweat broke out on the back of his neck. It hurt to breathe.

Rami burst back in with a tray of mugs. 'This is all very civilized,' he said with a grin, handing out the drinks.

Flynn gripped his mug and stared hard out of the window, trying to think of something else. The room seemed to be closing in on him, and his parents' faces had started shrinking into the distance. Hot liquid sloshed onto his hand.

Rami grabbed the mug and set it down on the table. 'Let's go and put our stuff upstairs,' he said abruptly.

Mum jumped up. 'I put new sheets on your beds this

morning but there's a blue stain on the back of one of the pillows. It's not dirty, it's just a stain. It's been there for ages. Someone once left a pen in their trouser pocket and I've never been able to—'

'That's fine, Mum! We'll be down in a minute,' Rami said, shepherding Flynn out of the room.

'OK, I'll go and check on dinner.'

Flynn burst into his room, breathing hard. The last of the evening sunlight slanted through the curtains, creating a golden puddle on the floor. Rami chucked the keyboard unceremoniously onto the bed.

'Sit down and lean forwards. Try and slow your breathing or I'll have to get you a paper bag. Just calm yourself down, Flynn.'

Flynn sat, head almost touching his knees. Patches of light danced dizzyingly on the faded green carpet. He gripped the edge of the sheets. The sound of his gasping filled the room.

'Cup your hands over your mouth. Stop panicking! You're just hyperventilating, that's all.'

'I'm going – I'm going to be sick.'

'No you're not – you're just breathing too fast. I'll get you a glass of water.'

Flynn closed his eyes, willing the dizziness away. Rami returned with a tooth-glass full of water and Flynn drank savagely, his hand shaking.

'OK, just calm down. Put your hands back over your mouth. That's it. Calm down.'

115

There was a long silence broken only by Flynn's muffled gasps.

Rami's hand was on his shoulder. 'What are you trying to do, hey? Give Mum and Dad a heart attack?'

'I didn't mean to. I told them about the concert when I shouldn't have – that's courting disaster. I told them I wasn't ready, tempting fate, and now it'll come true.' He was straining for breath again.

'Is this about the damn concert? Stop thinking about the stupid concert, Flynn. Nobody cares about it except you. We're here to celebrate Dad's birthday, remember? Get some perspective. It doesn't matter if you play in the concert or not. It's certainly not worth having a panic attack over. Tell Professor Kaiser you don't want to do it.'

'Why? Don't you think I'm up to it? Don't you think I'm ready? Professor Kaiser says I'm ready, so I must be ready. Don't you think I am? Why don't you think I am?' Dark spots danced before his eyes.

'Hey!' Rami was half laughing but his eyes betrayed a different emotion. 'What are you getting into such a state for? I don't know if you're ready or not – I haven't heard you play for months and I don't think I've ever heard you play the Rach Three. Professor Kaiser obviously thinks you're good enough but it's up to you, Flynn. If you don't feel confident enough just yet then that's fine. It's your call, OK?'

'I don't know if I'm ready. Maybe I'm ready but I don't know it. Maybe this is as ready as I'll ever be. Maybe—'

'Hey, how about we stop thinking about work for a bit? I've had a hell of a week, sounds like you have too. I think we both need a break. Think of this as a small holiday. Back with the folks, away from London. Let's relax and recharge the batteries.'

The room was filled with warm, stale air. He was going to suffocate. 'I have to practise, Rami. There isn't much time left. Where are my headphones? Did I leave them in the car? I left them in the car, didn't I? Did you see them in the car? Are you sure I brought them with me?'

Rami's hand grabbed his wrist, forcing him back. 'Flynn, get a grip. You're not going to practise now. Mum and Dad are worried enough about you as it is. You're here to see them, remember? You're getting all obsessive again. Don't. Come on, pull yourself together. Mum's been looking forward to this. Don't spoil it for everyone.' There was a sharp edge to his voice now.

Flynn looked at him desperately. 'But I can't stop thinking about it – you don't understand! I've got to practise or I'll – I'll—'

'Or nothing, Flynn. You know what your problem is? You're shattered, you haven't slept properly for ages and it's making you create mountains out of molehills. Let's go down to dinner, be pleasant and then go to bed. You'll be fine in the morning.'

'But—'

'No. Don't practise tonight. You're allowed some time off. Everyone's allowed some time off.'

Dinner was an interminable affair, drawn out by endless questions and lengthy replies, Rami regaling their parents with story after story about difficult, senile, or plain crazy patients. Dad went on about bowling, Mum about gardening, and night fell thick and fast behind the windows, increasing the close, fuggy atmosphere of the kitchen.

It was a gargantuan effort to force down forkful after forkful of stodgy food, answer in full sentences and feign interest in the myriad pointless topics of conversation. Flynn wanted to jump up, run, shout – move! Deep breaths were the only way to curb the restless energy inside him, despite Rami's anxious glances. His cheeks burned with the strain of it all.

Coffee and Baileys followed, prolonging the agony further still. He helped Mum clear, leaving Rami and Dad to discuss the proposed raise in doctors' pay, and took out his frustrations on the dishes in the sink. After a while, Dad joined him.

'How are you off for cash at the moment?'

Flynn pulled a face at the dishes. 'Not brilliant, Dad – everything in London is so expensive.'

'What happened to your idea of getting a part-time job?'

Flynn sighed heavily. 'I dunno, the piano lessons were a disaster – the kid just ran around the room the whole time and wouldn't listen to a thing I said.'

Dad chuckled. 'No, I didn't really see you as a

teacher, somehow. Look, I'll give you another small loan to keep you going till the end of this term, but this summer you're going to have to go back to work at the Red Cow and pay me back or I'm going to have the bank manager breathing down my neck.'

'OK. Thanks,' Flynn said.

'Flynnie, you were going to play us something!' Mum looked up eagerly from where she sat with Rami, discussing summer-holiday destinations.

Rami shot her a warning look with a brief, barely perceptible shake of the head.

'Or perhaps when you're feeling less tired, darling,' she back-pedalled quickly.

Flynn scowled at them. 'Goodnight then,' he said.

'Goodnight, darling. Have you got everything you need? I've put the heating on low, at about two, but you can turn it up to six if you're cold. It's the small dial on the left, remember. Just turn it. Not the one on the right – that will switch the whole thing off. Do you need an extra duvet? There's one in the cupboard in Rami's room if you need it. It's still rather cold here at night.'

'I'll be fine. Night, Dad.'

His father opened his eyes with a start. 'What? Oh, goodnight, Flynn. See you in the morning . . . Yes, I'd better turn in myself in a minute. That drink just went straight to my head.'

Flynn didn't bother turning on the light and undressed in the darkness, staring out at the moonless sky. He pushed the keyboard under his bed where he wouldn't be able to see it, trying to convince himself that one night would not make a difference, that perhaps if he got a good night's sleep then he would be able to practise properly tomorrow. He might even be able to concentrate for a change, he might even be able to get through the whole of the concerto without stopping suddenly and gazing, motionless, at a crack in the wall, allowing the hours to slide by.

There was nothing but baking-soda toothpaste in the bathroom, and rummaging through Rami's bag for Colgate he stopped when he saw his headphones, hidden beneath a pile of Rami's clothes. He hesitated for a moment, then went to brush his teeth, leaving them where they were.

'You know,' his mother said the next morning, 'if you decided not to play in that concert, we wouldn't be any less proud of you.'

Flynn had done nearly five hours of practice, from dawn until now, not bothering to dress or wash, a blanket over his head and shoulders. He had managed to sneak his headphones from Rami's Reebok bag without waking him.

Going to bed had been a waste of time. He could think only of the keyboard, lying accusingly unplayed under his bed, its angry aura radiating through the mattress on which he lay. He had woken after just a couple of hours of fitful, dream-filled sleep as the first rays of light oozed through the heavy curtains, making his heart jump and muscles tense with the thought of the day ahead. Now Mum was forcing him to eat breakfast, something he was reluctant to do even on a good day. The others were not even up yet. At her comment, Flynn looked up from the kitchen table with a start.

'What makes you say that?' he demanded harshly.

His mother, deliberately it seemed to him, did not look up from her whisking. 'I just wanted to make sure you knew, that's all.'

'Why? Don't you want me to?'

'I want you to do whatever you want to do.'

'What's that supposed to mean? Don't you think I can do it?'

His mother finally put down the egg whisk with a small sigh. 'I don't know, Flynn. I'm no Ashkenazy. The only thing I know is that you seem to be a bit overwrought.'

'So you think I'm going to make a mess of it.'

'Of course not! You got in a great state about your audition for the Royal College last year and you still got in.'

'Exactly. It's normal to feel under pressure for these kinds of things. If I want to make it as a concert pianist then I've got to get used to it.'

'Well there's pressure and then there's pressure.'

'What's that supposed to mean?'

'A little pressure might be good for one, but too much is not.'

'And you think I'm under too much pressure?'

'I'm not inside your head, darling. I can only tell you what I see. But I'm a bit worried about all this night-time practising and lack of sleep.'

Flynn took a sharp breath, ready for a belligerent reply, and then forced it back. His mother was only showing her concern and maybe she was right – maybe she and Rami were both right. Maybe he *was* letting things get out of perspective. Maybe he *was* going mad. He put his hands over his cheeks and rubbed his face hard.

'I just can't stop thinking about it,' he admitted desperately. 'I'm so tired.'

'Of course you are, sweetheart. You've hardly slept.'

He looked at her, her lined face now framed by greying wisps of hair, and felt as if the mother he had known as a child was now out of reach. She no longer had the answers. She could still show her concern but no longer had the power to put things right. He could try to share his problems with her but knew that, try as she might, she would not truly understand. The realization filled him with inexplicable sadness.

'I can't – I can't stop thinking about it,' he told her doggedly.

'I know. That's why I'm thinking it might be better to postpone it for another year.'

'You don't understand,' he said frantically. 'I can't just do that – it doesn't work like that. It's supposed to be an incredible honour that the Royal College has asked me to perform in the first place. I can't just pull out of it. And I certainly can't just say I'll do it another year. I may never get this kind of chance again.'

'Flynnie, they obviously think you're incredibly talented or they wouldn't have asked you in the first place. It may seem like a huge opportunity but no opportunity is so big that it's worth sacrificing your health for. There will be lots of other opportunities in your life, darling, this isn't going to be the only one.'

He ran his hands through his hair in frustration, wanting to pull it out by the roots. 'But don't you see? If I can't manage this, then how am I ever . . .? It puts the whole idea of becoming a concert pianist into jeopardy. It's not supposed to be a big deal! Like Professor Kaiser said, it would just – it would just be good experience. If I can't manage this then – then how am I ever going to be able to play professionally?'

'Sweetheart, you're not always going to feel like this. You're just going through a bit of a rough patch. As a little boy you were very laid-back about concerts and things. You were very confident, especially about your playing. You really loved those competitions. I don't remember you ever being worried about playing in front of an audience.'

He continued to run his hands through his hair, pressing hard against his scalp as if trying to manipulate his brain. 'So why – why am I like this now? I'm so – I know I'm obsessing about it. But I feel that if I don't, something terrible is going to happen. I feel like I should be practising all the time. Even now, just talking to you, I feel guilty. I feel like if I don't practise I'm going to – I'm going to go mad.'

'Flynn, just try and give yourself a break today. Go back to bed for a bit. You can afford to take a couple of days off.'

He stared at her, the blood rushing to his face, and entwined his fingers, jamming them together hard. 'No way.' His voice shook. 'There's no way—'

'Then, Flynn, you've got to call this off. If you continue pushing yourself like this, you're going to make yourself seriously ill.' Her voice was sharp and she suddenly looked frightened. He had said too much.

'Let's go for a cycle ride,' Rami announced after lunch. 'It's a beautiful day.'

Flynn opened his mouth to opt out but their father immediately voiced his enthusiasm and before Flynn could think of an excuse, Rami was organizing everything as usual, from borrowing the neighbour's bicycle to getting their mother to put her feet up and suggesting she invite Mrs Coats over for coffee. Flynn looked suspiciously from Rami to their father, suspecting that this had been pre-planned but, as it was Dad's birthday, he didn't have the heart to refuse.

They set off through the village – past the Red Cow, the church and Flynn and Rami's old primary school – the light wind almost balmy, the sky a brilliant blue. Compared to London, the village looked picturesque, almost quaint. Their father stopped twice in the high street to talk to acquaintances, and Flynn thought, I'm so glad I don't live here any more. Everyone knowing each other, everyone talking about each other.

Rami headed up the hill, calling back at them to hurry up, and Dad gave Flynn a conspiratorial roll of the eyes. As they reached the edge of the fields, they stretched out into a line, skimming the edge of the road. Rami was setting the pace and Dad was doing well to keep up as the smooth, flat tarmac allowed them to gather speed and the low fence beside them dissolved into a blur. Flynn looked out away from the road, across the fields with their perfectly rolled barrels of hay, to the sheep dotted beyond and the thin curve of the horizon where the forest met the sky. He heard the gentle notes of the second movement start up as if from an invisible orchestra, gifting the familiar English countryside with an air of plaintive mystery.

It is there, he thought. It is there in my head. I can hear it as clear and as pure as if I were playing it myself. It has become a part of me. I can forget the notes now. I can play with my eyes closed. I can play in my sleep. It is me and I am it. He could feel the smooth keys beneath his fingers and suddenly the music was not coming from an invisible source at all but from his own hands, each note resonating beneath his touch. *The fields are alive with the sound of music* . . . He laughed aloud.

The ground sprang up to hit him with a resounding crack. He felt himself bounce forwards. A brief moment of relief and then another crack as the tarmac came up to punch him again. The clatter of his bike falling behind him, a roaring in his ears – it seemed to take an age for everything to become still. The music had gone and he was left with the sound of the bike's wheels still spinning. He tasted dirt in his mouth and found himself staring at a scattering of small stones and a few tufts of grass. The road tilted away from him and he closed his eyes, trying to get his thoughts back.

'Flynn, for goodness' sake, are you all right?' He opened his eyes and his father's face swam into view.

He struggled to get up, to find the breath to speak. His arms stung.

'Hey, hey, you nutter. Have you broken something? Do we need to call an ambulance?' Rami's hand hauled him up to a sitting position.

Flynn grimaced from the grit in his mouth and spat into the hedge. 'I'm fine.' He rubbed his elbow where it hurt. His shirt sleeve was wet with blood. He examined his hands carefully. There was only a slight graze on his left palm. He breathed deeply, head reeling.

'Oh, look at you. I'll go home and get the car,' Dad said.

'No, I'm OK!' He struggled to his feet. 'I'm OK,' he repeated dully.

Rami handed him a tissue. 'You've cut your chin,' he said. 'Do you think you can get back on?'

'Yes.'

'What happened?' Rami asked him quietly when they had remounted. 'Hit a stone?'

'Yeah.'

They cycled home slowly. Flynn kept his eyes on the road ahead of him, trying to ignore the pain in his arms and knees. He did not hear the music again.

That evening, soaking in a hot bath, he gazed blindly at a crack in the ceiling, the warm water melting the dried blood on his elbows and chin . . . Mum had made her usual carrot cake, Dad's favourite . . . His scraped arms burned . . . 'This is happiness for me,' Mum had said, 'having my family all under the same roof' . . . Maybe the hot water would make him sleepy . . . Dad had looked weary but contented, Rami had taken some photos . . . His limbs ached, his mind hurt . . . He had played 'Happy Birthday' on the piano and then, later, some Scriabin . . . I want to sleep, he thought. I wish I could sleep . . .

He lay in his childhood bed, arm under his head, staring out through the open curtains. Sleep was light years away; the moonlight on the treetops, the faint curve of the fields, the orange glow from the street below causing his heart to pound. Shutting out the view was not an option – he felt he would suffocate alone with his thoughts. At least the window offered a distraction of sorts. His fingers twitched from the desire to play. Was it desire or was it simply fear of what would happen if he did not? He closed his eyes and felt hot tears pressing against the lids. Was he losing his mind?

I don't want to play, he told himself resolutely. I'm so tired, I just want to sleep. I must sleep or I won't be able to practise properly tomorrow. I must sleep or I'll go crazy. A moment's relaxation, a moment's distraction and his fingers had begun to move against the sheet. He didn't notice until the sound of the notes started falling into his head like shards of ice. No! He rolled over, pinning his hand beneath him, eyes wide, concentrating on the corner of the bedspread, willing the sounds away. He just wanted to sleep. Why wouldn't his mind let him sleep?

He did not have to play in the concert. Professor Kaiser might make life difficult for him but he could not force him, after all. Yet the idea of pulling out filled him with inexplicable dread. If he chickened out then what was he? Nothing. A pathetic dreamer who, at the end of the day, could not deliver. The laughing stock of the Royal College and an embarrassment to his teacher. André would never pull out of a concert. André would never let Professor Kaiser down. André would never doubt his abilities as a pianist, damn him, but continue to play concert after concert with effortless ease while Flynn choked and floundered and humiliated himself for all to see. He could not live with himself if that happened. Music was all he had, all he was good at – he could not fail at this. He had worked too hard; the investment of time, energy and money was too great. He would not let his parents down, he would not let his friends down. Damn it, he would not let himself down. This was his chance! If he was not grateful for it, did not seize it with both hands, then how could he expect to ever have a chance like this again?

Rami had told him that the concert didn't matter. His mother had told him the same. But that was nonsense – of course it mattered. It mattered not only to him but to them too. They wanted him to be successful. Mum wanted a son who had made it in the world. Rami had always been a high achiever – at school, at university, at medical school . . . Rami could say what he liked but he would hardly want a brother who was a failed musician, a jingle writer or pub player. Rami believed in him. Rami expected him to make it. They all did. And if he didn't? What if he didn't?

He had to get up, had to move. The walls were closing in on him, the air was stifling. He pulled on his clothes and grabbed his iPod, scrolling through the playlists to try to find something other than classical music. He found some rap he had copied off Harry last summer. He turned the volume up high, let himself out of the slumbering house and set off at a run. The noise blasted through his head, wrenching his thoughts away, his skinned elbows raw against his denim jacket. He sprinted up the road, through the deserted village, towards the woods. His breath came out in painful bursts – he was sobbing but did not care. He wanted to run, to run for ever, to escape . . . what exactly? He could run as long and as fast as he wanted but how would he ever escape himself? To be Rami, in an upstanding profession that was not only meaningful but implied intelligence by definition, to have his own home, to be solidly married, to want the things that were expected of him and to know that he could deliver . . . To be Harry, always confident, always entertaining, secure in the knowledge that he was good at other things besides music, to appear stressed about essay deadlines but have the ability to laugh about it, to be able to talk to anyone, mix with everyone . . . To be Dad, secure with a woman who had loved him for so many years, to fill his days with bowling and tennis, to be popular and well-respected, to know that he had made a meaningful contribution to the world and that he could now retire in peace . . . *To be anyone but me. Anyone but me!*

The pain in his side forced him to stop. He slumped against a tree, his sides heaving, gasping at the ground. Eminem screamed at him to kill his mother and suddenly he felt unbearably sick. He could not sleep like normal people did, could not play for an audience like normal musicians did, could not party the night away like normal students did. Instead, he frightened his brother with his outlandish behaviour, worried his parents by his obsessive practising, alienated his best friend by passing out drunk in his flat and ignored Jennah when she, ironically, appeared to be the only one who might possibly understand . . .

* * *

'Stop it.' Rami pulled off Flynn's headphones and stood there in his pyjamas, blinking blearily down at him.

'What are you doing?' Flynn protested.

'Telling you to go to bed. It's quarter to four, Flynn. You're going to be finished tomorrow and we've got a long drive back.'

'I can't sleep.'

Rami's eyes darted to his muddy trainers. 'Have you been jogging?' His words slowed in disbelief.

'I couldn't sleep,' Flynn said again. He did not have the strength to start an argument with Rami now, exhaustion pulled at his every muscle. But Rami was not going to let this go.

'What the hell are you trying to do?' he went on in an angry whisper. 'If you can't sleep then stay in bed and at least try. Or if you can't do that, then go and find something to read. But jogging? Are you out of your mind?'

Flynn reached for his headphones. 'Just leave me alone, Rami.'

'No! Do you think I'm going to stand here and watch you give yourself a nervous breakdown? Do you think I don't know how obsessed you're getting with your playing? Practising all day and all night! Sleep deprivation leads to insanity, Flynn. Is that what you're trying to do – drive yourself mad?' Rami was worked up now, wide-eyed and angry.

Flynn felt his throat tighten. He lunged for the headphones again and then let his arm drop as Rami jerked them away angrily. 'Fine,' he said numbly. 'Fine. Whatever you want. I'll go back to bed.'

Rami's look of annoyance suddenly turned to concern. 'I just don't want to see you overworking yourself like this,' he tried to explain, his tone gentler now. 'It's unnecessary, Flynn.'

Flynn nodded, defeated. He ached all over. His head hurt. His eyes hurt. He switched off the keyboard and shoved it beneath his bed. 'Goodnight then,' he said to Rami, pulling off his shoes and socks.

'What's going on?'

'Nothing, I'm just tired.' He fought to keep his voice steady.

'There's something else, isn't there?'

He brushed the back of his hand rapidly over his eyes, willing Rami to leave.

'Christ, what is it, Flynn? Has something bad happened?'

'Nothing, I said.' Fully dressed, he got into bed, face turned to the wall.

Rami lingered infuriatingly in the doorway. 'Why can't you tell me?'

Flynn could only shake his head, rubbing the sleeve of his jumper across his eyes. Go, Rami, he silently implored him. You can't help me, nobody can. You'll never understand. You have no idea what it is like to be inside my body, my brain, my mind! Trying to describe my life and feelings to you is like trying to describe colours to the blind, or music to the deaf. It's simply not possible. We may exist side by side, we may share the same blood, the same upbringing, but our minds exist in different worlds. You exist in the world of the rational, the world where every problem has a logical solution, every question has an answer. Can't you see that none of my problems have solutions, my questions can't be answered? Nothing in my irrational brain can be solved by your common sense, none of my pain can be shared by your structured emotions! In my world black is white, one and one never makes two and agony and ecstasy lie irrevocably intertwined. The only way to understand it is to share it and I would never wish this existence upon anybody, not even my worst enemy. You may try and sympathize, help and care with all your soul, but you will never, never understand.

'Shall I go?' Rami asked quietly.

Flynn nodded and Rami switched off the light and clicked the door closed.

CHAPTER SEVEN

Flynn hit the chords of the third movement as if he were beating a snake with a stick. Again and again, harder and harder, faster and faster, his fingers grappling with the keys as if with a will of their own. Eyes tightly closed, the music swelled and rose until he could no longer tell whether *he* was controlling *it* or the other way round.

'Feel the music, feel the anguish, feel the pain!' Professor Kaiser's voice rose above the chords as he paced the room, stopping now and again to hum along to a section, waving his arms about extravagantly to demonstrate the intensity of the piece, the power of the music.

'And more and more! And higher and higher! Swelling like a wave! Keep up the momentum, make it bigger. More, more!'

Flynn opened his eyes to a blur of fingers and tried to make sense of the thick fog of music as well as respond to Professor Kaiser's commands. His fingertips were numb, and his arms and shoulders ached. He bit his tongue hard to dredge up the last burst of energy. A final excruciating bar and then it was all over, hands on knees, head down and breathing hard, the final chord still ringing in the air.

'This is better, this is better. I can feel the passion now. You were leaving the notes and putting your mind only on the music – the emotion inside the music. *Gut, gut . . .*' Professor Kaiser paused by his industrial-sized window and gazed outside.

Flynn straightened up and pressed his hands to his face. His cheeks were burning to the touch and no doubt his ears were glowing too, as they always did after a lesson like this. Professor Kaiser claimed it was a testament to his concentration.

Flynn reached for his bottle of water and drank thirstily. He had been back in London a week now and was filled with a strange energy – an edgy, sleep-deprived buzz like a constant caffeine high that made it difficult to sit still.

Professor Kaiser turned from the window and gave him a rare smile. 'Do you want a rest?'

Flynn nodded gratefully and swung himself round on the piano stool, putting his elbows on his knees. Professor Kaiser moved away from the darkening window and sat down in his creaky chair. There was a quiet moment.

'By the way,' Professor Kaiser said, 'you're doing very well with that piece.'

Flynn looked up in surprise. So much praise in one lesson was a rare thing indeed.

'You *are* going to be ready, you know.'

Flynn looked down again in embarrassment. Was his self-doubt so transparent?

'What is worrying you?'

Stunned by this unexpected show of concern, Flynn pulled a face. 'Nothing.'

'It is sounding good, *ja*?'

'Yes, but—' He could not finish.

'But what?' Professor Kaiser's tone hardened suddenly.

'Nothing.' Flynn sat up with a quick smile. 'It's fine. Shall I go over the slow movement again? I think it still needs working on.'

'Have you heard about Jen?' Harry asked him between mouthfuls of instant noodles that evening.

'What?'

'She dumped Charlie.'

'Oh, that. Yeah, she told me last week.'

Harry scraped out the bottom of the saucepan with an irritating sound. '*So*,' he went on without looking up, 'what did you make of it?'

Flynn sifted wearily through the loose pages of lecture notes strewn over the kitchen table. 'I don't know. I didn't really give it much thought,' he lied. 'I've lost the article about Mahler now . . .'

'Here.' Harry peeled it off the bottom of his saucepan. 'Don't you think it's strange, though, just like that, out of the blue?'

Flynn gave a faint shrug, skimming the article. Writing a two-thousand-word essay on Mahler was no easy task when his every fibre resonated with Rachmaninov. 'I suppose so. Apparently there's some other guy.'

Harry gave him a sharp look. 'Really? Any idea who?'

'Nope.'

'Really?' Harry's lips twitched with the hint of a smile. 'No ideas at all? *Really?*'

Flynn dropped his hands down to the table with an irritated thud. 'Why are you quizzing me on this? Do you think it's you? It's not you.'

Harry looked as if he were trying not to laugh. 'I know it's not me, you moron. Besides, Kate and I are quite happy together, thank you very much.'

'So why are you so interested?'

'I'm not. Just thought *you* might be, that's all.'

'She didn't tell me who it was, Harry.'

'Bet she didn't.'

Flynn stopped writing mid-sentence and looked up with a frown. 'What's that supposed to mean?'

'Nothing,' Harry answered quickly. 'Just thought this might be your chance to – how can I put it? – swoop in, maybe.'

'Swoop in? Jennah fancies someone else, I just told you. Anyway, it's not as if I – I—' He ground to a halt and infuriatingly felt himself flush.

Harry looked to be biting back a grin. 'As if you—?' he prompted.

137

'I'm trying to write this essay,' Flynn protested quickly. 'You're not exactly helping.'

But Harry had that glint in his eye. 'You're not getting off the subject that easily.'

Flynn lowered his head and viciously filled the top of the margin with black ink. His cheeks burned.

Harry continued to scrape the bottom of the pan, watching him with amusement. 'Why are you getting so embarrassed?' he asked after a moment.

Flynn put down his pen and forced himself to look up. 'I'm not embarrassed!'

Harry started to laugh, then swiftly turned it into a cough. 'Just finish your sentence then. It's not as if you what?'

Flynn quickly averted his eyes. 'I can't remember what I was saying.'

Harry gave a sigh of exasperation but still seemed to be trying not to laugh. 'Stop playing all innocent! You've only had a crush on Jennah, like, *for ever*!'

'You don't know what you're talking about!' He glared at Harry hotly.

'Oh, come on,' Harry laughed. 'Isn't it time you stopped kidding yourself?'

'I'm not!'

'Look, how hard can it get? She's just broken up with her boyfriend. Go and ask her out!'

Flynn jumped up, the blood hot in his cheeks. 'I don't want to, OK?'

'You don't want to, or you're afraid to?'

'Drop it, Harry.'

'But why—?'

'Drop it, will you!'

'Fine!' Harry slumped back in his chair, an amused but slightly confused expression on his face. There was a silence. Then he looked at Flynn and shook his head. 'What the hell are you afraid of?'

Flynn slammed into his bedroom, heart pounding, as the irritating sound of Harry's tuning wafted through the wall. He dumped his books on the bed, sat down cross-legged in front of them, picked up his pen and took a deep breath in an attempt to gather his thoughts. Why had he allowed himself to get so rattled by that conversation? Why did he embarrass so easily and why was it that he was always so damn transparent? What was Harry trying to do? Did he think it was funny?

Flynn remembered the first time he heard about Charlie, the shock that one of the group had broken rank, then the realization that his dreams about Jennah – his stupid, childish, impossible dreams – would have to come to an end. Seeing Jennah with Charlie had been like a fist in the stomach, and Flynn had sworn to himself then that that was it, he wasn't going to let his emotions run away with him like that ever again. So he had forced himself to think of Jennah as his friend – only his friend and nothing more. And now – now he was over her. Harry was just talking bullshit. So what if Charlie was no longer on the scene? Jennah went for the tall, dark, mysterious type. She only thought of him as Harry's quirky sidekick – Harry's *crazy* sidekick if Harry had leaked information about the depression, the pills and the psychiatrist, which was distinctly possible.

He gazed at the Mahler article and tried to banish thoughts of Jennah from his mind. Despite every effort not to, he couldn't stop thinking about her break-up with Charlie. Who was she in love with? Another student? Somebody really good-looking, no doubt. Somebody really good-looking but also into music; somebody talented like André, or that Croatian trombonist, or – or— He racked his brain, trying to come up with a student that Jennah had been particularly chatty with recently, but came up with a series of blanks. She was always hanging around with him and Harry.

He threw down his pen. Why was it that he could never concentrate? He needed to get this essay over and done with so that he could get back to his practice. The deadline had already passed – he had been granted an extension courtesy of the concert rehearsals, but Myers was not going to fall for another excuse tomorrow! It was almost ten. His mind began to race. If he wanted to get in two hours' practice tonight and get to bed before one then he had to finish this essay in the next hour. He still could not remember what the Mahler article was about, despite now having read it for a third time. Gritting his teeth, he began reading it for a fourth . . .

Harry seemed to think he should ask Jennah out . . . The print danced before his eyes, he could not hear a single word inside his head. He tried to read aloud but his dull monotone made no sense. Reeling, he picked up one of the library books and tried to decipher his own pencilled scrawl . . . Being around Jennah made him feel awkward and breathless . . . He felt the adrenaline rise. Nothing was getting through. He couldn't even remember the essay title. He pressed the heel of his palms against his eyes. Don't think about her! Mahler, not Jennah. Jennah, Mahler; Mahler, Jennah. The names went around in his head like a crazy chant. He began to rip up the blank page into tiny pieces, letting them fall to the carpet like snow.

It was inconceivable that tomorrow he would be walking into the Royal Albert Hall to rehearse with the London Philharmonic Orchestra. Flynn was overcome with a feeling of dread so strong that his limbs seemed to be in a kind of torpor and his brain felt like it was working in slow motion. Everything seemed to be a huge effort; just sitting up on the sofa, gazing blindly through the living-room window at a couple of bare, ugly trees was absurdly exhausting, yet he had slept more in the last twenty-four hours than in the whole of the previous week, and knew that more sleep would bring little relief. He felt chilled to the bone but couldn't even be bothered to get up and turn up the heating or fetch a jumper. Anything in the least bit positive or proactive lay completely beyond his reach. In fact, after some reflection, he realized that the only two things he felt able to do were think – black and negative thoughts – and cry. The thoughts just kept welling up of their own accord – a constant, steady flow.

The pressure behind his eyes reminded him that tears were never far away. He managed to hold them back, but only through fear that Harry might suddenly walk through the door. It was suffering, in its simplest, purest form, and all he could feel was the pain, un-identifiable by its cause or exact location but present all the same, permeating his every pore. *I can't*. The two words seemed permanently lodged inside his head. I can't play tomorrow ... I can't go to the rehearsal, I can't tidy the flat, I can't go for a run and I sure as hell can't practise. He kept his eyes purposely averted from the keyboard in its corner but its mere presence weighed on him like a physical ache. Part of him hated the thought of anyone seeing him in such a pathetic state, even Harry, but another part of him wished for Harry's return in the hope that it might provide some relief, if only temporary, from his unbearable self.

He flushed the remaining anti-depressants down the toilet. Fat lot of good they had been. After the first flush, some of the green and white capsules bobbed irritatingly to the surface; he threw a wad of toilet paper over them and flushed again. The toilet gulped in protest, the cistern still emptying. Flynn bit his lip against a wave of violence and gripped the sides of the washbasin, head down, breathing heavily. He could feel the blood throbbing in his cheeks. He would not go under again. Would not go to bed with a bottle of alcohol and barricade his door. There was the big rehearsal tomorrow. There was Rami, never far away with his concern and his pep talks and his psychiatrists. Mum and Dad would make him leave the Royal College and come home. He had to hold it together. Had to get through the next two weeks at least, the rehearsals and then the concert. He had to show them, had to show himself that he could do it . . . But could he? That was the million-dollar question.

His legs felt unsteady. He lowered himself to the floor, one hand still gripping the edge of the basin, and drew his knees up to his chest. He must not give way now. This was just a temporary feeling – he was just over-tired, just a bit nervous about the concert. Why then did the mere thought of practice fill him with horror? Why did tomorrow overwhelm him with fear? Why did the pain of his own existence cause him to break out in a cold sweat? He was losing it, he was losing it again! But he mustn't let this happen. He couldn't go through this another time. He could not risk ruining this chance, could not make a fool of himself in front of everyone.

The vision of the Royal Albert Hall stage – the orchestra sitting behind the gleaming Steinway, instruments poised, waiting for his cue – flitted across his mind and a wave of sickness engulfed him. He dragged himself to his feet and walked blindly into the kitchen to pour himself a glass of water. He would not give in to this, he would not let himself fall apart. This time he would fight it, for there was too much at stake. He would keep his composure, he would go through the motions of an ordinary life, he would do it, he must.

He finished the water and looked around wildly for something else to do. He had to keep his mind occupied to prevent himself from thinking! He strode resolutely into the living room. The late-afternoon sunlight filled the room with a golden hue, illuminating the dust on the surfaces. Going for a run crossed his mind but the mere thought of looking for his trainers filled him with despair. The television was the only easy option to hand. He switched on the news and stared at the reader's face, willing himself to listen to the monotone. Such a simple task was excruciating.

Harry's arrival made him start. He did not know whether the breaking of his solitary confinement was a positive thing or not. Perhaps it would prevent him from thinking but it would also throw up the real test – making conversation, appearing normal, behaving as other people did. The task appeared almost impossible.

'Hi,' Harry said. 'You'll never guess what happened. Sally, that crazy redhead in HS, went over to Phil and slapped him, right across the face. It was hilarious! Turned out he'd been caught snogging her best friend. She marched out and all the girls started cheering. Phil was gob-smacked. Honestly, it had to be seen to be believed!'

Painfully, Flynn forced himself to make eye contact, to nod in response, gnawing savagely on his thumbnail.

'You look a bit red in the face. What have you been up to?' Harry grinned.

He could not even come up with a witty reply. 'Nothing.'

'What are you doing tonight?'

'Nothing.' It hurt to talk.

'I'm meeting Jen at her salsa bar in an hour,' Harry went on. 'I told her I had two left feet but apparently I don't have to dance. Kate's been wanting to go for ages. Clive and Nikki are going to be there too. And Jennah says I'm to drag you along on pain of death.'

Flynn looked at him hotly.

'I *said* you'd be practising . . .' Harry rolled his eyes with a weary shake of the head. 'I *told* her that with the big rehearsal tomorrow there was no way you'd be parted from the piano . . .'

Going to a noisy bar full of people would be horrific. Staying at home alone with his thoughts would be worse. 'I'll come,' Flynn said impulsively.

Harry looked suitably surprised. 'Really? Great, just what you need. A bit of real music before the heavy stuff in the morning!'

He knew about the rehearsal with the Philharmonic. God, they all knew.

'I'm going to have a shower and change,' Harry informed him. 'Jen will be pleased – she was complaining she hadn't seen you for ages.'

He departed, whistling, and Flynn returned to the television screen. He breathed deeply, trying to quell a rising knot of fear. What was he thinking, going out the night before his first rehearsal? But he clung to the desperate hope that maybe being around people would force this thing out of him, oblige him to behave rationally and purge this wave of blackness from his addled mind. He had to believe, had to be positive. Otherwise, alone with the long evening hours and the intolerable night ahead, he would go mad, he felt certain of it.

'Are you OK?' Harry asked him as they made their way down Bayswater Road, towards the bright lights and hubbub of Notting Hill Gate, cutting through the harassed-looking commuters spilling out of the tube station.

Flynn nodded, hands in his pockets to deter any further nail-biting, and managed a smile.

'Nervous about tomorrow?' Harry suggested with a sympathetic grin. 'Hey, it'll be great. I'm so jealous. You'll probably feel a bit stressed at the start but when you get into it, playing at the Albert Hall . . .' His eyes lit up. 'Wow. This really *might* be better than sex!' he laughed.

Flynn managed another strained smile, his eyes on the ground. He wondered whether he was going to manage to say anything again, ever. The paving stones in front of him blurred together in the fading light. The energy and determination of the passers-by amazed him. They all appeared to want something, looked as if they had somewhere important to go. He wanted to shake them for their assurance, for their place in the world.

The purple lettering of the bar came into view as they turned the corner. The beat reached out to greet them halfway down the road. A couple of semi-clad girls laughed loudly in the doorway. The place was heaving. Through the darkened entrance, Flynn could make out a mass of heads flashing with fluorescent purple lighting. Crossing his arms, he hung back, reeling. Waves of adrenaline crashed through him, turning his stomach. He was suddenly appalled that he had agreed to this.

Harry turned in the doorway and gave a brief smile. 'Busy, isn't it? By the way, I know you're broke, so drinks are on me.'

Flynn found himself staring back at him like a cat caught in headlights. Now was the time to open his mouth, to tell Harry he had changed his mind, to make some excuse and leave. But Harry pushed open the door and ducked inside. He had lost his chance.

The sight of Jennah, Kate, Clive and Nikki, holding drinks and chatting animatedly around a small table, rooted him to the spot. The urge to bolt was overwhelming. This was too much. He couldn't go through with it. He wouldn't be able to hold down a conversation, would be quite incapable of engaging in small talk with these people as if he were part of their group.

Harry, bounding ahead, was greeting everyone exuberantly with much cheek-kissing and back-slapping. Flynn hung back, trying to disguise his panic, trying to keep the terror from showing and, when Harry had finished, managed a brief smile and a vague 'Hi' at no one in particular. But, to his horror, the attention was on him.

'Hey, it's the elusive maestro!' Clive greeted him. 'All ready for the big concert?'

Flynn smiled and nodded, feeling his face burn. The heat from all the bodies was oppressive and it hurt to stand. He could not think of a thing to say. Harry came to his rescue, plunging in with the story about Sally's slap, which everyone seemed to find surprisingly amusing. But then Nikki edged her way towards Flynn and started going on about Eastern European music, sounding as if she had read too many books on the subject, and going on about the different inter-pretations of the Rach Three. She was bright-eyed and attractive, very intense and completely over the top. Flynn struggled to nod in the right places and string together some kind of coherent answer to her myriad questions. It was as if he were an extra in some crazy film.

None of this seemed real, somehow. The pounding music, the exuberant voices, the raucous laughter – it was all acting. No one felt so great they wanted to laugh all the time, no one had so much to say that they could not stop talking, no one liked people so much that they wanted to pack themselves into a couple of small rooms filled with heaving bodies. He wanted to tell them all to quit the joke, to stop pretending, to be honest and say what they really felt, to be real again. But was this not reality? Their reality, if not his? He did not belong, did not fit in and that was why he could not tolerate being here. But there was nowhere else. Nowhere else but alone – alone with his painful thoughts. Where *did* he belong? Not here, among this crazy, heaving mass of flesh, nor with his friends, nor with his parents. Not anywhere. He wanted to run and keep running, to try to find his place – a place where he felt comfortable, where he felt real. A place where he could stop hurting, far, far from all this.

'Sorry?' he said yet again, leaning towards Nikki. The music was deafening and conversation futile. Yet everyone else seemed to be chatting with ease, albeit at the top of their voices. Did he now have some kind of a hearing problem? Nikki repeated her question, leaning in close, her hair brushing against his cheek. Flynn pulled back quickly. Someone touched his arm and he almost lashed out. Managed to turn round instead and, with considerable relief, discovered Jennah, standing at his elbow.

'Come and help me get the drinks?'

He nodded, excused himself and followed her over to the bar. She stopped at the counter, turned and smiled. 'I hope you didn't mind me doing that. You looked like you needed rescuing.'

'Thanks.'

'How *are* you?' Jennah asked. 'I haven't seen you for ages.' She was wearing a black, knee-length dress and her arms were bare. Her eyes looked very bright in the half-light.

'I'm all right.'

'How was your dad's birthday?'

'OK.'

Jennah crinkled up her nose. 'Thanks for coming along, Flynn. I know you'd rather be practising but I really wanted to see you and, anyway, it's better to chill out the night before so that you're nice and relaxed for the rehearsal – or too hungover to be nervous, whichever way you want to look at it.'

Flynn almost laughed.

'Hey, I knew I'd get you to smile!'

The smile faded with embarrassment and he looked away.

'I've been worried about you. I hardly see you any more. You work too hard!' Jennah nudged him teasingly, making him flinch.

There was a silence. 'Is everything OK?' she asked.

No, it's not! he wanted to shout. I can't cope with this any more! I'm dying inside and I've got nowhere to go! Nobody understands me, not even my own mother, and just getting out of bed in the morning terrifies me! I'm sinking, sinking and there's no way out! But instead he gave a shrug and nodded.

Jennah cocked her head with a small smile. 'You'll have to do better than that!'

150

He looked at her, breathing hard, suddenly terrified that she was going to break in, see through and realize what was going on. He could not watch himself carefully enough, could not be sure he would not let something slip. 'Shall we get the drinks?' he managed.

Jennah nodded slowly and turned to lean over the bar. She did not turn back as she waited to be served.

Flynn found a chair on the other side of the table from Nikki when they returned. Harry was on the dance floor with Kate – so much for his two left feet. Flynn sipped his beer with mounting dread. Now that he had cut short his conversation with Jennah, he was exposed to either sitting alone and looking pathetic, or to being pitied and talked to. Neither was appealing. How soon could he leave? He tried to look interested in Harry and Kate's comical moves but he obviously wasn't convincing enough, because Clive started talking to him. Better than overzealous Nikki but Clive was loud, confident and cracked a lot of unfunny jokes. Clive too wanted to talk about the concert, and Flynn could not understand why until he realized that they did not know him well enough to talk about much else. He was not volunteering any free information, nor enquiring about them at all. Anyway, they probably knew him as the eccentric always holed up in the piano room . . . It was an effort just having to pretend to listen to what Clive had to say. The image of the concert hall flitted repeatedly across Flynn's mind. He was suffocating . . . Eventually, Clive grew tired of Flynn's catatonic answers and took Nikki to the dance floor. That was when Jennah reached her arm out across the table.

'What about it then, Flynn?'

The colour rushed to his face. 'No, I can't – I'm not – I really can't—'

'You liar! You're a great dancer. I haven't forgotten Kate's birthday!'

Another time, another life. 'You go,' Flynn said. 'Harry will dance with you – he looks as if he could go on all night.'

Jennah narrowed her eyes with a teasing pout. 'I don't *want* to dance with Harry,' she said.

'Don't stay sitting here,' Flynn said quickly. 'I'm going to go, I've got to go. Early start and all that.'

Jennah's face fell. 'You've only just got here!'

'I know but I'm whacked and I've got to – you know—' He didn't dare say 'practise' for fear of her reaction. Yet he had to leave urgently, before he spoiled the evening for Jennah, who clearly was not going to leave him sitting alone.

'Please don't go,' Jennah said, imploringly.

'Look, you can go and dance with Clive. Nikki's dancing with someone else,' Flynn said desperately.

'Flynn, stop it, I don't *want* to dance with Clive!'

She had almost shouted. He looked at her, shocked.

'If you're leaving, I'm going too,' Jennah said.

'Why?' His voice rose suddenly and he felt his eyes sting. He could not take this any more. What was Jennah trying to do?

She stared at him. 'Hey, I didn't mean – it doesn't matter, I don't really want to dance. I'd – I'd rather just chat with you . . . We could go upstairs and find a table where it's quieter or – or—'

Flynn shrugged, blinking hard. 'OK.'

'Or – or you could go.' Jennah looked flustered. 'Of course you don't have to stay, Flynn. I didn't – I didn't mean—'

He managed a faint smile. 'Stop babbling and come on then.'

She smiled, looking relieved, and followed him upstairs.

The upstairs lounge was mercifully empty, the music fading to a muted thud. They sat beside a large window filled with night, and Jennah put her feet up on the chair beside him. Flynn lit a match and began to burn a piece of aluminium foil from the ashtray.

'Pyromaniac.'

He let the match burn out and dropped it into the ashtray. Jennah nudged him with her foot.

'What's bugging you then?'

He glanced at her briefly. 'Nothing.'

'And the truth?'

'Everything.'

She winced. 'That bad?'

There was a silence. He felt his throat tighten and started biting his thumbnail. He couldn't meet her gaze.

Head propped up against her hand, Jennah gazed

across the table at him. 'Is there something in particular?'

His throat ached. He could not tell her. Wearily, he shook his head.

'The concert?' Jennah suggested.

He crumbled the burned match between his thumb and forefinger, staring down at it. He could not reply.

'*Why*, Flynn? Don't you know how talented you are?'

She sounded like she actually believed it. He swallowed hard.

She nudged him again with her foot. 'What are you stressing about, hey?'

He gave a wry smile. 'Only that I'll freeze. Only that I'll forget the notes and mess the whole thing up.'

'That's every musician's nightmare,' Jennah said. 'But you're too well prepared. It won't happen to you!'

'I'm so stressed, it probably will.'

'Everyone gets stressed,' Jennah said. 'It's normal, it's part of the deal. Coming on stage is like death – the first few bars are the worst, but once you get into it, the stress lifts. You're too damn concentrated to have time for it.'

'I know. I just don't think I'll get that far. At best it'll be a repeat of last year's scholarship audition. Professor Kaiser was furious with me for a month afterwards and that was just for a silly award. God knows how he'll react when I'm representing his precious department, not to mention his sacred teaching.'

There was a silence. 'You're thinking about it too

154

much,' Jennah said. 'It's one concert, Flynn. It'll be over before you know it.'

'But my parents are going to want to be there, and my brother. My parents still expect me to be the best – they don't know what it's like here. André's so much better than me and – and so are loads of people and – and Rami already thinks I'm a joke because all I do is practise, but he doesn't realize that I have to in order to keep up and if I don't then everything will fall apart and everybody will realize that I'm not really that good and I'll just be this huge disappointment to everyone and—' He broke off. Shallow breaths to fight back the tears.

'Oh, Flynn,' Jennah said quietly. 'How can you think like that?'

Her sympathy threw him. He wanted her advice, not her kindness. The pressure behind his eyes overwhelmed him.

'Hey—' Jennah sat up, her voice softly aghast.

He sniffed hard and brushed the back of his hand across his eyes, hating himself. 'I feel like I'm losing the plot here!'

'Flynn, it's not – you're not . . .' Jennah was floundering.

He dragged his fingers down his cheeks, holding his breath.

'Oh, Flynn—'

'It's OK. I'm all right.'

'Come here.' Jennah reached forwards.

'Don't!' He held her off with a raised hand. He had to pull himself together – she must not touch him. The evening had turned into a nightmare.

Jennah stared at him, wide-eyed.

'I'm fine!' He sniffed, rubbing his cheeks hard and managing a half-smile. 'I'm just tired. I can't sleep these days, it's doing my head in.' He forced a laugh.

'That's because you're stressed.'

'Yeah, I know, it's stupid. Anyway, I'm going to take off.'

A sudden look of panic. 'Flynn, wait – is Professor Kaiser giving you a hard time again?'

'He's OK. I'll see you in Aural tomorrow.'

'Yes, but hold on – do you want me to come with you to the rehearsal?'

'God, no, it'll be so boring! I'll see you tomorrow, OK? Say bye to the others for me.'

'Flynn, wait—' She jumped up suddenly, her expression desperate. 'Just tell me. Tell me one thing I can do.'

'About what?' A shrug and a laugh. 'Everything's fine. Honestly.' He gave her a smile and turned away.

CHAPTER EIGHT

On the steps of the Royal Albert Hall. The elliptical building bulged with importance, its curving stone and terracotta façade with its domed skylight jutting out against an overcast sky. Flynn had walked past it unseeingly every day on his way to university, been inside it for countless concerts, yet today he saw it for the first time, monstrous in its importance like a Roman amphitheatre, ready to have him fed to the lions.

He walked slowly up the wide flight of steps, his shoes making a gentle shuffling sound against the concrete, his legs moving with a will of their own, as if transporting him to his execution. He saw himself as from a distance – a lone figure making its way towards Prince Albert on his pillar, moving automatically, body functioning of its own accord, ferrying him to his doom. But it didn't matter, because his body knew what it had to do and it continued steadily up the steps and in through the doors, down the hall and past the deserted ticket offices, past the cloakrooms and up the stairs, his footsteps suddenly muffling into the carpet. The bag containing his score and a bottle of water was on his shoulder. His expression, a little on the serious side, was carefully set to give nothing away.

Professor Kaiser was waiting for him outside the stage entrance, dressed in an impeccable dark blue suit, his steel-rimmed glasses perched importantly on the bridge of his nose. Strains of the closing bars of Vivaldi's 'Winter' drifted out of the auditorium. Katherine Morden, Yehudi's top violinist.

'They have been rehearsing now for two hours, so they should be finishing soon. The orchestra will be nicely warmed up, so for you it is perfect to be second.'

Flynn managed a wan smile.

'Did you sleep well?' Professor Kaiser seemed to startle himself by the force of his tone.

'Yes, of course,' Flynn replied automatically.

He relaxed. '*Gut, gut*. You need to have much energy for this. Radin is a very brilliant conductor, but of course his expectations can be high. Don't forget what I said – if he asks you to do something and it's not completely clear for you, you must ask, always ask. He makes many quick, sharp decisions. If you don't understand something, don't get worried if he seems a little annoyed, just take a deep breath and ask him to explain it again, *ja*?'

Flynn nodded, silent.

Professor Kaiser's expression relaxed for a moment. 'And try not to look so fearful, Flynn. This is a rehearsal only, *ja*? It is not supposed to be perfect.'

158

Flynn excused himself and went to find the toilets – there was a lot of talking going on inside the auditorium and it sounded as if Katherine's rehearsal might be coming to an end. After washing his hands, he scooped water onto his burning cheeks, acutely aware of his shallow, rapid breathing, the painful thudding in his chest. He gripped the side of the counter and tried to slow his breathing. *Calm down. You won't be able to play like this. For God's sake, calm down.*

He dried his face and looked up at his reflection: the flush gave him an almost healthy look; the violet shadows beneath his eyes did not. He tried to smooth down the wayward wisps of fair hair and sucked in his lower lip, staring into his own eyes. The eyes stared back. There were no secrets there, no magical power he could unlock. They were just his eyes – wide, blue, frozen, terrified . . . It was just him, Flynn, alone inside his head. Only he could play now, only he could walk onto that stage. Only he could remember the music, only he could tell his fingers what to do. The next hour rested on him. It was up to him and him alone. He was entirely responsible for what was to come. He ached with the greatness of the task ahead. *Don't mess it up, Flynn.*

The feeling of sickness rose again as he joined Professor Kaiser at the back of the stalls. Katherine was playing with great confidence as the piece reached its crescendo. The members of the orchestra looked serious, intense and thorough, the aura of effort, purpose and determination permeating the auditorium. They were making great music and they knew it. There was nothing amateurish about this rehearsal – they could have been playing at the Last Night of the Proms.

Two men and a woman sat in suits in the fourth row, the elusive Dr Wells, Director of Music at the Royal College, among them. The piece came to an end and the orchestra members were given leave to disperse. Radin and Katherine left the stage to join the three suits, and Katherine's violin teacher ambled from the back of the stalls to join them, greeting Professor Kaiser and whispering 'Good luck' to Flynn as he passed. He was smiling – Katherine had done well.

'Now, remember, cantabile for the middle section. Make the melody light and build with the left hand. Do not let the final section run away with you, focus on the tempo. Don't forget, the orchestra have to keep time with you and not you with them.'

Flynn nodded and took a sip of water. His throat felt so dry he feared he would soon be unable to speak.

'If something goes wrong, just keep going and don't stop. Wait for the conductor to tell you to stop. It is always up to him.'

'Yes.'

Katherine and her teacher were about to depart, gathering up belongings, thanking the conductor, moving towards the exit. Flynn could hear nothing but the pounding of his heart, could see the beat through his shirt. Goose bumps rose down his arms and back, the lights seemed to grow brighter and his vision began to blur. Terror pulsated through him, the overwhelming desire to flee, the sense of utter incapability at the sight of the Steinway. In desperation he turned to Professor Kaiser but could not speak.

'Try and enjoy yourself!' Professor Kaiser said with a smile. 'Come on, it is our turn. Let's go.'

Flynn got up and followed Professor Kaiser down the aisle, surprised that he did not fall. He forgot his bag and had to go back for it. He could not even keep track of his own belongings – not a promising start. He could feel his cheeks burning again as they reached the front and approached Radin and the suits. Professor Kaiser seemed to know them all and greeted them with jovial handshakes and cheerful hellos.

'I didn't know I was getting one of yours, Hans,' Radin said with a smile. 'This should be fun.'

'This is Flynn Laukonen, a very promising young student of mine.' Professor Kaiser beamed.

Flynn stepped forwards and shook hands with the suits, unable to meet their eyes.

'So, Rachmaninov's Third. Not lacking in ambition, are we?' Radin said.

Flynn pulled an embarrassed face.

'How do you feel about playing in the Albert?' the Director of Music asked him.

'I'm pleased.' His voice was barely audible even to his own ears.

'And what year of study are you in at the Royal College?' the woman asked.

'First.'

'Laukonen, that sounds Finnish,' said the Director of Music.

'Yes.'

'That would explain the complexion. Were you born here?'

'Helsinki.' He did not dare speak up for fear of them hearing his voice shaking.

'I remember visiting Sibelius Park in Helsinki once,' Radin chipped in. 'Pretty place.'

The members of the orchestra began to trickle back in, sit down, tune up and fiddle about with the music on their stands.

'Come up and get the feel of the Steinway,' Radin suggested.

Professor Kaiser raised his eyebrows and gave him an encouraging nod. Flynn followed Radin up the wooden steps and onto the stage. He suddenly needed to pee.

Flynn sat down at the piano, adjusted the stool with sweaty palms, wiped his hands on his trouser legs, played several arpeggios and ran through a couple of technical exercises. The keys were very shiny, as if they had just been polished. He could make out his reflection in the glistening ebony in front of him. The lights here were brighter than ever, burning holes in his head. He took out his score and placed it closed, along with his pencil, on the stand. He took out his bottle of water and managed three sips, hoping his hand was not shaking too visibly. From the edge of his blurred vision, he could see that all the orchestra members had come back on now, rustling music sheets and talking. Radin tapped his baton on the edge of his stand and there was sudden silence.

'Right, on to our second piece now, please. It is my pleasure to introduce Flynn Laukonen, pianist.'

Flynn glanced over at the blurred mass of heads and instruments and managed a quick smile. There was a silence. A heavy sense of expectancy.

'Flynn, if you could give us an A,' Radin said evenly.

He played an A, then a D. The mass of sound that followed was overpowering. He did not know if he should play the notes again. Looked behind him at the first violinist for guidance. But the orchestra was only a blur of faces, of eyes, of lights.

'We'll start with the first movement and play it through from beginning to end, without stopping. Then we will go back over any trouble spots,' Radin announced, walking over to the rostrum.

Flynn took a deep breath and concentrated on the pale blue pattern on the cover of his closed score. It seemed to be made out of little dots. He had never noticed that before. Little dots on a cream background, clustered into the shapes of flowers. It was hard to breathe. His heart was thumping as if it were about to burst. His fingers didn't feel warmed up properly and now he really needed to pee.

Radin was flicking languidly through the pages on his stand. There was a faint shuffling as some of the orchestra members got comfortable and adjusted their stands. Then screaming silence, the air hot and heavy, everyone watching him, waiting.

The flowers are made out of dots, he thought. The flowers are made out of dots. He wiped his hands on his trousers one last time and screwed his eyes shut briefly. He exhaled slowly. He turned his head. His eyes met Radin's. Flynn gave a brief nod. Radin raised his arms and held them, suspended in the air. The violinists raised their bows. Radin's arms came crashing down.

Flynn started playing before even being aware of his cue. The notes flowed and he was filled with an over-whelming sense of unreality, of detachment, as if he were simply a member of the audience, listening to all this and just sitting back, not playing at all. He felt sure that if he lifted his hands from the piano, the music would continue on its own. He could not be responsible for all this, there had to be somebody else behind the stage, pulling the strings. Then the tempo began to quicken and he watched his fingers gather speed of their own accord. He looked up at the conductor to get his cue, and the violins in the front were a mass of buzzing bows, and Radin's arms were plunging dramatically through the air. The music was extra-ordinary, overwhelming, larger than life, and he could not believe he was a part of this. The orchestra swelled and then died and his notes rang out, clear and smooth. He felt as if his fingers were trying to keep up with the music, as if his hands had a life of their own.

But the tempo seemed to fade unexpectedly after bar thirty-two and, momentarily disorientated, he came in late. The music was obliterated by his racing heart and he struggled to hear it again and focus, focus on the music ahead. This time he lifted his head and stared at Radin, who thankfully half turned his head and gave him a nod for his cue. And then Flynn was plunging again, through the thick fog of black and white notes, of light and dark, life and death.

The music began to build and he tried to stay in the present and not think about the dramatic finale, the series of impossibly fast chords he still had to get through. He could barely hear himself through the rising wave of strings and wondered whether he should be playing forte instead of fortissimo, thinking that if he could not hear himself, then nobody else would. But he didn't dare change it now. And then the wave began to swell and he could barely follow the music, and he could not think or see, only hear. Now it was no longer just his hands that were playing but every inch of his body working to bring out the music, higher, faster, greater, deeper. He could only hear himself playing and could only think of getting to the end, desperately reaching, clawing out for safety. And then suddenly he had reached the final chord and, as the sound echoed through the air, he let his arm drop and, heaving for breath, was finally still.

He became aware of the faint sound of clapping from the stalls and straightened up and looked across at Radin, who was flicking back through the score. The shuffling and murmuring started up from the orchestra. His face was on fire and his arms felt weak, lifeless, incapable even of lifting the bottle of water from the floor. Hands on his knees, he chewed his bottom lip and stared down at the innocent-looking keys, the source of his torment only moments before. He did not dare glance towards his audience.

'Good,' Radin said, and the orchestra was quiet. 'Now for the real work. Bar thirty-two, what happened there?'

'I lost tempo,' Flynn replied, his cheeks burning.

'Let's try it again, shall we? Dum, dum, dum, two, three and in.'

Flynn nodded, swallowing.

'We'll take it from the G sharp.'

Which G sharp? There was more than one! Flynn panicked for a moment but then the red fog lifted as the orchestra gave him his cue. He watched Radin like a hawk for his re-entry and got it right. Relief flooded through him.

Radin held up his hands. 'Good, good, thank you.' He turned back to Flynn. 'That sounded a bit tentative, you need to come in with conviction.' He hummed the first few notes and punched his fist in the air for emphasis.

Flynn nodded, feeling desperate. They played it again, still less than perfect. He felt thrown by the orchestra dying away before his re-entry. He had never heard it played that way before. He wished Radin would move on – if they went over it too many times he would start thinking about the notes and it would then become a sticking point, a terror spot, causing him to freeze. Professor Kaiser always let him absorb changes before going back to them. Pushing a point was counter-productive. It almost always ended up getting worse.

They must have spent half an hour on that re-entry alone. It got so that Flynn stalled in the end, forgetting his notes. Radin did not look too impressed but finally had the wisdom to let it go. They moved on to the melody of the middle section.

The late-morning sunlight exploded like a flashbulb in his face. 'That wasn't so bad!' Professor Kaiser buttoned his coat against the chill breeze and patted Flynn's shoulder as they descended the concrete steps. 'You survived it.'

Flynn managed a weak smile and nodded. He was drained, an empty shell, a heap of exhaustion. He could not find the energy to speak, his legs were numb beneath him.

'The first time you play a new piece with an orchestra

is always difficult,' Professor Kaiser went on. 'It takes some time for getting used to the other musicians and to the way the conductor interprets it. There are some things we must work on still but we have three more rehearsals to go, so there is nothing to worry about.'

Flynn nodded again.

'You seem as if you need some food.' Professor Kaiser smiled suddenly. 'Let's go to the café on the corner and I will buy you lunch.'

Flynn could not eat, still saturated with adrenaline, still reeling from his inability to get the timing right on bar thirty-two.

'Don't worry about that now,' Professor Kaiser told him. 'You were just a little nervous. You didn't have trouble with that part before.'

That was just it. He was inventing problems where none existed. How many more problems could he create before the concert? The possibilities were endless.

He sat with a cup of coffee and a sandwich but could consume neither. Professor Kaiser bit into a large prawn baguette and the smell turned Flynn's stomach. All he wanted to do was go home now, go to sleep for the rest of the day, but it was not even twelve and there was a whole afternoon of lessons to get through, including a lesson with Professor Kaiser at one.

'We only have two weeks left before the concert, so I think it would be a good idea for you to come for a lesson every day,' Professor Kaiser said. 'That will help us to get through all the points that Radin spoke about.'

Flynn nodded numbly. There was too much work to do, Professor Kaiser was saying. He was not ready.

'I have a free period at eight thirty,' Professor Kaiser said. 'How is that for you?'

Flynn nodded again. He had lectures at nine but what did that matter?

'You are not much wanting to talk, are you?' Professor Kaiser commented with a wry smile.

'Sorry,' Flynn said.

He strode home through the park. He needed to move, to focus on something else and put as much distance between himself and the rehearsal as possible. He didn't want to keep seeing Radin's intense expression – the small frown brushing across his face as Flynn mistimed his entry, the fleeting look of exasperation touching his eyes as Flynn missed the accent on bar twenty-three. But the scenes played out again and again on the screen inside his head as he relived every painful detail, every minute embarrassment, every humiliating moment, unable to change a single thing. He thought about going running, but running would only occupy his body, leaving his mind stuck with the film inside his head. He was trapped – even in the middle of Hyde Park's expanse of rain-soaked grass and trees and sky, he could not escape the stifling, narrow, painful confines of his own mind.

Flynn left the windy Bayswater street and, the moment he stepped into the narrow entry hall and slammed the front door behind him, his world kaleidoscoped into the five small rooms of the flat and it was an effort not to scream. Kicking off his trainers and stepping over the dirty washing on the kitchen floor, he put the kettle on and turned the radio up loud. Anything, anything to distract himself from himself. He was humming along to the radio, making coffee, kicking Harry's washing out of the way. Everything seemed so normal – *he* seemed so normal. If anyone came in right now they wouldn't suspect anything was wrong. Yet his mind seemed to be fragmenting, like a mirror spiderwebbing with cracks. He felt as if he were at some kind of junction; what he did now could have huge repercussions – should he try to hold on or just let himself fall apart?

His mind was running, running, running, words were coming so thick and fast he couldn't keep up, there seemed to be so many possibilities. The window, for instance, opposite him above the sink – he could punch it, he could wash it, he could throw the frying pan through it, or he could ignore it. Four choices, many more, and that was with only one object. There was a knife on the drying rack, and a plate, and a large glass jug. There were probably a hundred things in this room alone. The possibilities were endless. A normal person would ignore it. He *should* ignore it, but yet it beckoned to him in some way, loud inside his head. He picked up the jug, hurled it to the floor and watched it shatter into a thousand pieces. Then he sank to his knees, gazing at the broken shards of glass winking in the light of the afternoon sun.

CHAPTER NINE

For the next three weeks, Flynn went to his daily lessons with Professor Kaiser and missed his first hour of lectures. He practised through the night, snatching a few hours' sleep towards dawn. It was no good going to bed earlier – his thoughts encompassed him until he burst from his covers, sweaty and frantic, and went back to his keyboard. He used the kitchen tactically, to avoid Harry. He tried not to be too monosyllabic around Jennah but avoided her too. He skipped lectures to practise, but nobody complained. He went to three more rehearsals at the Albert. The concert date approached.

'Am I allowed to come to this concert then or not?' Rami wanted to know.

Flynn twisted the telephone cord around his fingers, watching the tips turn purple. 'If you want.'

'Of course I want! Can I bring Sophie?'

'I suppose.'

There was a silence. 'Flynn, are you really not going to invite Mum and Dad?'

'No.'

'Do you realize how hurt they're going to be?'

'They'll get over it.'

Rami was silent.

He had not slept for two nights and now Harry was tuning at the crack of dawn. Flynn flung back the covers and stomped into the living room. Only just managed to resist the overwhelming urge to grab the cello and smash it over Harry's head.

'Sorry, did I wake you?' Harry greeted him.

Flynn glowered. 'No.'

'You look rough. Were you practising again last night?'

'Yeah.'

'I know it's only two days away but be careful, you don't want to burn yourself out.' Harry returned to his cello, played a very flat A and twisted the pin.

'It's too fast, it's too frantic,' Professor Kaiser shouted above the music. 'Control, Flynn, it's all about control. You must put in the passion but you must never, never lose the control.'

'I am in control,' Flynn said desperately.

'Play it again. I want to hear it again. You are letting the music run away with you now. You had this bit yesterday – remember how you played it yesterday. Don't get carried away!'

* * *

173

Jennah caught up with him in the hall, her cheeks flushed, her smile bright. 'How are you feeling?'

'Fine.'

'Really? Not too nervous?'

'I'm fine!' he snapped.

'OK.' She looked hurt for a brief moment, then recovered. 'I can't wait. I know it's going to be fantastic.'

'Thanks.'

'You're going to be great. Everyone knows how good you are.'

The phone was ringing, the flat was empty. The sunlight had turned golden – it was nearly evening already. Twenty-seven hours to go. The phone continued to ring and ring. Harry had forgotten to switch on the answering machine.

'Hello?' He grabbed the receiver on the twelfth ring.

'Flynn, it's Rami. I'm calling from work.'

'Why?' An emergency at the hospital? Perhaps he would not be able to make it after all?

'Look, don't get upset, it's not the end of the world, but I was on the phone to Mum this morning and, um – well, they're coming to the concert tomorrow night.'

'*What?*'

'Don't overreact, Flynn. I know it's rather last-minute but apparently Professor Kaiser invited them. Dad rang him about – about you, actually – and when Professor Kaiser heard that you hadn't invited them, he invited them himself.'

'*What?*'

'Look, Flynn, I'm being paged. I'm going to have to go. Don't worry about anything. They're coming here tomorrow morning and I'll drive them over in the evening. You won't even know they're there. I'll make sure they don't drop in on you, so you won't have to see them until after the concert. Maybe afterwards we can go out for a meal or something.'

'Hi!' Harry came in sideways, manoeuvring several bulging Tesco bags through the narrow doorway. 'I bought some food for tonight.'

'Why?' Heart still thudding painfully from Rami's phone call, Flynn looked at him wide-eyed from the arm of the couch.

'I thought I'd make a curry.'

'Who for?' His voice began to rise.

'Kate and Jen. Didn't I tell you?'

'You invited them over?'

'Yes! Why are you shouting? I'm not deaf.'

'Why? Why did you invite them over?'

'Calm down! Jennah wanted to pop by to wish you luck and Kate doesn't believe I can cook, so I wanted to show her.'

'Why does Jennah need to wish me good luck? She's already wished me good luck at least six times! And why does Kate have to come? Why can't you go there?'

'For heaven's sake, stop yelling! Surely I'm allowed to invite *my* girlfriend back to *my* flat, for crying out loud!'

Harry was not easily rattled but now his eyes widened in outrage.

'Why tonight? Why does it have to be tonight? I'm not spending the whole evening making stupid small talk to bloody Jennah and Kate!'

Harry's voice was low, angry. 'Hey, easy, Flynn.'

'Fine, you have dinner with them but count me out!'

'Fine, I will! Just because you're miserable all the time doesn't mean everyone else has to be too! Perhaps if you just made an effort for a change, perhaps if you weren't always so damn self-involved, you wouldn't feel so shitty!'

Flynn stared at him, the blood hot in his cheeks. It was sobering to see Harry so angry.

'For God's sake,' Harry went on, 'you never want to do anything any more – you never come out to the pub, you never just hang around with us after lectures. It's no wonder you feel depressed – anyone would be, cooped up indoors all the time, practising all day.'

Flynn felt a small pain start at the back of his throat. 'D'you really think I have a choice?'

'Of course you have a choice!' Harry exclaimed. 'Nobody's chaining you to the piano! Nobody's forcing you to be miserable all the time! You could have dinner with us tonight, you could come out with us once in a while, you could practise a reasonable amount of time and start sleeping again, like a normal person!'

'You have no idea what you're talking about!' Flynn yelled. 'You have no idea what it's like! I'm sick of this! I'm so fucking sick of feeling like this all the time!'

'Feeling like what? Are you stressed about the concert? Come on, mate, you know you'll be fine.'

'It's not the concert!'

'Then I don't understand—'

'I'm not asking you to understand! I'm asking you to leave me alone!'

'OK then! I'll tell Jennah and Kate you don't want to see them. See how that makes them feel. Maybe *then* Jennah will finally stop lusting after you!'

Flynn stormed out of the room. He crashed into his bedroom and threw himself face down on his bed, breathing heavily into his pillow. Red blotches flashed behind his closed lids against a sea of darkness. His pulse raged in his ears. Waves of sickness flooded him. It hurt to breathe. He had never yelled at Harry before but now suddenly he hated him. Suddenly he hated them all. He hated them for their normality, their shared kindness, their naïve generosity, their simple acts of goodwill. But most of all he hated them for not understanding.

His heartbeat faded to a dull, painful thud, his breathing still snatched and ragged. He rolled onto his side and gazed over at the curtains. Another night and another full day. Alone. His parents would be coming, eager and excited. Mum would be all emotional, Dad beaming with pride. He closed his eyes, wished desperately for sleep, but knew his bed could no longer offer him that refuge. It was now just a place of torment, of crazy thoughts and restless meanderings, of bitter frustration as the hours crawled by.

After a while, he was aware of the sound of crockery from the kitchen. Harry was going ahead with his curry. Flynn fought back a fresh wave of fury. There was something wrong with him that he should explode at his flatmate just for inviting a couple of friends over. There was something wrong with him that he should feel like yelling at the slightest provocation. There was something wrong with him that the prospect of performing in a concert should fill him with such horror. Was he going mad?

Then, as the thudding of his heart began to die down, a new thought occurred to him. What was it that Harry had said before Flynn charged out of the room? *Maybe Jennah will finally stop* lusting *after you?* He looked down at the white, crumpled sheet, the patch of golden sunlight staining the bed. What a joke. Not in a million years would anyone lust after him – least of all Jennah. He was a loser, a screw-up, a faker who hid behind hours and hours of practice to make up for his lack of talent, then freaked out at the thought of playing in public. What was Harry *doing*? Having a laugh? Jennah would have scoffed at Harry's outrageous suggestion, would have pitied Flynn for entertaining the idea even for a second, would wrinkle up her nose at the mere thought of being attracted to such a socially

178

inept weirdo. But Jennah wasn't like that . . . Jennah would never be so unkind . . . Jennah would only feel sorry . . .

Flynn pressed his hands against his face and felt hot tears trickle between his fingers. He wanted everything to go away. He wanted everything to stop. As long as he lived, he would never escape himself. How much more could he endure? Another fifty years, another sixty? How could he endure the weeks, the months, the years, when he couldn't even get through the hours? It was only a matter of time. Only a matter of time before he reached the end of his tether and found himself incapable of carrying on for another day. He would not make it through a lifetime. Not like this . . .

How easy it would be to end it all now, he thought. If he did it right here, right now, he would not even have to bother about the concert. He might be unable to change the pain of his existence but that did not mean he was forced to endure it. He would not live like this any more. There was always another option, always another option. Either he would defeat the pain or he would bow out. Sitting on his bed in a pool of evening sunlight, Flynn contemplated death while, in the next room, Harry started cooking to the beat of Kiss FM.

'Do you want to give me a hand with this?'

Harry showed no surprise when Flynn returned to the kitchen nearly an hour later, showered and changed, wearing a sheepish smile.

'OK. What shall I do?'

'You can do the carrots.'

'Ooh, such responsibility.'

Flynn started chopping and was silently grateful to Harry for not probing. While he had been sitting on his bed in a pool of late-afternoon sunlight, a new emotion had suddenly thrust itself over him – fear. The sudden realization that all that lay between life and death was the catch on his bedroom window, the sudden realization that following his thoughts to their logical conclusions would lead him to jump, the sudden realization that it would be so easy to smash himself down onto the concrete four storeys below. The phrase *He is a danger to himself* suddenly held new meaning. How easy it would be to turn into a murderer, *his* murderer. And suddenly he was scared. Scared of his own company. Scared of himself.

Harry threw open the window to let out the cooking smells, and the cool touch of blue-grey dusk floated in on a blanket of birdsong. It was almost summer, supposedly a time of such hope and promise, bringing with it every reason to be happy. He was going to have dinner with friends and then tomorrow he would do a final run-through. In the evening he would play in a concert and he would be all right, everything would be all right, he would *will* himself to be all right. He wasn't going to think of his bedroom window, he wasn't going to think of his smashed-up body lying in the morgue, he wasn't going to think how unbelievably quick and easy it

180

would be to die . . . A cold sweat broke out across his arms and back from the effort. He was mad, he knew that now. He was so mad that he was frightening even himself. Normal people didn't go to pieces about playing in a concert, normal people didn't start screaming because their friends were coming to dinner, normal people didn't think about hurling themselves out of a window at four o'clock on a sunny spring afternoon.

At the stove, Harry was humming, a beer can in one hand and a wooden spoon in the other. Harry was thinking about his curry, about Jen and Kate coming over for dinner, about a chilled weekend of football and practice lying ahead. Flynn wanted to be like Harry. He wanted be normal and cheerful and relaxed. If he couldn't be normal then he could *pretend* to be normal. Perhaps it might work . . . It *had* to work . . .

Flynn grabbed the four-pack from the fridge. 'D'you want a beer?'

'Please. Have you finished with those carrots?'

'These carrots?' He flicked a piece at Harry's head.

Harry grinned. 'Now don't get childish, Flynn.'

Flynn flicked another piece over.

'You want a fight? If I send this curry in your direction, things could get nasty!'

'Ooh, I'm *scared*!'

Flynn set the table at lightning speed. 'OK, done. Give me something to do – carrots really aren't challenging enough.'

'It's more or less ready. You can taste it if you want

181

and tell me if it's OK.' Harry pulled himself up onto the counter and picked up his beer. Flynn went over to the stove.

'Is Rami coming tomorrow?' Harry asked.

'Yeah, and so are my parents but, you know what, I don't care, I don't care, I don't care!' He took a deep swig of beer and laughed. 'I've actually got to the point where I don't care about a single thing! I'd recommend it, it's utterly liberating!' He sang along to Justin Timberlake, and Harry gave him an uncertain smile.

'Surely it's a good thing that your parents are coming?'

'I don't care, I don't care, I don't care!' Flynn sang.

Harry laughed. 'OK, point taken. Perhaps you should stop stirring that curry now before you pulverize it into soup.'

'Curry soup, we can have curry soup! Hey, aren't you meant to put beer in curry? Liven it up a bit?' He lifted his can over the pot.

'Hey!' Harry's laughter held a hint of alarm. 'Don't you dare.'

Flynn began to tip his can threateningly. 'Do I . . . ? Do I . . . ?'

'Flynn, put it down—'

Flynn started to laugh at Harry's growing concern and splashed a little more beer into the curry than he had intended. Harry was off the counter in a flash, elbowing Flynn out of the way. 'Keep away from my food!'

Choking with laughter, Flynn grappled with Harry, grabbing him by the shoulders. The laughter hurt his throat, made him want to retch, but it seemed to fool Harry and maybe, if he tried hard enough, he might even end up convincing himself too. Harry hung onto the side of the counter, red in the face, as Flynn tried to hook his leg and knock him to the ground.

'Flynn, you nutter, stop, get off, this is going to end badly!'

'For you, I think!'

The bell went, saving Harry from a humiliating defeat.

'You get it.'

'No, you get it.'

'Give me your beer can then.'

'Fine, take it!'

'Thank you, I will!'

Voices in the hall – Jennah and Kate. Harry was taking their coats, ever the gentleman, asking them about their day.

'Mm, smells lovely,' Jennah said, coming into the kitchen. Her hair was windswept, her smile very bright. 'I didn't know you guys could cook! Hi, Flynn.'

'It's the only thing that Harry *can* cook but, yeah, this is really good curry.' Flynn went over to the stove, dipped his finger in and sucked it. 'Kind of tastes of beer, though.'

Harry's eyes latched onto the newly opened beer can in Flynn's hand and widened. 'You didn't!'

Flynn started to laugh again as Harry leaped over to the stove.

Jennah and Kate exchanged amused glances. 'What's going on?' Jennah asked.

Harry grabbed Flynn's wrist and tried to wrestle the beer can out of his hand. 'How much did you put in? How much did you put in?'

'Oh, just a drop!'

'That's an interesting recipe!' Kate began to laugh.

'No, no, no!' Harry was red in the face. 'There was not meant to be beer in the curry!'

Jennah gave Flynn a grin. 'Are you trying to sabotage Harry's culinary efforts?'

'No, improve. It's a good tip, adds a certain *je ne sais quoi*! Let's go and put some decent music on.' He swung round and headed for the living room.

'I'm gonna kill him,' he heard Harry mutter behind him.

Moments later, Jennah followed, glass in hand, and sat down on the couch. Flynn emerged from beneath the side table, pulling piles of CDs out with him. 'What d'you fancy? I've got Bob Dylan, Aerosmith, Queen, Manic Street Preachers, U2, Kylie – Harry's, not mine – REM, Meatloaf, Oasis—'

'I really don't mind.'

'Massive Attack, Coldplay, Travis, Lauren Hill . . .' He continued to reel them off, chucking each CD case into the middle of the floor as he finished with it.

'Or how about some hip hop? We've got Doctor Dre, 50 Cent, Eminem, Notorious B.I.G.—'

'Flynn, Flynn, I really don't mind!'

'You've got to choose! What about Snoop Dogg, Gang Starr, Obie Trice, Missy Elliott—'

'OK!' Jennah leaned forwards and snatched one off the carpet. 'What about this one?'

'No, you picked it randomly. You have to put some thought into this. Choosing which music to listen to is a very important decision, especially when you've got friends round, especially when you're eating. Choose the wrong music and you could get severe indigestion. Huh – see, did you ever think of that? D'you want to end up with a stomach ache?'

'All right, all right. Let's have Queen then – definitely goes with curry.'

'Are you sure? Because if it's the wrong choice . . .' He tailed off, looking at her, breathing hard. He seemed to have forgotten the rest of his sentence. He started chucking the CDs back under the table. Spun each one so that it hit the bottom of the wall with a satisfying thud. Once he had started, it seemed imperative that he give each case the same treatment. The trick was to get each CD to land on the pile. If he missed he had to start again. His jaw ached with concentration. As the last CD spun out of his hand he turned to face Jennah. She watched him, her folded arms resting on her knees, chewing the corner of her lip.

'*What?*' Flynn demanded, his voice sounding very loud.

185

'Nothing,' she replied.

Flynn looked around for the Queen album. Then he began to laugh. Jennah's eyes widened.

'Oh no, d'you know what I've done?' He was laughing so hard he could hardly speak.

Jennah smiled uncertainly.

'I've chucked the CD back under the table! Oh, shit, it's back to square one!'

'You know what, I'd actually rather we didn't listen to any music right now,' Jennah said suddenly. 'Why don't we go and see if Harry needs a hand?'

'No, no, come here, come here, you've got to come here—' He grabbed her arm and pulled her down onto the carpet beside him. 'You've got to help me find it. It could be anywhere. It could be right at the back. This could take a very long time—'

'I'll help you in a minute, OK?' Jennah said, pulling away. 'I'm just going to see Harry.'

Reluctantly, Flynn let her go and dived back under the table.

Sometime later, he felt someone kick his leg. He emerged from beneath the table to find Harry standing over him.

'I'm very busy,' Flynn replied. 'You'll be impressed. I'm arranging them alphabetically – by artist, not by title. Actually, by artist's last name, then first name, then title.'

Harry's eyes were narrowed. 'Why the hell are you

trashing the living room? We're about to sit down for dinner!' His voice sounded almost angry.

'OK, OK, I'll finish this later.' Flynn got up and followed Harry. But the thought of the half-finished pile of CDs made him feel on edge.

In the kitchen, Kate and Jennah were seated at the table, deep in conversation. They broke off quite suddenly as Flynn and Harry came in.

'Oh, wow, this curry smells of beer. What did you put in it, Harry?' The sight of the curry made him want to laugh again.

Harry gave a small sigh, raised his eyebrows and started to dish up.

'Who wants another beer? What are you girls drinking? *Coke?* Oh, for goodness' sake. Another beer, Harry?'

'No, thanks. And you'd better go easy, Flynn.'

'Why? I think being hungover for the concert tomorrow would be an excellent idea. What was it you said, Jen? Too hungover to care? But, hey, being drunk would be even better. Then I can roll my head and sway about like flaming André and I'll actually look the part!'

Kate laughed. Harry and Jennah did not.

'Oh, you two are unreal,' Flynn protested. 'So serious! It would be funny if I was drunk, wouldn't it, Kate? Then I'd trip on the steps, start playing "Chopsticks", and fall off the piano stool.'

'Tuck in, guys,' Harry said, passing out the plates. 'Don't let it get cold.'

187

'Yeah, cold beer curry, horrible!' Flynn exclaimed.

Harry gave him a long-suffering look.

The curry was actually quite nice, despite the beer. Kate started talking about some presentation she was giving at her Music Theory class the following week and Flynn struggled to suppress the urge to laugh. A sense of unreality had descended over him. The table, the meal, Harry, Kate and Jennah, the darkness gathering behind the half-open window, the muted strains of Mariah Carey on the stereo. He took a deep breath – how could he have considered leaving all this when there was so much? It was working, it was actually working – a wild sense of crazy well-being was shooting through him. Even though he was still on his first beer, he felt drunk – the kind of drunk that makes you want to climb onto the table and swing from the chandelier and sing and dance.

Jennah was talking, fiddling with a strand of long brown hair as she spoke. The deep flush of her lips stood out against her pale skin. Her knitted green jumper was a little too long in the arms, the sleeves almost covering her hands, the colour matching her eyes. She looked so beautiful, it hurt. How could he fail to embrace life, to absorb all this beauty, to revel in the fact that he was alive on this gentle evening in May with all his life ahead of him, stretching out like a blank canvas, waiting, ready . . . ?

Twenty-three hours to go; he had passed the

twenty-four-hour mark without even realizing it. But it was of little importance now, for the world was a stage and its people merely players. They were acting here, they would be acting tomorrow, and for every day that followed. Actors in a beautiful play – a play where life was good, a play that knew no fear, nor pain, nor sorrow. The despair could not touch him now, he would not let it touch him again. He would play the game, he would not seek more. This was enough, this was more than enough. He was lucky to be alive . . .

Harry put down his fork. 'I think I should propose a toast.'

They raised their glasses.

Harry's eyes met Flynn's and he gave him a little smile. 'To the worst kitchen assistant but undisputedly the RCM's greatest pianist, best of luck for tomorrow, not that you'll need it.'

'Cheers!' Jennah and Kate exclaimed together.

'Thanks,' Flynn said.

They put down their glasses and resumed talking again, but it was difficult to make out what anyone was saying. The air seemed to be filled with a loud, thick hum and the room had begun to blur around the edges. Flynn didn't seem to be able to distinguish what he had just been thinking from what he had just been saying. The thoughts and words and words and thoughts were getting all jumbled up in his head. Had he thought to himself that Kate was going to mess up her presentation or had Kate been saying she was afraid she was going to

189

mess up her presentation? Had he been thinking how much he wanted to kiss Jennah or had he told Jennah he felt like kissing her? Suddenly he needed to move, to get away, to knock over all these people and kick down the walls. But if he did that, then the ceiling would collapse and they would be crushed right here, where they sat. Great chunks of brick and plaster would come tumbling down – they would be knocked unconscious first, then covered with white powder as the blood ran down from their temples. Who would be the first to die? Flynn looked up at the ceiling. He realized that he didn't even need to move to make the walls crumble. His thoughts were powerful enough. The light shade had already started to sway.

Jennah touched his arm, making him jump. 'What are you staring at?'

He looked at her, his eyes wide. She was smiling, unaware, unafraid. He did not know how to tell her. Harry and Kate were talking blissfully. He did not want to scare them. He whispered something to Jennah.

'What?' With a tentative smile, she leaned in closer.

'I think we should go,' Flynn said.

A look of surprise. 'Where?'

'Next door. This room's not safe.'

Jennah started to smile, then stopped. 'What do you mean?'

He looked meaningfully up at the light shade and then back at her again. With a puzzled look, Jennah raised her eyes. The light shade continued to sway.

'Do you mean that light shade? I don't think it's going to fall, Flynn.'

Flynn gave a barely perceptible shake of the head. 'Not the light shade, everything.'

Jennah began to smile again. 'Is this your idea of a joke?'

'No, you've got to believe me. Come on, if we go the others will follow.' He got up and grabbed his plate and glass. Jennah stared at him, then slowly stood up too.

'Hey, where are you going?' Harry exclaimed.

There was a silence. Harry and Kate were staring at them. Then Jennah suddenly said, 'We thought we'd be more comfortable next door, it's – it's a bit cold in here.'

Harry looked disbelieving. 'Is that meant to be a hint or something?'

'No, no, you've got to come too,' Jennah said quickly.

Flynn could tell they were exchanging confused glances but he could not wait any more.

In the living room they gathered around the coffee table on the couch and armchairs, balancing plates precariously on their laps. Harry was looking perplexed and staring at Jennah. 'Shall I lend you a jumper or my jacket?'

'No, no – in here it's fine.'

If one ceiling gave way, wouldn't the next one fall too? Flynn looked up at the light shade. It was still. As he looked down, his eyes met Jennah's. She glanced away, but not before he had seen the fear in her eyes. She knew they were in danger too. He could not eat any more, adrenaline coursed through his veins. The orange glow of the streetlamps reached the tall windows. One more night. Would he survive? Could he survive? He might smash everything to pieces. He might just end it all, right here, right now.

Harry and Kate were chatting again. Jennah was gazing strangely at him, oddly subdued.

It's all right, he wanted to tell her, *we're safe in here. I won't knock down the walls.* But he was not, *could* not, be sure.

'So what are we up to tomorrow night?' Harry suddenly asked.

Jennah looked over at him. 'What do you mean?'

'Well, after the concert,' Harry explained. 'We're going to have to do something to celebrate, don't you think?'

'We could go to a club!' Kate exclaimed.

'Why don't we just chill out with pizza and a DVD?' Jennah suggested.

There was a pause. 'What do you want to do, Flynn?' Harry said.

Flynn shrugged. People, more people, but tomorrow would never come. They were talking about after the concert, not before it. The concert was the bridge. He would have to cross it in order to reach the other side.

'What if it goes badly?' he said suddenly. 'Then we won't have anything to celebrate.'

Harry looked up in surprise. 'It's not going to go badly.'

'You don't know that.' Harry's optimism was suddenly infuriating. 'What, do you have some kind of ability to see into the future? You actually have no idea how it's going to go, do you? You have absolutely no idea at all.'

'It's going to be fine,' Harry said.

'Stop saying that – you don't know!' He was aware of his voice beginning to rise. 'You don't know because it's got nothing to do with you! *You* don't have to do anything, *you* don't have to think about anything!'

'Hey!' Harry protested. 'What are you trying to—?'

'You're right, Flynn, he doesn't know,' Jennah said hurriedly. She took a deep breath. 'Harry just thinks – we all just think it's going to go well because we know how good you are. But you're right – we don't know what's going to happen. And if it doesn't go as well as you hoped, then we'll still celebrate. It's not as if any of us have ever been asked to play at the Albert Hall, so we'll still be impressed, whatever happens.'

Flynn felt the heat rush to his cheeks. 'But you won't be impressed, you won't be impressed!' He began to shout. 'The third movement is a complete mess. I've got no control – I let the music run away with me and my fingers can't keep up. You try and play a piece you're crap at in front of three thousand people! You try and *then* tell me what it feels like!'

'Flynn, I'm sure you're not—'

'No, no! Don't say I'm not crap at it because you

193

don't know, you don't bloody know! You're just saying what you think is the right thing to say, you don't care about the truth!'

'But I'm not – I didn't mean—' Jennah broke off suddenly, her eyes filling with tears.

'Leave it, Jen. He's going to go off on one whatever we say.' Harry's voice was infuriatingly measured. He put his hand reassuringly over Kate's.

'Don't bloody patronize me!' Flynn yelled at him.

'Back off, Flynn, you're so going to regret this tomorrow,' Harry said.

'You think I care about tomorrow? I don't give a shit about tomorrow! I don't give a shit about anything!'

'Fine. Then how about you stop shouting for a minute because at this rate you're going to give us all a headache.'

'Maybe you're just a bit nervous about the concert,' Kate suggested in a rather high-pitched voice. 'That's – that's normal.'

Flynn ran his hands savagely through his hair. 'I'm not nervous!' he shouted desperately. 'I'm not nervous about anything! I don't care about anything any more!' Furiously, he jumped up. He had to move, had to throw off this horrific feeling before it overpowered him again. 'Nothing matters,' he said, walking aimlessly around the room. 'You're wrong, you're wrong. Nothing matters!'

Jennah's face was pale. 'That's right, Flynn, it doesn't matter – nothing matters that much. Just don't think about it. You can only do your best.'

'My best, my worst, my in-between. Nobody knows, you don't know, I don't know.' He gave the bookcase a vicious kick and then another. 'It's up to the music – it's always up to the music!'

'Kate, Jen, why don't you go and finish eating in the kitchen,' Harry suggested, his voice infuriatingly calm.

The girls took their plates and left hurriedly.

'You hate me, don't you?' Flynn said raggedly. 'You hate me because that's the second time I yelled at you today.'

'No, I don't hate you. I'm just worried about you.' Harry leaned against the closed door, eyes wide behind his specs. 'What the hell is going on?'

'Why are you worried? You're thinking about tomorrow, aren't you? You're worried about tomorrow!'

'No, I'm worried about you right now!'

'Why? Why? What's going to happen to me right now? People are in danger, everyone's in danger all the time. I thought the ceiling was going to fall. It's not going to fall, is it? Because if it is, you've just told Jennah and Kate to go back into the kitchen and they'll be killed—' He paused, gasping for breath. 'And then if the ceiling collapses in there, we'll be next, d'you realize that? Do you? If one ceiling goes, they'll all go and we'll be crushed by the bricks and our skulls will be smashed to pieces and we'll all die!'

Harry moved towards him, hands raised. 'Jesus, Flynn, calm down. No one's going to die!'

'You don't know that! You're not God, you don't

know anything!' He had started to shout again, he could not help himself. The walls seemed to be closing in and everything seemed shrouded in a sinister haze. The blood burned in his face. It seemed impossible that any of them would survive. 'Nobody knows anything. We're all pawns in someone else's game! You can only pretend not to care, pretend not to care about anything! And it's all a lie – everything's just a lie!'

'Why don't you stop pacing and sit down for a minute?' Harry suggested. 'I'm going to give Rami a call—'

'Don't you dare do that again!' Flynn grabbed the phone out of Harry's hand and flung it against the wall before Harry even had time to begin dialling. There was an almighty crash.

Harry looked vaguely stunned. 'Don't get violent—' he began, his voice faltering. Then the door opened and Jennah appeared in the doorway, her eyes wide with fright.

'Oh God, Harry, what's going on?'

'I think you and Kate had better go.' Harry had his eyes on Flynn and did not turn round.

'I'm not getting violent!' Flynn shouted. 'That's only a phone, isn't it? It's a machine, it doesn't have feelings! Did it hurt you? Did I throw it at you? D'you think I'm going to hurt Jennah, is that why you want her to go?'

Jennah came in and quietly closed the door. She approached him slowly, arms by her sides. 'I know you'd never hurt me, Flynn. I know you'd never hurt anybody.

But why are you getting so angry, hey? We're all your friends here, we all care about you, we hate to see you so upset.' Her eyes were huge with concern, her face white.

Flynn stopped, leaning against the wall, breathing hard. He had ruined the evening, ruined his friendships, ruined everything. If he kept on going, he could ruin it all. Tomorrow would never come . . . He turned from them both, went over to the window and flung it open.

The evening breeze felt cool on his face, the sky was made up of shades of inky blue, the branches tinged with silver in the moonlight. He couldn't think any more, couldn't be. All he could do was shout, hurt, destroy. He wanted only to break down this interminable life, this excruciating existence, and shut out all the pain . . .

As he swung his legs over the windowsill, he heard Jennah scream.

Harry's hands grabbed him by the shoulders, dragging him backwards, down off the sill and onto the living-room floor. His head banged against a table leg. Harry gasped and grunted, wrestling him hard.

'Get off, get off!' Flynn yelled.

'Stop it! I'm going to punch you if you don't stop it!' Harry was shouting.

'Leave me alone, just leave me alone!' Harry had him pinned down with all his weight, and Jennah was sitting on his legs. He was nailed to the ground, cheek pressed against the carpet.

'Get off me!' Flynn raged. 'Let me go!'

'Kate, use the phone in the kitchen – that one's broken!' Harry shouted.

'What? Where? Who do I call – the police?'

'Speed dial seven, ask to speak to his brother, Rami. Tell him to come straight away.'

'No!' Flynn yelled.

Harry shifted his weight a little and Flynn tried to shove him off. Harry swore at him and sat on his back.

Kate returned a moment later. 'He's on his way,' she said shrilly. 'He said he was on call in north London so he wouldn't be long.'

Flynn struggled as hard as he could, gasping and grunting.

'Are you sure you're not hurting him?' Kate whispered.

'I don't care if I am!'

'What happened?'

'He's just being an idiot. Close that window, Kate.' Harry's voice shook.

There was the sound of the window closing.

'Are you OK, Jen?' Harry's voice again.

No reply.

'Jen?'

A muffled sob.

'His brother's a doctor,' Harry said. 'He'll know what to do.'

* * *

198

Sometime later the doorbell went. Kate's feet went to get it, Kate's feet returned with Rami's.

'What the hell's going on?' Rami demanded.

'They won't let me go!' Flynn yelled. 'Get them off me, Rami, get them off me!'

'Hold on, old chap. What on earth's going on, Harry?'

Whispering voices. 'Get off me!' Flynn raged.

More whispers. Then Rami's hand on the back of his head, Rami's face leaning down, wide-eyed, sweaty, a little out of breath.

'OK, listen, mate. I'm going to ask them to get off you on one condition. That you sit up and *only* sit up, not stand. If you stand up then both Harry and I will knock you to the floor and we'll have to start all over again.'

'Why?' Flynn yelled. 'Why?'

'It's for your own good. Now is that a deal?'

Flynn felt as if he were choking, desperate to get the weight off him. 'OK, OK!'

'I need you to promise, Flynn.'

'I promise!'

Rami straightened up and, a moment later, Flynn felt the weight lift from his back and legs. He struggled to get up but Rami held his wrist, pinning his hand to the carpet. Flynn threw himself backwards, banging his head repeatedly against the wall until Harry grabbed his shoulders to stop him.

'Leave me alone! Why can't you all just leave me alone?' Flynn screamed at them.

Rami was giving instructions to Jennah to find something in his medical bag.

'What are you doing?' Flynn yelled at him.

Rami was tearing something open with his teeth. 'I'm just going to give you a small shot.'

'You've got to be joking!'

'Nothing horrid, just to help you calm down,' Rami said, taking out a needle.

'No way! Get off me, I'll kill you!' He tried to get to his feet but, in an instant, Rami was behind him, pulling back his arms, forcing him onto his knees.

'Harry, grab his arm! Here, here, this one! Keep your hand still, Flynn, otherwise we'll have to pin you down again. I mean it!'

Flynn twisted his neck and looked desperately up at Harry, towering above him, his knee pressing against Flynn's back. Harry bit his lip and looked away. They had gone mad, all of them. They were ganging up on him. This was Harry's revenge and Rami was helping him. They must hate him, they must hate him so much. As he felt Rami grab his wrist, he let his head fall to his knees. The needle went in. It hurt, life hurt. He had failed. He wanted everything to end.

A long moment seemed to pass. The only sound was his own ragged breathing. He didn't lift his head from his knees. Maybe if he sat still for long enough it would all go away.

'OK, listen, this is what we're going to do,' Rami said at last. 'You're going to come downstairs, get into the car with me and we're going to drive back to Watford.'

Flynn lifted his head. 'No!' he began to protest.

'Actually, Flynn, this is not open to discussion. If you won't come back with me, I'll have to take you to hospital.'

'I'm not going to hospital,' he said desperately. 'You can't make me! Just let go of me, just leave me alone!' He tried to pull away, but his arms felt weak.

'Flynn, if we call an ambulance, they'll section you.'

'Why? They can't do that! They can't!'

'They can and they will because right now you're a danger to yourself.'

Flynn put his forehead back on his knees and bit his thumb hard. He just wished he could go back in time to before the argument, before the dinner, before Rami's phone call, before this morning's practice. How could the events of one day have ended in this?

'Don't call an ambulance,' he whispered.

'Are you going to come back to Watford with me?'

He nodded. Defeated.

The sides of the car were closing in. Flynn gripped the door handle as Rami drove on regardless.

'What is it now?' Rami asked.

'This car is going to crash.'

'No, it's not, we're perfectly safe,' Rami replied evenly. 'I'm a very good driver.'

'Can't you see that the sides are buckling?'

'They're not, you're just imagining things. Look outside, look at the lights, focus on the lights.'

Flynn pressed his forehead against the window and watched the streets flash by in a haze of orange lampposts, brightly lit restaurant interiors, blinding headlights and warm yellow windows. He unfocused his eyes, allowing the lights to blur like colours on a Catherine wheel.

Rami's house looked unfamiliar in the dark. He could not get out of the car.

'There's something wrong with my legs.'

'It's just the sedative. Come on, stand up – lock your knees.'

With a concentrated effort, Flynn pulled himself out of the car. The ground tilted dangerously.

'I'm going to fall, you know.'

'No, you're not, lean on me.'

Sophie looked startled to see them. 'I thought you were working very late tonight,' she said with a surprised smile. 'I was about to go to bed. Hello, Flynn, I haven't seen *you* for a while. Are you all right? You look—'

'Slight change of plan, Soph,' Rami said quickly. 'Flynn's not very well – I'm going to take him upstairs.'

Sophie shot Rami an alarmed, questioning look. Flynn sagged against the banisters. The walls were shaky here too. But Rami's hand was on his shoulder, propelling him up the stairs.

The guest room was canary yellow with daisies painted above the skirting board. They had bought matching curtains since Flynn had seen it last. He sat on the edge of the crisp sheet and put his head in his hands. Once in this position, he felt himself begin to tip forwards and had to put a hand on the carpet to stop himself from falling to the floor. 'Jesus, Rami, you've knocked me out,' he heard himself slur.

'I think you needed to be knocked out for a bit,' Rami said. 'Come on, get into bed.'

'I can't.'

He felt Rami pull off his trainers. 'Come on, you can do the rest. I'm going downstairs to see Sophie. I'll be up in a minute, OK?'

Flynn managed to nod and rolled onto his back as he heard Rami close the door. He stared up at the ceiling and slowly realized that for the first time in ages he was not thinking about very much at all. There were just two things he had to do – get undressed and get into bed. With heavy hands he unzipped his jeans. Kicking them off took an eternity and getting beneath the covers without actually standing up again was another monumental task. His body sank into the mattress; bed had never felt so good. But as he let his eyes close he felt the walls approaching. For a moment he could not reopen his eyes and terror flooded through him. As canary yellow filled his vision once again, relief descended.

Rami returned. 'Would you like a hot drink and would you like Sophie to make you a sandwich?' he asked.

Flynn shook his head.

'Are you sure?'

Flynn shook his head again. 'The walls here aren't very strong,' he mumbled.

'Don't start on that again. You know it's just in your mind,' Rami said quietly.

Flynn rolled onto his side and rubbed his eyes. 'Don't go.'

Rami shot him a look. 'Come on, you're exhausted and I've got to get up at seven. We'll talk tomorrow.'

'You've paralysed me.' His voice shook.

Rami smiled slightly. 'I haven't *paralysed* you. You're just reacting strongly to the drug because you haven't slept properly for days.'

'Don't go,' Flynn said again.

Rami sighed deeply and gave him a small smile. 'OK, let me get my newspaper and say goodnight to Sophie.'

Rami returned some time later carrying a small desk lamp, a mug and the newspaper. He plugged in the lamp, switched off the overhead light and sat against the wall, spreading the paper out over his knees. Then he looked up. 'Why are you still awake, matey?'

'I don't sleep any more,' Flynn whispered.

'Closing your eyes would be a good start.'

Despite his heavy lids, it did not appeal. The darkness held terrors, the walls would start approaching again.

'Rami?'

Rami lowered his paper and looked up. 'Mm?'

'I'm so sick of it.' He felt his throat constrict.

'I know. Things got too much. Sometimes that happens.'

'Not the concert – everything.'

'You're not well, Flynn. Don't worry about it now, we'll sort it out in the morning.'

'But I've really had enough.' It hurt to talk.

'Come on, you're exhausted,' Rami said. 'Things always seem worse at night. Just try and get some sleep.' His face looked drawn, his eyes worried and weary.

Flynn watched him as he returned to his paper and the contours of his face began to dance and fade. The bright yellow bulb of the desk lamp started to retreat like a setting sun. He knew his eyes were closing but he no longer had the strength or the inclination to stop them.

This is peace, he thought. This is the suspension of life, of feeling, of being. I have missed it so much.

CHAPTER TEN

Flynn had no idea how long he had been lying there, staring at the bright glow of the yellow curtains before realizing he was awake. It took him several more minutes to work out where he was and what he was doing there and to remember that today was the day of the concert and that yesterday something had happened that filled his brain with a deep, painful fog, causing his eyes to close and his thoughts to grind to a halt. Despite the strong feeling that he had been asleep for a very long time, he felt strangely weary and empty. He could tell that, behind the closed curtains, the sun was already high in the sky. He sensed that there was a lot to do – practise, a final run-through with the orchestra and, although he did not even know what time it was, it did not really seem to matter. He needed to pee, but getting out of bed would mean starting his day and he did not feel ready for that, not yet.

It was faintly reassuring to know that, beyond those curtains, people were rushing about, already well into their daily activities, while he was just lying here, still foggy with sleep, choosing to delay the point when he made the transition from night to day. His senses were still pleasantly numbed by his long night and for the moment he didn't care about very much at all. It seemed absurdly wasteful to be lying here when it was already so late and there was clearly so much to do, yet he continued to do just that, letting his eyes move slowly around the edges of the room, thinking how calm and uncluttered and peaceful it was.

Morning sunshine filled the kitchen like a scene from a family film, lighting up the beech cupboards and sparkling against the Formica. Sophie stood at the sink, broad-hipped and no-nonsense in black trousers and a floral blouse. She turned as the door hinge creaked, and smiled broadly, her auburn hair scraped back into a pony tail, her face pink and cheerful, her large collection of silver bangles jangling against her wrists. Rami had met her at Watford General four years ago. To this day, she was the only person in the world whose opinion seemed to matter to him.

'Hi, Flynn! Come in and have some breakfast.'

He struggled to meet her gaze, trying to banish thoughts of the night before, faintly horrified at the idea of what she must think of him. 'It's OK, I'm not really hungry.'

'Come and have some juice then. Sit down anyway.'

He got himself over to the kitchen table and sat, at a loss for anything better to do. She looked at him and his heart started to beat faster. He wanted to go back upstairs but it was too late – now he was trapped and there was no sign of Rami.

'Orange juice?'

He nodded. Sophie's smile was very bright but her eyes were watchful. She probably thought he was mad too, was waiting for him to lose it again. Despite the smell from the percolator filling the room, she had not offered him coffee, no doubt following Rami's instructions.

'Did you manage to get some sleep?'

Her tone was too gentle and he nodded, cringing inwardly, sipping his juice to give himself something to do.

'Rami's on call today. He had to go out suddenly but he should be back in about an hour.'

What was he going to do for an hour? Sophie must have sensed something because she added, 'You can call him on his mobile if you want.'

'It's OK.' He looked down at his glass and tried to concentrate on the specks of pulp floating just beneath the surface. There was a silence. Normally this was when Sophie would ask him about the Royal College, life in Bayswater, whether he and Harry were behaving themselves. Today she said nothing.

'Can I offer you some toast? You must eat something.'

'I'm really not hungry.'

She looked away, suddenly at a loss. He felt guilty for his lack of appetite.

'What you need is a good holiday,' she said suddenly,

smiling brightly again. 'Too much work and too little play – that's not right at your age! Have you got plans for the summer?'

'Not really.' He wished he had something more interesting to say.

'Spain's an affordable place for a summer holiday,' Sophie ploughed on. 'Have you found yourself a girlfriend yet?'

'No.' He gave a small smile to show that it did not matter, but a dangerous smile to warn her that she was not to pursue this particular topic of conversation. But Sophie's eyes just widened in surprise.

'Really? You *must* be working too hard then, Flynn. What's a drop-dead-gorgeous guy like you doing without a girlfriend? What about that pretty friend of yours I met at the Christmas concert – the flautist?'

He shrugged hotly. 'Just a friend.'

'Oh, shame, I told Rami I was sure something was going to happen there!'

Flynn stared down at the table, willing her to stop chatting. 'Can I go next door and watch TV?' he asked in desperation.

'Of course you can!'

'The concert!' Flynn jumped to his feet as soon as Rami walked through the door. 'I've got a lesson at one and a rehearsal at three.'

'I rang Professor Kaiser first thing this morning and told him you wouldn't be able to make the concert.'

Flynn stared at his brother, stunned. He knew he should care, but at this moment it seemed like too much of an effort. 'It's not a dentist appointment, I can't just cancel. What did Kaiser say?'

'He was fine about it, Flynn.'

'I don't believe you. What did you tell him?'

'I told him the truth,' Rami said.

Flynn continued to stare at him, his head beginning to throb. 'Jesus,' he whispered.

'Don't look at me like that. It's not the end of the world. I can't stop you from playing in the damn concert. If it means so much to you, you can always call him back. But I honestly don't think you're in the right frame of mind to go through with it tonight.'

Flynn's emotions were numbed. He knew he should be feeling horror and outrage at Rami's uninvited intervention but he only felt a strange sense of sadness. The fight had gone out of him.

'Do you know how many weeks of practice I've put in?'

'I do know and I think it's one of the reasons you're in this state now.'

'What about Mum and Dad?'

'I told them not to come, obviously.'

'Did you tell them why?'

'I didn't give them the details, Flynn, OK? Look, it's not such a big deal. There'll be other concerts – this one was not the be-all and end-all.'

Flynn felt a faint, distant spark of irritation at Rami's

210

flippancy. 'I'll never be able to see them again,' he said. 'I'll never be able to face Harry and Jennah again, d'you realize that?'

'Quit the melodrama. Of course you will.'

He let himself fall back onto the sofa. 'No, they think I'm insane. It'll be all around uni. Everyone will know there's something wrong with me.' The realization descended like an invisible weight and the inevitability of it filled him with a crushing sadness.

'Come on,' Rami said suddenly. 'I'm taking you out to lunch. And then we're going to pop by the hospital.'

Slowly, Flynn levelled his gaze with Rami's. His reactions were dulled – it was taking him an inordinate amount of time to think about anything. 'Why?'

'We need to try and sort you out, old chap.'

Getting in the car, sitting in traffic, talking to strangers, seemed way beyond his capabilities right now. He rested his chin back on his raised knee and returned his gaze to the television screen. 'I'm OK now,' he mumbled.

'That's debatable. Come on, get your shoes, it's a beautiful day.'

Flynn gave a faint shake of the head, his eyes fixed on *Trisha*.

'*Flynn.*'

'I'm not going.'

'You're not going to sit here like a vegetable all day, either. Come on, you *want* to feel better, don't you?'

'I don't care any more.' It was true. Happy or sad,

211

ecstatic or wretched, he just *was*. And that would continue till he died. He just had to find a way of coping with the time in between. The waiting.

Rami lifted the remote and switched off the television. Flynn found himself gazing at his distorted reflection in the black screen.

'Come on,' Rami said.

Flynn got up slowly, too tired to argue. He followed Rami out of the house and into the car. Rami turned on the stereo and rolled down the window. A warm summer breeze floated through. Everything was too loud, too bright; the roads too busy, the people too rushed. He felt as if he were in his own bubble, separated from everyone and everything by a transparent screen.

They sat outside a small café at a table set on the pavement. The Mediterranean feel to the busy high street, basking today in summer sunshine, jarred him. Rami tucked into a large plate of pasta while Flynn toyed with the garlic bread.

'Can you believe this glorious weather?' Rami was saying. 'It actually makes winter feel like a distant memory. I thought you were going to *eat* that.'

'You can have it.'

'No, I ordered the bread for you. Why don't you have a sandwich then?'

'Don't feel like it.'

'You're a nightmare to take out to lunch, do you realize that?'

Flynn smiled faintly.

Rami grinned back. 'Idiot.'

A silence. Then Flynn asked, 'Are you and Sophie, you know, happy together?'

Rami thought for a moment, then nodded. 'Yes, we are. Why?'

'Just wondered.'

'It's not always easy,' Rami went on. 'In fact, living with another human being can be bloody difficult. But you learn a lot – learn to compromise, learn to talk things through, learn to listen to each other. The rough times you learn to weather, and the good times can be pretty amazing.'

Flynn nodded and looked away.

'Is there someone you've got your eye on?'

'No.'

'Really?'

Flynn shrugged and chewed his thumbnail.

'Bet there are a lot of fit girls at the Royal College.' Rami gave a teasing smile.

Another shrug. 'What's the point?'

Rami smiled. 'You'll realize what the point is the first time you fall in love.'

'But what if she doesn't – you know—?'

'Feel the same way? Then you charm her, of course! Win her over!' Rami laughed.

There was a silence. Flynn scratched his cheek.

'Is that what's happening to you?' Rami asked.

'No . . . Dunno . . . Rami?'

'Yes?'

'Am I always going to feel like this?' He bit his tongue hard and stared at his plate.

There was a silence. Then, 'No, no, of course not, Flynn.'

Flynn looked at him, his eyes hot. 'How the hell do you know?' It hurt to talk.

'Because we're gonna get you better.'

'How?'

'By finding you an excellent psychiatrist.'

'So do you . . . do you think I'm going mad?'

A pause, a silence. Rami looked at him searchingly, suddenly serious. 'I'm not sure exactly what's wrong, mate.'

Flynn had his answer. He gave a small nod, managed a wry smile and looked away.

'Anyway, what does mad mean exactly?' Rami added quickly. 'Aren't we all a little mad? Don't we have to be somewhat mad just to go on living, to go on hoping?'

'That's not what I mean.'

'I know . . . I know what you mean. But madness is just a derogatory term for mental illness and mental illness affects a staggering twenty-five per cent of the population in this country. People just don't talk about it because it's got this stupid stigma attached to it and that's only because most of them don't understand it, and they're pathetically frightened of what they don't understand.'

'Do you think I'm mentally ill then?' Flynn persisted.

Rami hesitated, his eyes not quite meeting Flynn's. 'Well, I'm not a psychiatrist, I can't—'

'*Do* you?'

'I – well I think it's a possibility.'

Dr Stefan had the air of a man who had seen it all before. Rami had insisted that he was a first-class doctor and renowned as an excellent diagnostician. Flynn did not like him. He exuded an irritating aura of quiet, weary, unshakeable self-confidence. He used words sparingly. It was a shock for Flynn to find himself suddenly confronted by someone who spoke even less than he did. It threw him. Dr Stefan appeared to relish silences and felt no need to fill them. He asked questions and then sat back, fully prepared to wait as long as necessary for the answers.

Yet for some strange reason that he could not define, Flynn felt forced to take notice of him when he did talk. There was something so calm and deliberate about the man's tone that it made you sit up and listen. It was difficult not to respect him and impossible to ignore him. He looked unshockable. And perhaps it was this that caused Flynn to finally begin to talk, to start recounting the bizarre ups and downs of his recent life. Flynn talked to Dr Stefan because Dr Stefan looked as if he had all the time in the world and did not much care whether Flynn opened his mouth or not.

Soon, Flynn's life as he knew it had shrunk to almost nothing. He seemed to exist only within the constraints of his daily routine – the confines of his brother's house, the hospital café, the psychiatrist's office. After waking each day around twelve, the sun already high in the sky, he would meet Rami for lunch at the hospital, then go to his appointment with Dr Stefan, then take the bus back to the house to watch a diet of soaps and game shows until evening. There seemed little for him to think about and even less for him to do. He didn't even know if he liked it.

Every day Rami would ask him how he felt – sometimes he felt OK, or he felt lousy, or he felt nothing at all. The only thing he knew with any kind of certainty was that he could not go back to university, to Professor Kaiser, to Harry's flat and to his friends. He wondered if he could even call Harry and Jennah his friends any more: how would he ever face them again?

Rami and Sophie seemed to be taking turns doing hospital shifts. They couldn't always work like this or they would never see each other, so he guessed they were taking it in turns to babysit him. Flynn knew he should feel grateful, or at least touched by their concern, but instead he felt infuriated. It was difficult to understand how he could have failed so spectacularly at everything. Barely a year into university he had demonstrated catastrophically that he could not cope, not only with the pressures of playing but with the art of living. His body felt as if it had been hijacked by emotions he couldn't control, his life had turned into a joke and he felt afraid of all the things he had once enjoyed. He had tried to sort himself out but had failed, so now his only choice was to hand over to others. His life was no longer his own. And he couldn't understand where it had gone.

They sat side by side on the leather sofa, Mum nervously stirring her coffee, Dad looking uncomfortable against the brightly coloured cushions. Flynn sat opposite them in the armchair, toying with the remote control.

'I really think you should come home for a few days,' Mum said for the third time. 'Just to give yourself a rest from that university and that over-demanding professor.'

'He *is* having a rest,' Dad reminded her gently. 'He's staying here and Rami's got him seeing a good doctor.'

'Yes, but Watford's still almost London. It's all this fast-paced, hectic lifestyle—'

'He just needs a break from university for a while, and from the piano, both of which he's getting here,' Dad said. 'And Rami's found him a really good psychiatrist at his hospital.'

'But are you *eating* properly, are you *sleeping* properly? What brought all this on, Flynnie? Was it the concert?' Mum's face was drawn and she looked tired. She appeared a lot older suddenly, upset and bewildered. She was frightened, she didn't understand. They had never gone through anything like this with Rami. Rami had always been sensible, calm and independent. There had been no crises with Rami, so where had they gone wrong with Flynn? 'Did something happen?' Mum persisted. 'Is there something you're not telling us?'

Flynn whacked his knee repeatedly with the remote, refusing to look up, afraid that if he did he would start shouting at them and not be able to stop.

Dad laid his hand comfortingly over Mum's. 'Maybe this is something for Flynn to talk to the psychiatrist about. That's what the man's there for.'

'But we're his parents, Matti! What could have happened that is so bad he can't tell us?' There was a catch in her voice and Flynn forced himself to look up, flinching at the sight of the tears in his mother's eyes.

'Nothing happened, Mum. I just got over-tired, that's all.'

'But you've been very depressed! Rami said that you've been very depressed and when you came back for the weekend you couldn't stop talking about that concert!'

'I was just tired, that's all. I'd been working too hard and hadn't been sleeping enough.'

'But why were you having to work so hard? You're only eighteen! I blame the university – I blame that professor! That's why I never wanted you to go to music college – those sort of places are just forcing houses!'

'There's no point blaming anyone,' Dad said. 'These things happen. As Flynn says, he's just been working too hard and sleeping too little. At least he realizes it and is having a good rest now.'

* * *

'I think the time has come to start you on a course of medication,' Dr Stefan announced at the end of the following week.

Flynn gave him a look. 'Anti-depressants don't work.'

'Anti-depressants are very successful at treating depression,' Dr Stefan countered. 'But I'm not sure that you're just suffering from clinical depression, so I want to try you on something else. I think you would benefit from a mood stabilizer.'

'What's that?'

'It does what its name suggests. Helps regulate your mood swings.'

'So, I'm *not* depressed?'

'Not all of the time, no. It would appear that you're suffering from a form of bipolar disorder, Bipolar Two, which would account for your depression and many of your other symptoms.'

'Bipolar *what*?'

'Disorder. Commonly known as manic depression: fluctuations of mood, from severely depressed to, in your case, mildly manic. I could be wrong, but it looks that way to me.' Dr Stefan sat back in his chair, cleaned his glasses and glanced out of the window as if they were having a conversation about the weather.

Flynn stared at him, jarred.

'You seem to be rapid-cycling,' Dr Stefan went on. 'That means that your moods change very fast, within days, sometimes even hours. We'll need to carry on with our therapy sessions. Medication is rarely the answer on its own, but it should kick-start you into feeling better and we'll take it from there. I'm going to start you on some lithium. It can make you feel slightly unwell to begin with, a bit drowsy and nauseous, but that should soon wear off. I'll start you on a low dose and we'll build it up slowly and see how you get on.'

Rami had been on the phone for the last twenty minutes. 'Are you sure it's necessary?' he kept on asking.

Sprawled out on the sofa, arm behind his head, Flynn gazed at Chris Tarrant waving a cheque to his sweating contestant and tried to catch snippets of Rami's conversation with Dr Stefan. The prescription lay on the kitchen table. He'd had to give Dr Stefan permission to discuss his condition with Rami and now Rami was going on about the benefits of sodium valproate versus carbamazipine versus lamotrigine . . . For some reason he seemed thrown by the lithium.

Rami finally got off the phone, came back in and sat down next to Flynn's feet, running his hands through his hair in a gesture that Flynn had not seen since Rami's days at medical school.

'Which European city hosted the 1992 Olympic Games?' Flynn asked him.

'I dunno – Madrid?' Rami gazed unseeingly at the television screen. 'Well, Doctor Stefan seems pretty certain that lithium is the right drug for you, so perhaps you'd better give it a try—'

'It can't be Madrid, that's not one of the options.'

'I don't know then, but Flynn, listen—'

'It's Barcelona, I'm sure it's Barcelona. Oh no, the stupid woman's going to go for Berlin. *It isn't Berlin!*'

'Flynn, just listen a minute, will you?'

Flynn's smile faded. 'I *am* listening, but it isn't Berlin.'

'Did Doctor Stefan mention possible side-effects?'

'Yeah, feeling sick and feeling tired.'

'Well hopefully it won't be too bad but with all medication there are side-effects and the important thing is that you persevere. Doctor Stefan can always lower your dose if you're feeling bad but you have to give the drugs a chance – this kind of thing can take several weeks, even months, to have an effect, so you'll need to be patient.'

'Why were you asking Doctor Stefan about those other medications? What's wrong with lithium?'

Rami appeared to hesitate fractionally. 'It's – it's a powerful drug. It can be difficult to get the dosage just right and you'll need to go for regular blood tests to check the lithium levels in your blood. The therapeutic level is often precariously close to the toxic level and the side-effects can be pretty lousy to start with.'

'What if it doesn't work?'

'Then he'll try you on something else. There are other mood-stabilizers, not just lithium.'

'What if the other stuff doesn't work? What if nothing works?' It was an effort to keep his voice steady.

'There are lots of different medications out there.

Sometimes it's a question of trial and error. You try one thing, then you try another. You lower the dose or increase the dose or you try different combinations. But lithium works for most people, Flynn. I'm hopeful it will for you.'

'What if it's not bipolar disorder? What if it's something else? What if it isn't an illness at all? What if it's *just me*?'

'Doctor Stefan knows what he's talking about, Flynn. It fits. To be honest, bipolar was something that crossed my mind too.'

Flynn glared angrily at his brother. 'That's stupid. I'm never manic.'

A small smile touched Rami's lips. 'Not now you're not. But you can get pretty hyped up. You're just not aware of it. According to Harry, you stay up all night composing, you go running for miles and miles, you practise for days on end—'

'That's just energetic and inspired!' Flynn protested.

'Well, you're more energetic and more inspired at times than most people. Put it that way.'

'So I *am* mad.'

Rami seemed to hesitate for a moment, then his face broke into a smile and he ruffled his brother's hair. 'Mad as a hatter,' he said. 'Always have been.'

And so he started taking lithium, that warm evening in May, at his brother's house in Watford, sitting on the edge of the bath with a tooth-glass in his hand, gazing down at the white pill nestling in his palm. He was supposed to have been playing in a high-profile concert, was supposed to have been out celebrating with his friends, was supposed to be a student in London and out partying every night. But instead here he was, diagnosed with a mental illness, taking pills to try to regain his sanity, and normality, as he knew it, had disappeared.

Flynn watched the last blob of butter melt on his toast and steadied his head on his hand. He was aware of Rami and Sophie watching him covertly across the table but could not bring himself to take a bite or even think of an excuse to get out of the kitchen. Day five of the lithium diet and things had not got any better. His face had a heavy-lidded, puffy look of resigned exhaustion and the sight of food turned his stomach. He wanted nothing more than to crawl back into bed.

'Just try and eat half of it,' Rami was saying. 'Half a slice of toast is not going to make you throw up.'

Flynn shook his head faintly, struggling to keep his eyes open.

'When are you going back to see Doctor Stefan?' Rami asked.

'Dunno.'

'What d'you mean, you don't know? You must have made an appointment with him!'

Flynn rubbed his face. 'Just leave me alone, Rami.'

'Why don't we all go for a walk?' Sophie chipped in brightly. 'It's a beautiful day!'

He went to the park with them because he did not have anything better to do. The sun was high in the sky, filling the air with a bright, white light. It was supposed to be summer now and there were boys in shorts sailing boats on the lake, little girls in summer dresses pushing dollies in prams, and pregnant mums in flip-flops waddling after toddlers playing in the sand.

Sophie, holding Rami's hand and swinging his arm exuberantly, suggested they have an ice cream. Rami resembled an American tourist in his khaki shorts and stripy T-shirt with his sunglasses hanging off his collar, carefree and smiling. Flynn could only think how he was spoiling their rare day off together and wished he could just disappear.

He felt cold despite his thick jumper and could not stop shivering. He was a mess: everything about his dishevelled, drugged, unhappy appearance was an embarrassment; he was a misfit and an eyesore in this whole happy-clappy scene. Rami and Sophie only wanted him to lighten up, smile occasionally, chat to them and try to act vaguely normal, tasks which seemed completely beyond his reach. An impenetrable fog seemed to encompass him, rendering even the simplest functions – standing, walking, looking, listening – unbearable. He craved the shelter of the car. Better still, the hideout of his bed – a bunker and a safe house against the harsh sun, the blue sky and the loud, bright-eyed people spilling out of everywhere, filling the park with their tangible, boisterous happiness.

They sat down on a bench, watching the remote-controlled boats weaving around the ducks on the pond. 'Shall I get you a hot drink to warm you up?' Rami asked.

Flynn shook his head. His shivering had intensified, but he could not tell whether he was feeling cold or just frightened by the sight of all these people, all this life, reinforcing the aching emptiness he felt inside. Rami got up to get coffees for himself and Sophie while Flynn, elbows on knees, continued to stare at the sunlight dancing on the water, the little wavelets lapping against their concrete shore. He flinched at the touch of a hand on his back.

'It *will* get better, you know,' Sophie said.

He rubbed his cheek in embarrassment, jarred by her show of concern.

'The first few days on a new drug are always horrid but the side-effects will have worn off by next week and then I'm sure you'll begin to feel yourself again.'

Flynn forced a wry smile. 'That's hard to imagine.'

'You'll be back at uni in no time and it will be as if none of this had ever happened.'

Flynn continued to rub his face. He doubted that somehow.

'I know Rami can be a bit of a pain sometimes,' Sophie went on doggedly, 'but he's a good brother to have in a crisis. He'll drag you to all the top doctors in the country until you feel better again. He won't give up till you're back to your usual, cheerful self . . .' A pause. 'He adores you, Flynn.'

Two small boys were trying to fix a propeller on their motorboat with a piece of string. The younger one held it in place while the older one carefully tied the string into a single knot, his eyes narrowed in concentration. Flynn stared at them, biting his tongue against the threat of tears.

At the end of the week he went for a blood test. Rami drove him to the hospital and sat with him in the waiting room, because he was likely to get lost just walking down a corridor. They had to wait for nearly an hour. Rami read the paper. Flynn stared at the top right-hand corner of a black square of lino. When his name was called, Rami had to nudge him.

The nurse was talkative and irritating. She put the needle into his left arm but couldn't get at the vein. She put the needle into his right arm with no success either. Then she made some joke about him not having any veins as she tried taking blood from the vein on the back of his hand. As the nurse inserted the needle, the dark red blood finally shot up the thin tube.

This sucks, Flynn thought. This really sucks.

CHAPTER ELEVEN

'Harry called again.' Rami lowered his paper as Flynn walked through the door, dropping his rucksack to the floor and collapsing into the armchair. 'That's the third time this week,' Rami added.

Flynn let his head fall back and rubbed a hand over his damp, burning face. 'It's boiling outside!'

'You've been here almost a month. He's going to think I'm keeping you hostage. Perhaps you should call him back.'

'It's too hot. I don't like it here when it's hot. England's supposed to be a cold country.'

'Shut up about the weather for a minute and listen to me. Are you going to call him back?'

Flynn sat up reluctantly and began untying his laces. 'I don't like speaking on the phone.'

'Then go and see him. Jennah's been trying to contact you too. Perhaps you should go back for a bit. Sounds like they're missing you.'

Flynn's eyes narrowed in annoyance. 'Don't be stupid.'

Rami sighed and folded his paper. 'Flynn, it's been

nearly a month. You're only seeing Doctor Stefan once a week now. Don't you think it's time you tried going back to uni?'

Flynn felt his pulse quicken. 'What?'

'Don't look at me like that. You know Sophie and I love having you here. And you can always come and stay whenever you want. But I can see you're beginning to get bored. You have your own life – the Royal College, your music, your own flat, your friends . . . Don't you miss all that?'

'No.'

'Are you worried things are going to go back to how they were before?'

'No.'

'Because they won't, Flynn. You're better now, you're far more stable. You're being treated for bipolar, you're on medication, going to therapy. You don't need to hide out here any more. I think you're well enough to go back.'

Flynn stared at him hotly, trying to come up with a reply that would not brand him in the role of clinging younger sibling. There was a silence.

'Are you worried about your friends' reactions?'

Flynn flushed at his own transparency. 'No.'

'Harry and Jennah know about the bipolar, Flynn.'

'*What?*'

Rami cleared his throat, looking slightly uncomfortable. 'You know that they called several times asking to speak to you. They've been very concerned about you, obviously. You were really unwell at that point, so I had to explain.'

'You didn't have to! You could have said I had glandular fever or – or *something*!'

'I don't think they would have bought that, not after the episode with the window. It's better they know the truth.'

Flynn ran his hands through his hair distractedly, mind reeling. 'Jesus, Rami! They'll think I'm mad! They'll think – they'll think—'

'They'll think you've been ill, which you have,' Rami said quietly. 'It'll be all right.'

They manoeuvred into an unlikely parking space, just metres from the front door, and sat in silence, engine still humming. 'D'you want me to come in with you?' Rami asked.

'No.'

'OK, I'll pick you up on Friday for your appointment with Doctor Stefan and you can come back and have dinner with us afterwards.'

Flynn nodded, gnawing his thumbnail.

Rami dug into his pocket and pulled out four crumpled £20 notes. 'Here's some cash to keep you going. Try at least to remember to eat.'

'Thanks.'

Rami gave him a playful shove. 'Sod off then!'

The flat was empty. It was Sunday afternoon so Harry

was probably out with Kate. Flynn didn't know if he felt disappointed or relieved. But as he put the key in the lock and heard Rami drive off behind him, a wave of abandonment washed over him, like being left on the first day of school. He found himself walking aimlessly around the living room and kitchen, his heart thudding, quickly averting his eyes from the pile of letters addressed to him on the counter. He was afraid he was going to lose it again. The kitchen phone had been removed from the wall. He found it in the living room, in the place of the one he had broken. The closed piano lid looked dusty and the sight filled him with fear. He had no idea what to do. At Rami's he hadn't been doing anything much, but he couldn't do 'nothing much' here. The end-of-year exams were only a few weeks away and the closed piano lid was like an accusing scream.

Harry stopped dead in the doorway, keys dangling from his hand, his face breaking into a slow grin.

'Blimey, it's you!'

Flynn smiled self-consciously. 'Hi.'

Brushing the hair from his eyes, Harry perched on the arm of the sofa, staring at Flynn and still grinning. 'I didn't know you were coming back today. This is a surprise! We were beginning to wonder whether we'd ever see you again! Rami hasn't been volunteering much information.'

Flynn could not think of anything to say.

'Hey, it's good to have you back. The flat's been lonely without you and Aural's been seriously dull without you there to wind up Peterson.'

Flynn smiled faintly.

'Are you OK now?' Harry asked, suddenly looking uncomfortable.

'Yeah.'

Harry was examining the floor. 'Rami mentioned that you . . . that you'd been ill . . . Anyway, I'm just sorry that I didn't realize . . . a-and that I wasn't any help.' He glanced up awkwardly, then jumped up. 'Hey, shall I call Jennah? She's been asking me every day if I've heard from you.'

'OK.'

Harry bounded off into the kitchen. Flynn sat back and switched on the TV. Perhaps it wasn't so bad to be back after all.

He came out of his stupor but found himself in an area he couldn't quite define. Had the despair lifted or had he simply entered a realm where every emotion was dulled and every painful thought was hijacked as it went through his mind? The torpor of depression had somehow lifted, but he wasn't back in the real world yet. This seemed to be some kind of temporary stage, like that transition between sleep and wakefulness, where the emotions all ran together and thoughts had their own absurd logic. His mind felt sluggish yet anaesthetized and his thoughts had slowed but were still tinged with darkness. He had crawled out of the abyss, for now at least, but still had a way to go.

At university, people he barely knew came up to ask him how he was feeling. No one mentioned the concert, not even Professor Kaiser. The Rach Three was abandoned and they went back over some old Mozart. Harry gave him a pile of photocopies. Lecturers were exceptionally nice to him. Everyone was talking about exams. Flynn continued taking his lithium. It was working, Dr Stefan said. Flynn no longer felt like running in the middle of the night; no longer tried to write operas. Nor did he want to knock himself out with alcohol and sleep all day. He was able to go through the motions of being a normal student for the first time in ages. But he felt dead inside.

BrainTeaser seemed to hold a new fascination. As dry and repetitive as it was, it allowed him a certain refuge from the jarring emotions of the soaps or the bolshie glitz of the pop-star wannabes. It permitted him to remain in his torpor, hypnotized by the scrambled letters . . . Flynn could not remember ever having watched so much TV before, apart from when there had been some big sporting event on perhaps, but since his stay with Rami he seemed incapable of doing much else. There seemed little point in practising now, not just some silly little Mozart pieces, neither was he particularly interested in reading through Harry's huge pile of notes. Running was out of the question – his first day back at the Royal

College had left him feeling utterly drained. Exhaustion pressed down on him like a powerful, invisible force and even sitting up had become an effort.

On the phone, Rami kept assuring him that the exhaustion was a side-effect to the lithium which would soon wear off, but it was impossible to know where the depression ended and the lithium began. So much for the wonders of modern medicine. Rami kept insisting he had to give it time, but Flynn couldn't help wondering if he would ever feel normal again. The feelings of panic and horror seemed to have dulled but he felt as if he were only barely existing. Everything had become an unbearable effort, even thinking, while Harry rushed around infuriatingly, bouncing from one activity to the next in a tireless whirl of energy. In the hour since his return he had managed to cook himself dinner, eat it while retelling anecdotes from his day, wash up humming to the radio, call Kate for twenty minutes and had now started cello practice in his bedroom. During this time, Flynn had remained glued to the sofa.

BrainTeaser ended; a kids' cartoon began. Flynn could not be bothered to lean forwards and pick up the remote from the coffee table.

Harry returned, loosening his bow. 'I'm going to meet Kate and some friends down at the pub. Coming?'

'No, thanks.'

'Go on. Half an hour?'

Flynn gave Harry a look, astonished that Harry

should think he might possibly change his mind. Obviously Harry did not realize that only holding a gun to Flynn's head could have made him walk out of that door.

'For goodness' sake!' Harry exclaimed. 'Aren't you bored out of your mind, just watching TV all day?'

Flynn shrugged. 'Beats anything else.'

Harry let out his breath and shook his head in a gesture of defeat. He put on his jacket and left. Flynn returned his gaze to the television screen.

By Thursday, Flynn had his television viewing all planned out before he had even left class. By mid-afternoon it was all he could think about – longing to be half lying on the sofa, feet up on the coffee table, channel-surfing his way through the evening, cocooned away from all the talk and music and exam papers and practice, from prying questions and false concern and fake friendships, from the noise and rush and clatter that seemed to fill the outside world. It exhausted him, all of it. His own company was as much as he could bear.

'Did you ask Doctor Stefan whether he would consider cutting your dose before your exams?' Rami asked him over dinner on Friday.

'Yeah,' Flynn replied, his mouth full.

'And?'

Flynn swallowed. 'He said he would look into it if I didn't go high before the end of the month.'

'OK, well that's something.'

'I don't want him to cut the dose,' Flynn said acidly. 'I want to stop taking the bloody stuff altogether.'

'Lithium is a tricky drug to prescribe,' Sophie said. 'If the dose is too high it can completely muffle you and make you feel exhausted but if the dose is too low then all your symptoms can come back. I expect the psychiatrist will have to do a bit of fine-tuning before he finds exactly the right level.'

'Great,' Flynn said sarcastically with his mouth full again.

'Well at least it's not affecting your appetite any more!' Rami exclaimed.

Saturday afternoon was all football and racing. At least it made a change from *Blue Peter* and *Newsround*. It was almost four and Flynn had only been up for a couple of hours, sprawled on his front in his T-shirt and tracksuit bottoms, the sunlight plunging in through the open window. Harry burst in from orchestra practice – loud, sweaty, breathless from lugging his cello up the stairs.

'More TV?' he said, a hint of exasperation in his voice.

'Better than bloody orchestra,' Flynn muttered, returning his gaze to the screen.

'That's debatable,' Harry replied, sitting on the keyboard stool and yanking off his trainers. 'Oh, come on, let's *do* something. Kate's away all weekend so you've got to keep me company! Let's – let's go to the lido!'

'You've got to be kidding.'

'OK, I know, let's have a game of pool!'

'I'm *not* going outside,' Flynn said in a voice that left no room for argument.

'Oh, for fuck's sake!' Harry suddenly shouted. 'It's a beautiful day! How can you just sit there?'

Flynn glowered at him.

'Isn't your medication supposed to be working by now? I know Rami said that the lithium would take a couple of weeks to get you back to your normal self but you're still exactly the same as before!' Harry's cheeks were flushed suddenly.

'This *is* my normal self,' Flynn said drily. 'The bloody lithium's not going to change my personality, for Christ's sake.'

Harry stopped. 'This isn't your normal self,' he said quietly.

'How do you know? Who the hell said it was up to you to decide who I am and who I'm—'

'OK, OK.' Harry held up his hand and backed out of the doorway. 'Excuse me for talking. Enjoy your evening. Don't do anything too wild.' He slammed out of the room.

But sometime later that evening, as Flynn was dozing off in front of a re-run of *Friends*, Harry came in with Jennah, brandishing DVDs. 'I figured that since you've become such a slob, we might as well join you,' he said.

Flynn looked at Harry over the back of the couch. He wore a sheepish, lopsided smile, and Flynn knew that this was his way of trying to make up. Harry never stayed angry for long. But Flynn almost wished that he had – Jennah's sudden appearance jarred him and even spending the evening watching DVDs with them seemed like a monumental effort.

Jennah laughed. 'I think everyone needs to slob out once in a while.'

'Well, once in a while maybe, but the Slob King here has taken it to an entirely new dimension.' He grinned at Flynn's scowl.

Jennah laughed again. Her hair looked different, slightly curly with a strip of burgundy material tied around her head. Small diamonds hung from her ears. She looked like she might be wearing make-up. Flynn peeled himself off the couch and busied himself with cold drinks and snacks.

'So what DVDs did you get?' Harry asked Jennah.

Jennah reached into her bag. 'Well, I couldn't find a compromise. So in the end I got *Bridget Jones: The Edge of Reason* for me and *The Matrix Revolutions* for you guys.' She held them up proudly.

'Oh, you star, I never got round to seeing *The Matrix Revolutions*!' Harry exclaimed.

'God, I knew you'd say that. Back me up, Flynn. You'd rather watch *Bridget Jones*, right?'

Flynn smiled and shrugged awkwardly.

237

'Don't be stupid, that's a chick-flick!' Harry exclaimed.

'Well I think since I'm the guest and, more to the point, since I'm the one who actually got them out, I should decide,' Jennah declared.

'And I think that since I will no doubt be returning them, as well as *paying* for them, *I* should decide,' Harry countered.

Jennah narrowed her eyes playfully. 'Oh, listen to spoiled little rich boy.'

'We're going to watch them both so what difference does it make?' Harry argued.

'Exactly. We may as well start with *Bridget Jones*.'

'Or *The Matrix*.'

They looked at each other and started to laugh.

'Flynn's going to have to decide – there's no other way,' Jennah declared.

Harry held up the two DVDs. 'Go on then,' he said.

'I don't mind,' Flynn said, turning away.

'You have to help us out or it'll come to blows!' Jennah exclaimed.

'*Bridget Jones* then,' Flynn said, and disappeared into the kitchen.

'Traitor!' Harry called after him.

Rinsing his glass pointlessly in the sink, Flynn breathed deeply, trying to quell a mounting knot of frustration. Why was it that whenever Jennah came round, Harry always turned into this entertaining charmer and he into a monosyllabic idiot? It was always the same! The more gregarious and expansive Harry became, the more tongue-tied and awkward *he* did. And now things were even worse because Jennah thought of him as some kind of freak. No doubt she was waiting for him to start raving on about falling ceilings or jump out of the window. They were both waiting for him to lose it again.

When he returned to the living room, Harry had taken up residence in the armchair, legs slung over the armrest, watching the trailers.

'I hope this is *Bridget Jones*,' Jennah said.

'Would I dare put on anything else?' Harry pulled a cushion out from behind his back and placed it strategically behind his head. 'Wake me up when it's over.'

Flynn sank back into the sofa, grateful for the opportunity to sit in front of the TV again. But Jennah's presence beside him was an obstacle to total immersion. The brush of her bare arm against his as she reached for her glass, her small explosions of laughter at each funny line . . . She was so – well – reactive. The small sounds that escaped her, betraying her every emotion, were more riveting than the film itself. Pizza arrived and Flynn was grateful for the distraction. By the time Renée Zellweger and Colin Firth were left snogging in front of the courtroom, dark was falling outside.

By then, though, it was almost twelve and no one felt much like watching *The Matrix*, not even Harry. He hung upside down off the side of the armchair, complaining about his back.

'Coffee, anyone?' Flynn asked.

'Yes, please,' Jennah replied.

'Harry?'

'No, I'm knackered. I'm going to hit the sack. Jen, I take it you're spending the night?'

'I'll get the night bus—'

'Don't be daft. You can have the couch.'

'OK. Thanks.'

Flynn went to make coffee in the kitchen.

'Night, Flynn!' Harry called from the hallway a moment later.

Jennah was sitting on the opened-out sofa bed in one of Harry's oversized T-shirts when Flynn returned. He handed her a cup, glanced away from the unnerving expanse of leg and, after a moment's hesitation, sat down on the piano stool.

There was a moment's silence. 'Flynn?'

'Yes?'

'I owe you an apology.'

He looked at her in surprise. 'What for?'

'I didn't realize . . . Even though we talked and stuff, I didn't realize you were feeling so bad . . . I didn't even realize you were ill . . .'

Flynn shook his head quickly, embarrassed. 'Oh, forget about all that—'

'The night of the dinner party, I couldn't stop crying,' Jennah said. 'I felt so guilty.' There was an awkward silence. Then she gave a small smile. 'Didn't your mother ever teach you not to make girls cry?'

240

Flynn gave her a look. 'No. Just not to get them pregnant.'

Jennah started laughing. Then she said, 'I miss you, Flynn.'

He raised his eyebrows.

'I mean I miss *you*, the non-depressed, non-silent you. I miss the way you get excited about crazy things and get all worked up about, I dunno, a piece of music. I miss how we were when we went on holiday, just mucking around and cracking each other up and laughing at Harry. Remember the time when Harry wanted to buy some stamps and we told him the word for stamps was *vache* and so he walked into the corner shop and asked the shopkeeper for a cow?'

Flynn started to laugh. 'God, we were silly.'

'But happy,' Jennah said.

Flynn stopped laughing. 'Yeah.'

'I miss that,' Jennah said.

'Me too.'

'How are you finding university?' was the first question Dr Stefan asked on Friday.

Flynn gave an exaggerated shrug. 'Fine. Nothing much happened this week. I managed to act fairly *normal.*' He laughed. Dr Stefan did not. Flynn started to bite his thumbnail.

'How does it feel to be back at your flat?'

He shrugged again. 'OK.'

'What about your music practice?'

'It's OK too.'

241

'You're going to have to do better than that.'

Flynn gave an exaggerated sigh. 'Uni's OK – we've only got revision lectures now and I'm managing to catch up. Professor Kaiser's easing off on the practice because of exams.'

'What about your friends?' Dr Stefan asked.

'What about them?'

Dr Stefan adopted an expression of weary patience. 'How did you feel about seeing them again?'

Flynn pulled down the corners of his mouth. There was a silence. Dr Stefan watched him.

Flynn shrugged.

Dr Stefan continued to watch him. Flynn began to flounder. He glanced at Dr Stefan, then glanced away again.

'It doesn't have to be this difficult,' Dr Stefan said quietly.

'What do you want me to say? It was fine!'

'Before you can begin to recover, Flynn, you need to feel,' Dr Stefan said quietly. 'By pushing your feelings aside, you're denying yourself the very essence of who you are. You sit there and tell me about your week as if you are talking about somebody else. In an attempt to cope with your own life, you plunge from hyperactivity to depression without any idea of the feelings that have caused you to feel like this in the first place.'

There were children, children and whole families, strolling across the grass with babies in buggies or kids on bikes. Flynn found himself watching them covertly, especially the children. There were two boys on bikes who couldn't have been more than seven or eight. Perhaps they were brothers. They looked so happy. From this brief snapshot their childhood seemed idyllic and Flynn wondered whether he and Rami had appeared that happy at their age. Had they mucked about with bikes and footballs and sticks? Of course they had – Dad was always taking them to the local park and he remembered being given his first bike when he was three. They must have appeared as happy and as carefree as those boys, back then. So why did he watch these children play and feel such sadness? Was it because he was looking at something he'd once had – living in the moment, finding excitement in the little things, feeling safe and loved? Would he ever feel like that again? And why, if this had once all been his, had he turned into the miserable wreck that he was now?

It was almost inconceivable that there had been a time, only last summer, when he had gone backpacking across France and Italy with Harry and Jennah, sleeping on dodgy youth-hostel mattresses and crying with laughter at Harry's deplorable French accent. There had been sunburned arms and blistered feet, endless maps, condom jokes, truth-or-dare on long train journeys, ganging up on Harry to try to embarrass him ... *Was I really there?* he wondered. *Could that really have been the same me?*

* * *

He walked in the park in the evenings to catch that hour when day turns into night – black trees silhouetted against a turquoise sky, the blanket of cloud turning into soft pink fields and hills, illuminated by the dying sun. This was the only time he knew what heaven must look like; the only time he believed heaven existed and he wished he could be transported up there to walk across those fields of clouds, towards the sinking sun. The soft breeze smelled of summer, lifting his shirt and stroking his skin and wrapping itself around the trees. In the surrounding streets, he found himself glancing through windows at living rooms and kitchens, all looking so comfortable, so welcoming, so tidy, and he wished he could go in and be part of those houses, those lives, those families. It was not as if he didn't have his own home to go to, his own family to care about, so it made no sense. But it was as if stepping into another house would mean he could be somebody else for a while, live another life and escape himself.

I would give anything to escape myself, Flynn thought, just for a day, just for a minute even. Just to know what it was like to think differently, to feel differently, and to not be me.

And the lithium continued to wear him down, slowing his fingers, his thoughts, his mind. Professor Kaiser tolerated his sluggish playing with some kind of bewildered horror, Harry got used to him as a permanent fixture on the couch and Rami called every week to check up on him. The crooks of his elbows were bruised purple and yellow from the weekly blood tests. And despite what Dr Stefan had said, there didn't seem to be any emotions to run away *from* any more; he felt nothing but a dull sort of apathy, a meaningless void, empty of both pleasure and despair.

'I want to stop taking this,' Flynn announced the following Friday morning. He had been rehearsing that one line all morning, preparing to deliver it in a firm yet reasonable tone. He glared at Dr Stefan, his jaw set, trying to gauge his reaction, ready to fire a counter-attack against any words of persuasion. But Dr Stefan adjusted his glasses, sat back and said nothing.

'I feel sick all the time, I can't think, I can't read, I can't even follow a TV programme. It's like I'm retarded or something. And I'll never, *ever* be able to play the piano again, so what's the point? I may as well be crazy like before!' He had vowed to stay calm but now his voice was rising and he forced himself to stop, breathing hard. Please, he wanted to say. *Please* tell me I don't have to keep taking this. *Please* tell me there's another way, an easier way for me to feel normal again.

'I can't make you take lithium,' Dr Stefan replied in his deliberately slow way. 'But I am going to ask you to, just till the end of the month. Then, if you're still feeling tired, we'll talk about lowering your dose back down again.'

'Why?' Flynn almost shouted. 'It's not working! I feel worse, not better! I look like a zombie!'

'That's how most people feel when they first take lithium,' Dr Stefan answered calmly. 'With any new drug, it takes the body time to adjust. But your body will adjust and, when it does, the side-effects will begin to wear off and the lithium will begin to take effect.'

'How do you know? You said lithium didn't work for some people. It's not working for me!'

'Till the end of the month,' Dr Stefan said evenly. 'If there's no change by then, we'll try cutting the dose.'

'That's another ten days! What do you care – you're not the one taking it! That means I have to endure another ten days of hell, walking around like an idiot, bumping into things, forgetting the end of my sentences, feeling only half-alive! How am I supposed to believe this is going to work if it makes me feel like this? Why should I believe a word that you say?'

Dr Stefan smiled slightly. 'Because, Flynn, this is the most animated I've ever seen you. I would venture to say that you're beginning, just *beginning* to see the light at the end of the tunnel.'

Flynn narrowed his eyes in contempt. 'Well if that's the case, then, to quote Robert Lowell, it must be the light of the oncoming train.'

Dr Stefan threw his head back and roared with laughter.

Later that evening while he was watching *Coronation Street*, there was the sound of the key in the door. Voices in the hall. Flynn felt himself tense. Then Harry and

Jennah burst in, loud and merry from an evening spent in the pub.

'Here's square-eyes!' Harry exclaimed.

Flynn sat up reluctantly.

'How's it going, couch potato?' Jennah sat next to him and teasingly ruffled his hair. She pulled out a six-pack from a plastic bag. 'Look, we decided if you wouldn't come to the party, we'd have to bring the party to you!'

Flynn hunched forwards, elbows on his knees, and rubbed his eyes, unable to say anything for fear of sounding ungrateful. He wished they would just leave him alone with his TV programmes. They should have stayed at the pub in the company of others, having a good laugh, doing their own thing. He didn't want their pity. He couldn't stand this.

'We've got a pizza in the fridge,' Harry was saying. 'I think I need some food to soak up the booze. Who's hungry?'

Flynn stood up quickly. 'I'll leave you to it,' he said. 'I've – I've got revision to do.'

Jennah jumped up and blocked the door. 'No way, it's Friday night!' she exclaimed. 'Anyway, since when have you turned into a swot?'

Harry laughed.

Flynn backed away from them both and sank back down on the couch, defeated, too tired to protest. It was an effort to think. Getting out of the living room suddenly seemed impossible. All he knew was that he could not be around people right now, could not think of a single thing to say, could not bear to have to smile and look happy and interested and understanding. Harry and Jennah were loud and exhausting . . . This whole room was exhausting. He just wanted his bed . . .

'Wake up!' Harry gave him a painful shove.

He started violently. 'What?'

'God, you really are in a trance!' Harry exclaimed loudly. 'I asked you if you wanted a beer!'

'Yes – I mean no.'

Harry and Jennah started laughing together. Flynn tried to smile. And then put his hands to his face and burst into tears.

There was a long, shocked silence, heavy with embarrassment. Paralysed with shame and exhaustion, Flynn sat with his hands clamped over his face.

'Oh, Flynn—' Jennah breathed.

He could sense them looking at each other, not knowing what to do. He should just leave and put an end to their discomfort. But he couldn't even move. Instead he just sat, sobbing foolishly into his hands.

'Crikey.' Harry's voice now, cracked and awkward. 'I said something stupid, didn't I? I'm always putting my foot in it. Born with a foot in my mouth, my mum always says, but I didn't mean to – um – oh, shit . . .' Harry tailed off, lost for words. Harry was never lost for words.

Flynn felt Jennah sit down beside him and put her arm round him. 'Hey, we were being stupid and thoughtless, we're sorry,' she said softly. 'I'm sorry.'

248

Flynn found that he couldn't stop crying. Now that he had started, he was crying about everything, everything that had happened from the moment Professor Kaiser had asked him to play in the concert, till now. It was all flooding through him – the hope, the elation, the despair and the sadness. The sadness, always the sadness . . . Would it ever leave? He held his breath to try to stop the tears, thought he would choke, and the sobs redoubled.

Jennah stroked his back. 'It's no big deal, Flynn, it's OK. You're just going through a really rough time at the moment.'

'I'm telling you, it's all these bloody essays, they're enough to give anyone a nervous breakdown! I was practically crying myself last night . . .' Harry's voice tailed off awkwardly again.

'Oh, listen to him.' Jennah gave Flynn a squeeze, a smile in her voice. 'At least by the end of the month we won't have to hear Harry moan about another essay ever again! That's something to look forward to, hey, Flynn?'

He dragged his sleeve across his face, nodding silently, struggling hard to stop the onslaught of tears.

'Oi!' Harry exclaimed in mock outrage.

'In fact it might just be easier if we agreed to do all of Harry's essays for him until the exams,' Jennah went on. 'At least that way we'd get some peace!' She gave Flynn another squeeze. 'What do you think? We could take turns. We'll make him pay us, of course.'

He managed a smile, fists pressed against his eyelids, sniffing hard.

'In pounds or sexual favours?' Harry wanted to know.

'Well I can't be certain, Harry, but I should imagine Flynn would prefer the money.'

Flynn managed a brief laugh against his sleeve.

'Hey, don't knock what you haven't experienced!' Harry exclaimed.

'There are some things in life which one would prefer not to,' Jennah countered, her arm oddly comforting round Flynn's shoulders, and they carried on with their ridiculous charade until he managed to stem the tears and pull himself together again. He felt absurdly grateful towards them both.

That night, he stopped taking his lithium.

CHAPTER TWELVE

'*Hör zu.*' The next day, Professor Kaiser sat down at his desk and rubbed his hands together. 'I have a proposition to make to you – but you must understand you do not have an obligation to take it.'

Flynn scratched his cheek and surveyed him from the piano.

'It is only a suggestion,' Professor Kaiser went on, removing his glasses and beginning to polish them. He looked a little nervous. 'There is no pressure for you to say yes . . . but I did not want to refuse without asking you first.'

Flynn smiled slightly. 'Are you going to tell me what it is?'

Professor Kaiser cleared his throat. 'I – well, the Royal College has been asked to put forward two students for the London International Piano competition at the end of August. So naturally I thought of you.'

Flynn held back a smile. 'Really? Who – me and André?'

'Yes. But I know, it's quite soon after your . . . uh . . .'

Flynn grinned. 'That's OK, I can do it this time. The Rach Three?'

'Naturally. It is time we returned to it. There's been a big improvement in your playing the last few weeks and I sense Mozart is beginning to be boring for you.'

'You can say that again!'

Professor Kaiser gave a rare smile. 'Flynn, you must think about it. We do not have to decide until after the exams. Do not get worried about it – it is completely for you to decide. If you think it might be enjoyable then that is good, but if you don't then it does not matter.'

Flynn lined up the shot, drew back his cue and smacked the black cleanly into the bottom right-hand pocket. Then he straightened up and told Harry about the competition.

Harry started to say something and then stopped, mouth half open. He looked unsure how to react.

'It won't be like last time,' Flynn told him.

'Are you sure? I mean, I think it's great, but do you . . . are you . . . ?'

'Going to go crazy?' Flynn smiled. 'I hope not. I'm better now.'

Harry hesitated and then grinned. 'Well, congratulations then! You lucky sod!'

Flynn drained his glass and leaned against the window sill as Harry circled the table like a bear on the prowl. Another group of students came in noisily and the music started to pound. Flynn caught sight of

Jennah over by the bar and tried to catch her eye but she was deep in conversation with some long-haired percussionist.

Harry, having lined up an easy shot, hit the ball too fine and swore. With a smile, Flynn picked up his own cue. Minutes later he had cleared the table.

'Harry said you had some exciting news.'

Leaning against the wall, Flynn was puzzling over whether it was an ant or just a speck of dirt floating in his beer when Jennah approached.

He gave an embarrassed smile and shrugged at the floor.

'It's nothing much.'

'What *is* it?' Jennah asked eagerly.

'I might be playing in the London International Piano competition this summer,' Flynn said quickly.

Jennah grabbed his arm. 'Really?'

'Mm.'

'Oh, Flynn, that's fantastic! How exciting for you!'

He smiled at her reaction. Not a hint of concern crossed her face. 'Yeah, well, I guess I may as well give it a go, see if I can redeem myself after last time.'

'Of course you can, of course you will! Oh, wow!' Suddenly she leaned forwards and kissed him on the mouth. For a moment, he closed his eyes and felt as if he were falling, as if the world had opened at his feet. Then abruptly he found himself stepping back, pulling himself away, banging his side against the pool table, and the ground closed under his feet again.

Jennah stared at him and bit her lip, her eyes wide.

He gripped the edge of the table, breathing hard, reeling, the heat rushing to his cheeks.

'Sorry,' Jennah said, a horrified look beginning to spread across her face before she turned and disappeared into the crowd.

Freestyler . . . The music pounded in his ears, filling his head and blasting any thoughts of Jennah out of his mind. A white-hot energy exploded through his veins. He could run again. His feet felt light on the pavement. It was too early for rush-hour traffic along Bayswater Road but the sun was already rising in the sky.

I'm going to play in a big competition, he thought. I'm going to win. I'm going to show André once and for all. I'm the Royal College's top pianist. He ran up the incline to the top of the hill, barely out of breath. At the top he spun round, arms outstretched, laughing at the sky. He was alive again. His body was fizzing, his mind was buzzing, and the manic beat of the music made him want to leap and shout. The air around him felt electric. Anything is possible, he wanted to shout at the sky . . . ANYTHING. D'you get that, God? Nothing will stop me now. I know I'm damn good. Nothing can knock me down. You won't slow me down with pills. You won't slow me down with anything.

He ran along the Serpentine, scaring a gaggle of geese back into the water. The boat huts were deserted.

The sky was turning from pale grey to dark blue. It was going to be a beautiful day. The early-morning breeze was already turning balmy and his T-shirt was beginning to stick to his skin. He felt as if he could run for ever. He would run for two hours straight, till eight, then he would have a shower and grind through some Czerny until his first lecture at ten. And he wouldn't think about Jennah. He wouldn't think about her kissing him last night in the pub. Had the kiss been some kind of joke? Or had it been an act of pity prompted by Harry telling her that Flynn fancied her? He ran harder. He would forget it had happened. He had to forget it had ever happened.

'Hey,' said Rami.

Arriving home after the last lecture, Flynn discovered Rami sitting in his car with the door open, a newspaper spread out over his lap, his horn-rimmed reading glasses giving him a quizzical look.

'What are you doing here?' Flynn asked in surprise.

'And hello to you too!' Rami exclaimed. 'I had to pick something up in town so I thought I'd drop by.' He carefully folded his newspaper and put his glasses away. 'But there was no answer when I rang the bell so I figured that either you and Harry had both died from revision overload or you'd gone to the pub to escape it.'

'I had a late lecture,' Flynn said. 'I dunno where Harry is. D'you want to come in?'

'Well I'm not going to sit in the car all evening!'

* * *

In the kitchen, Flynn filled the kettle and pulled out two mugs.

Rami sat himself down at the kitchen table. 'So, the revision's going OK?' he asked.

'Yeah, yeah, it's fine.' Flynn pulled himself up onto the counter as he waited for the kettle to boil. 'D'you want some toast or something?'

'No, no, I've just eaten. So . . . you look well. How are things?'

'Fine.' Flynn gave a shrug and smiled.

'Cool, cool. So . . . you're still seeing Doctor Stefan?'

'Yeah, yeah.' Flynn drummed the heels of his trainers against the cupboard doors and looked over at the kettle.

'And the lithium?'

'What about it?' Flynn jumped to the floor as the kettle finally began to boil.

'You're still taking it, aren't you?'

'Yeah, yeah.' He concentrated on pouring the hot water into the mugs. There was a silence from behind.

'You *are* still taking it, aren't you?' Rami's voice had changed.

Flynn swung round. 'Stop giving me the Spanish Inquisition!' he snapped. 'Did you come round to say hi or to give me the third degree?'

'I came round to say hi *and* to see how you were. Mum said she hadn't heard from you in ages.'

'Well, as you can see, I'm fine,' Flynn retorted, setting the two mugs angrily down on the table.

256

Rami said nothing.

'What?' Flynn demanded.

'You've stopped taking it, haven't you?'

'Why is this your business?'

'*Haven't you?*'

'Yes, OK, I have! Several weeks ago if you must know! And I feel absolutely fine.'

'Flynn—'

'No, you listen. The lithium made me feel like shit, all the time. All I ever felt like doing was watching TV.'

'That's because your body was still getting used to it. The side-effects can be dire at first. But they wear off!'

'So? What's the point in me waiting for the side-effects to wear off if I don't even need it in the first place?'

'But you *do* need it, Flynn. Can't you see how much calmer you've been since you started taking it?'

'If by calmer you mean half-dead, then I agree with you!'

'You're missing the highs,' Rami said. 'Doctor Stefan said that might happen. But, Flynn, the highs didn't mean anything, they were caused by a chemical imbalance in your brain, and they made you strung out, unable to sleep, violent even! Don't you remember what it was like? The panic attacks, the obsessive practising, the flipping out for no reason, trying to throw yourself out of the fucking window, for God's sake?'

'At least then I felt *something*!' Flynn shouted. 'At least then I felt alive!'

'Oh, and when you crashed?' Rami had started to shout too. 'When you crashed the day after and couldn't even get yourself out of bed, did you feel alive then?'

'No but on lithium I feel like that all the time!'

There was a silence. Rami slumped back in his chair, suddenly looking drained. 'That's not true,' he said. 'On lithium you were tired, granted, but that was a side-effect, it was wearing off. You told me even the professor had commented on an improvement in you! Isn't that why he asked you to play in that competition? And on lithium you were functioning – you were down because you were feeling so tired all the time, but it wasn't like the depression before, was it, Flynn? You were able to get up in the mornings, go to lectures, practise a reasonable amount. You were even eating again! Couldn't you have given the lithium just a bit more time?'

Flynn took an angry gulp of his scalding coffee. 'I don't need these drugs,' he said quietly. 'You don't understand. The doctors have got it all wrong. I've felt fine since stopping the lithium. Neither up nor down. Just, you know, *normal.*'

Rami gave a small, tired laugh. 'And what's that when it's at home?'

'They've got it completely wrong,' Flynn went on. 'If I really had bipolar, I should be manic or depressed again by now. And I'm not. I'm really not.'

'I know you're not,' Rami said.

'So you see!' Flynn exclaimed. 'I can't have bipolar then, can I?'

'It's not that simple,' Rami said.

Flynn shot him an angry look.

'If a person with bipolar stops taking their medication, they don't instantly become ill again,' Rami went on. 'In fact, they could stay symptom-free for quite some time. But you can be sure that it will return, sooner or later, and probably with twice as much force.'

There was a long silence. Flynn felt a small pain start at the back of his throat. 'I don't believe you,' he said finally, his voice uneven.

'I would never lie about something like that,' Rami said.

'I haven't got bipolar disorder!' Flynn exclaimed. But even as he said it, he realized what he really meant was that he *wished* he hadn't got bipolar disorder, which wasn't the same thing at all.

The next day, it was a struggle to sit through lectures, his muscles still tingling from his morning jog. He hadn't been able to get Rami to leave until promising that he would make an appointment with Dr Stefan to talk things through. But in reality he had done no such thing. He would prove Rami wrong. He would stay well without the lithium and Dr Stefan would have to admit that his diagnosis had been a mistake. It was all a question of willpower. It was up to him, not the stupid chemicals in his brain.

The Historical Studies lecturer was droning on about opera at the end of the twentieth century. Flynn had revised that last night. He knew it now. It was a waste of time to go over it again. He leaned back in his chair and gazed out of the window.

At two minutes to twelve he was packing his bag and disappearing up the aisle as the lecturer asked if there were any questions. As Flynn bombed out of the exit, he felt a hand on his arm.

'Flynn, hold on—' It was Jennah, clutching a pile of books. She looked as if she had been waiting for him. Flynn backed away.

'I just – I was just wondering if I could speak to you for a minute?'

He felt his heart start to pound. 'I've really got to go—'

'Please, it'll only take a minute.'

'Later, OK?' He turned and hurried down the hallway.

'Are we supposed to have read the whole of *Musical Structure and Design*?' Harry wanted to know.

'I think so. As well as *Harmonic Practice in Tonal Music*.' Clive let out a weary sigh.

Flynn and Harry were having lunch with a group from their Stylistic Studies class. Kate came over with her tray to join them, squeezing in beside Flynn. 'I had my Aural practical this morning,' she told him.

'Did it go all right?' Flynn asked with his mouth full.

'I dunno. It was hard. *Three* different key signatures!'

'Yeah, it's always a pig.'

260

'Did Jennah find you?'

'What?'

'She was looking all over for you this morning. I told her you were in Historical Studies with Harry.'

'Oh, right. Yeah, she did.'

'Is she OK? She seemed kind of upset about something.'

'Probably just stressed.'

'Probably.' Kate started to laugh. 'And you should go easy on the Pro Plus, Flynn.'

'What?'

'Your leg! You're jiggling the whole table!'

'How on earth can you work like this?'

Flynn had beaten Harry home and taken possession of the hi-fi, which was now belting out hip hop as he sat on the living-room carpet, surrounded by wads of paper, highlighters and piles of books.

'Music helps me concentrate,' Flynn said.

'You call this music?' Harry flopped onto the couch with a groan. 'Just think of it – in two weeks this will all be over. If only I could hibernate until then . . .' He closed his eyes. 'Seriously, Flynn, you're going to have to turn it down or the neighbours are going to complain.'

The phone started to ring, barely audible beneath the beat of Dr Dre. Harry got up and went into the kitchen.

A moment later he returned.

'It's for you.'

'Who?'

'Jennah.'

'Oh, tell her I'm – I'm out.'

'What? Why?'

'I'm busy working, can't you see?'

Harry gave him a long look and went back to the phone.

The exam fortnight passed in a blur. Flynn didn't manage much sleep but it wasn't because he had too much work, he just didn't feel tired. It was fantastic. He was able to cram through the night, even managing to squeeze in a few hours' practice before dawn.

At seven, Harry would emerge, pale and sleepy, yawning and groaning at the prospect of a full day's revision ahead. Flynn would leave him to his toast and textbooks and go for a run before returning to have a shower and attack the piano.

His penultimate exam was a doddle and he finished his Historical Studies paper with a whole twenty minutes to spare. That night he found himself boasting to Harry about how easy it had been. He grabbed his lever-arch file and started showering his lecture notes out of the living-room window until Harry went ballistic.

'What the hell are you doing? You could kill someone!'

'It's just paper!' Flynn laughed. 'No more HS! No more crumbling Myers! Woo hoo!'

Harry slammed the window closed. 'You're crazy! The neighbours will call the police!'

'Let's *burn* our notes then! I know, we can have a bonfire!'

'Flynn! Our next exam is at nine o'clock tomorrow morning! Stop being such a—' He broke off as Flynn grabbed Harry's file from the coffee table and made off with it to the kitchen.

'Give that back to me now! I mean it, Flynn. What if I have to retake the damn module? Don't you dare set fire to my notes!' Harry wasn't laughing. He made a desperate lunge for the file as Flynn wrenched open the kitchen drawers, hunting for the lighter.

Flynn tried to kick Harry off, choking with laughter, and upturned the cutlery drawer onto the floor with a deafening crash.

'For God's sake, it's one o'clock in the morning! The neighbours are going to come pounding on the door! Would you stop – *please*!' Harry's cheeks were crimson as he tried to wrestle the file from Flynn's clutches.

'Let go! Let go!' Flynn yelled, whooping with laughter as he waved the lighter around, attempting to ignite the lever-arch file. 'Careful, Harry, you're going to be next. You'll be Guy Fawkes sitting on top of the bonfire! Whey-hey, it's burning, it's burning! Look at it go!'

Flynn's head snapped backwards. There was a massive jolt of pain and his eyes throbbed crimson.

The lever-arch file lay open on the floor, spewing out

sheets of printed lecture notes and biro scrawls across the lino.

Harry stood frozen, his back pressed against the cupboard door. His chest and shoulders rose and fell rapidly and his left hand squeezed the knuckles of his right fist. His eyes were wide and he seemed to be gasping.

Flynn felt himself sway. He took one step backwards and crashed into the saucepan stand, then his hands found the wall behind him and he slid down it to the floor.

Harry took a tentative step forwards. 'Are you OK?'

'Ow,' Flynn said in reply. It hurt to talk. His top lip stung and when he touched it his fingertips came away smeared with red. He felt as if a hot, throbbing balloon was being blown up inside his mouth. He looked up at Harry, his eyes watering. 'Ow,' he said again dizzily.

Harry looked white. 'I'm s-sorry,' he stammered. 'I didn't mean to punch your mouth, I'm really sorry. But you were – you were going completely crazy again! You were trying to set fire to my head!'

'Just wanted to make a bonfire . . . to celebrate . . . you know . . .' It was increasingly difficult to talk and his voice was muffled and indistinct. Now he felt like he had a hot boiled egg jammed between his front teeth and top lip. He swallowed what tasted like a mouthful of blood.

'Oh, fuck.' Harry sat down heavily on a kitchen chair and ran his hands through his hair. 'I really didn't mean to get your mouth – I freaked out – Flynn, I'm really sorry.'

''S OK,' Flynn replied, touching the pulpy mess of his upper lip. He suddenly felt tired and slightly sick. Right now a bonfire seemed like too much of an effort.

Harry suddenly jumped up and rummaged in the freezer and pulled out a large bag of peas. 'Here, take this, hold it against the swelling . . .'

Flynn took the bag of peas and stared at it in confusion.

'Hold it to your lip, here, like this.' Harry kneeled down in front of him and pressed the icy bundle to Flynn's face.

It hurt like crazy. Flynn coughed and blood splattered onto his jeans.

'I'm sorry,' Harry kept saying, and his voice shook.

On the morning of the last exam, Flynn was towelling his hair in the bathroom when Harry barged in.

'Hey, don't you knock?'

'Sorry, sorry. I thought I left my watch in here. Have you seen it?' Harry looked frazzled, still half-asleep, hair on end.

Flynn gave the surfaces a quick scan. 'Nope.'

'This is all I need! I can't do the exam without a watch! D'you think they'll let me take my alarm clock instead?'

'Not if it goes off halfway through!' Flynn laughed at

the thought and gave Harry a playful punch. 'Hey, this is our last day, our last exam! Whey-hey!'

Harry pulled away. 'Shit, look at your lip, it's still huge—'

'I think it gives me a kind of sexy, smouldering look!'

Harry flashed him a sheepish grin. 'You're a loon, did you know that?'

'Hey, this is our last day, our last day, d'you realize? Summer holidays, here we come!'

'Don't say that yet – we've still got this lousy Theory exam—'

'I feel like pancakes. D'you want a pancake? I'm going to make some pancakes.'

'Don't be daft. We've got to be at the exam hall in twenty minutes.'

Flynn laughed. 'Yeah, loads of time!'

He was halfway through mixing the batter when Rami called.

'Just ringing to wish you good luck for your last exam.'

'I don't need luck – this one's in the bag! Theory's a piece of cake! And after this it's freeeeedom!'

'Flynn, listen to me for a minute. Harry told me about what happened. Are you all right?'

'I'm fine, I'm fine! It was only a bit of fun and, don't worry, I'll get my own back on him!'

'OK, good, but listen. Did you talk to Doctor Stefan about—?'

266

'No, it's fine! I haven't had time, but it's fine. I'm feeling fine and—'

'Flynn!'

'I'm not hyper, just excited! Today's the last exam and I've got three months' holiday and Harry and I want to go away. We're going to go busking in Scotland—'

'Flynn, listen to me—'

'I am, I am, I am, but I'm not hyper and I'm trying to make pancakes with one hand and it's not exactly easy!'

'Then stop making pancakes and listen!'

'I can't! I can't stop. I'm going to be late. I feel like eating pancakes for breakfast. I'm sick of toast – toast's boring! I'm sick of cereal too! Cereal's just—'

'*Flynn, will you listen to me!*'

Flynn put down the frying pan and stopped uncertainly.

Rami inhaled deeply. 'You need to go back and see Doctor Stefan about your meds. Today, after your exam. D'you hear me? It's important. You're getting high again.'

Flynn emerged from the exam hall into brilliant sunshine. He wandered through the throng of students, looking for Harry. He found him by the wall, rolling up his sleeves, a relieved look on his face. Flynn held up his hand with a grin. Harry slapped it hard.

'It wasn't too bad, was it?' Jennah approached with a tentative smile. Harry jumped forwards and gave her a big hug. 'It was fantastic. I got the question on

267

Stravinsky's "The Rite of Spring"! I can't believe it's all over!'

'I know. It's a great feeling.' Jennah drew back from Harry's hug, smiling. There were dark shadows beneath her eyes. She looked at Flynn. 'Oh my God, what happened to your lip?'

'I walked into a doorframe,' Flynn replied.

Harry opened his mouth as if to protest and then lowered his eyes to the ground.

Jennah glanced uncertainly from Harry to Flynn. 'What's going on? What really happened?'

'Well actually—' Harry began.

'Nothing.' Flynn cut him off sharply. He leaned against the wall, hands in his pockets, unable to meet her gaze. Harry tactfully moved away towards another group of people.

Jennah was looking at Flynn carefully. 'Are you OK?' she asked him.

He gave a small, dismissive shrug. 'Fine.'

'I haven't seen much of you lately. I – I sort of got the impression you were avoiding me.'

Flynn shook his head, looking away from her and into the crowd.

'Well . . . I'll see you around then.'

He nodded and she turned away, head lowered, walking quickly down the road.

CHAPTER THIRTEEN

'Jennah came round looking for you.' Harry greeted Flynn the moment he walked through the door. Harry was watching the tennis, feet up on the coffee table, arms folded over his chest.

'What?'

'I told her to come back around seven. You'll be here then, won't you? She heard you were going home at the end of the week and wanted to catch you before you left.'

Flynn stopped in the doorway and swore.

Harry's eyes narrowed in disbelief. 'Surely you weren't going to leave without saying goodbye?'

Flynn leaned back against the doorjamb, hands in his pockets, banging his head repeatedly against the wall in frustration.

'You're treating her like shit, do you realize that?' Harry said quietly.

Flynn stopped his head-banging and stared at him.

'The least you could do is talk to her,' Harry said. 'She's got the message loud and clear that you don't want to go out with her. She just wants some reassurance that the two of you can still be friends, like before.'

'Well it can't be like before, can it?' Flynn shouted, and slammed out of the room.

There was nowhere to go. He felt tired, so tired again. The fire had left him as swiftly as it had arrived and he was left a burned-out shell, hollow, brittle, empty. Now that the exams were over it seemed as if there was nothing more to look forward to; nothing more but the long, hot, excruciatingly dull summer back in Sussex, where all there was to do was mow the lawn, work behind the bar at the Red Cow and practise. He had thought about spending the summer here in the flat but Harry was going to join his parents in Brussels before jetting off to somewhere in the Caribbean, and Mum was insisting he came home for a while. Then would come the waiting – waiting to find out whether he had passed his exams, wondering what on earth he was going to do if he hadn't. And then, of course, there was the London International competition, looming at the end of the holidays, casting a shadow of fear over the whole summer. And he couldn't even think of that, he couldn't even think of that now, because it made him want to throw things and smash things and scream at everyone.

After everything that had happened, Harry was sure to have changed his mind about them going to Scotland together – a real shame because his parents had been going to lend them their car. And it took all the energy he had not to think about Jennah. Every time he felt his mind drift towards the touch of her hand, the smell of her hair, her smile, Flynn felt as if he were starting to fall, in slow motion, off the edge of a cliff, and the only thing he was aware of was fear.

He lay face down on his bed, fully clothed, one arm dangling off the side, his finger tracing the pattern on the carpet. He couldn't sleep, couldn't be bothered to get undressed and into bed for that matter, but felt too tired to move. From the hallway, Harry called out that he was off to see Kate. Flynn just grunted in reply. He heard the front door slam, contemplated the long evening ahead and thought about the three boxes of lithium tablets in his bedside drawer. He was sure there were enough there to kill a horse . . . He could either lie here all evening, or start packing for Friday, or end it all right here, right now. His heartbeat quickened at the thought. Would it take a long time? Would it hurt? He wouldn't be found until tomorrow afternoon at the earliest, when Harry started getting concerned. Maybe not even then . . . Twenty-four hours. More than enough time . . . But he couldn't do it. He was too afraid. Or was he? Other stuff scared him more. Living, for example.

He sat up and took the packets out of the drawer. Pulled the blister packs out of their boxes and lined them up on his bed. He could take all the pills out and arrange them into groups of four. Then fill a pint glass with water in the kitchen and take them four at a time. Six blister backs, so seventy-two pills. Seventy-two divided by four ... Eighteen, something like that. Eighteen swallows, it wouldn't take very long. But just looking at the packs of pills lying on his bed was making his heart race – what if he changed his mind halfway through? He would need to get himself drunk first. There was some gin somewhere in the kitchen. Perhaps he should go and drink that first, then decide ...

The shrill of the doorbell startled him out of his thoughts. He froze, hoping whoever it was would give up and go away. Then he realized it might be Rami, come to drag him back to Dr Stefan's. Flynn sat immobile on his bed, breathing rapidly, the blood drumming in his ears. The doorbell went again, this time longer, more urgent. Still he didn't move. The bell went a third time. Damn, damn, *damn*. He was going to have to open the door. His hands shook as he shoved the pills roughly back into their boxes. Clawing his hands through his hair in frustration, he went out into the hall.

It was Jennah. He was hugely taken aback. Relieved that it wasn't Rami, but absolutely thrown at seeing her there. Then he dimly recollected Harry saying something about her coming round at seven ...

'Flynn, are you all right?'

'Yeah.' He leaned heavily against the doorjamb, blinking at her.

'Sorry to be so insistent but Harry said you would be in and I really, really need to see you.'

'Oh.' He continued to gaze at her dully, struggling to make the transition between the pills on his bed in his darkened bedroom and the bright afternoon sunshine lighting up Jennah's hair.

'Were you sleeping?'

'No.'

'Well—' Jennah chewed her lip, looking flushed and slightly desperate. 'Can I come in, just for a minute? I know you really don't want to speak to me but you don't have to. I just wanted to explain a couple of things to you before you left for the summer.'

'All right.' He stepped back, defeated.

Jennah sat on the couch. Flynn perched on the edge of the armchair, elbows on knees, chewing his nails. He had offered her a cup of coffee. She had declined. Now there was nothing but silence stretching out between them. Flynn felt as if he were teetering on the edge of a pool of icy water, waiting to be pushed in.

She looked up at him with a strained smile. 'So, what's going on?'

He shrugged with a feeling of dread. 'Nothing.'

'You seem really angry at me about something.' Jennah's smile was artificially bright and there was a slight tremor in her voice. 'You've been going out of your way to avoid me recently and I think I know why but – but I was wondering if there was any way of getting things back to how they used to be? I – I miss you, you know.' She bit her lip hard, her eyes suddenly bright with tears.

Another long silence. Flynn stared at the tree outside the window. 'Are you even listening to me?'

His eyes snapped back to her and he rubbed his cheek hard, aching with embarrassment. He could hardly look at her, could barely tolerate her presence and as sure as hell couldn't talk to her. He wanted to say he was sorry, wanted to tell her it was not her fault, wanted to let her know that she was better off without him as a friend anyway, but the words remained painfully lodged in his throat.

'What's the matter?' Jennah was still trying to smile but her voice had an edge to it now.

He continued to rub his cheek, looking at the floor.

'Why won't you talk to me? Why won't you even *look* at me?'

'I'm just not in the mood to talk right now.'

'But you're never in the mood any more! You've been ignoring me for the past three weeks, ever since I – I got carried away at the pub. Oh God, I know I shouldn't have kissed you, Flynn. I know it was really embarrassing for you and – well – really embarrassing for both of us. But I didn't – I didn't plan it, it wasn't deliberate, it just happened, and ever since then I've been trying to apologize to you but you keep avoiding me! I just want you to please, please forget about it! I know it's stupid to pretend it never happened but I promise I'll never do it again. I just want to go back to how things were! I *never* realized I was risking our friendship. I *never* thought you'd be so angry you wouldn't want to talk to me!'

'I'm not angry,' Flynn said desperately, flushing at her words and turning away to try to avoid her furious gaze. 'I don't feel like talking to anyone right now, I'm just tired.'

'Why?' Jennah's voice was frantic. 'Is it your illness?'

'No!'

'Then I don't understand! Why are you acting this way? Why are you acting so weird just because I tried to kiss you? It was just a stupid heat-of-the-moment thing! Why do you have to let something so silly ruin our friendship?'

'I don't know, OK?' Before he even knew it, Flynn had jumped to his feet and started to shout. 'I can't tell you because I don't know! I can't answer any of your questions! So why don't you just leave me alone? I don't want to speak to you. I didn't ask you to come here, so stop going on!'

Jennah stood up too, her eyes wide and frightened. 'I didn't mean to make it worse, Flynn, I just wanted – I just wanted us to stay friends.'

'Well we can't, OK? So go! Just leave me alone!'

Jennah stared at him, her eyes flooding with tears, and left.

As he heard the front door close, he sank down onto the sofa, his heart hammering. He bit his thumb hard, struggling to get a grip, his breathing exploding in short gasps. He knew he was losing it again but was determined to fight back. He needed to calm down so that he could think. He must think so that he could work out what to do. He sat motionless on the couch for what must have been an age . . . As the screaming tension in his muscles began to fade, it slowly dawned on him that he had done something truly, truly awful.

He looked over at the DVD player to see the time. He had been sitting there for nearly an hour, in some kind of a trance. Jennah would be home by now. He needed to call her. He needed to apologize. He needed to find some way of explaining his behaviour, of getting her to realize that he didn't really mean it. He had hurt her. He needed to find a way of taking it all back . . . He would have to explain the bipolar to her. He would have to tell her that he had stopped taking his medication and that she was right, he was ill again. And that the reason he'd been ignoring her wasn't because he was angry that she'd kissed him, it was because he was – he was . . . something else. He couldn't find a word for it. Something like a fist would reach down inside his chest and take hold of his heart and squeeze and hurt and force him to feel a long-ing . . . a wanting so powerful and so painful that he didn't think he could bear it. And if he let it happen, if he let the glass bubble that had surrounded him for so long shatter, he would start to feel again.

He looked up at the window, breathing hard. Maybe he should call her and ask if he could go round and talk to her and tell her what was going on. And then maybe she wouldn't look so sad any more, and then maybe they could just hang around together like they used to and everything would be OK. He picked up the receiver. His hands started shaking as he punched in the numbers and he found himself gripping the receiver painfully hard, feeling his racing pulse in the palm of his hand.

It went straight to answerphone. OK, so Jennah had switched off her mobile. He hung up and called her home number. Someone picked up on the fourth ring.

'Hello?' Sounded like Jennah's mother.

He swallowed hard. 'Hi. Is Jennah there, please?'

'I'm afraid she's out. I was expecting her back for supper half an hour ago so she should walk in any minute. Can I ask who's calling?'

'It's Flynn. I–I'll try calling back later.'

'Oh, Flynn, didn't she come round? She told me she was going out to see you.'

'She did, she did come round. But then she left and I – I just forgot to tell her something.'

'Oh! When did she leave? She assured me she would come straight home because her aunt's coming round for dinner.'

Flynn's mind started to race. Should he lie and cover for Jennah? Had Jennah not gone straight home because she didn't want her mother to see she was upset? Had she gone to see a friend?

'Flynn, are you still there?'

'Yeah, I'm – um – I'm just' – he rubbed his cheek furiously – 'I'm just – um – thinking—'

'Is everything OK? You sound a bit bothered.'

'No, everything's fine. She left about an hour ago. I'll – I'll call back later.'

He replaced the receiver and ran his hands through

his hair. OK, so Jennah hadn't gone straight home, it was no big deal. She had probably gone to see a friend. It was fine. Jennah was often late home. Her mother didn't sound worried. It was only nine o'clock. Maybe Jennah had forgotten about her aunt and decided to go out for the evening. Maybe she'd gone to the pub with some friends. That would be a good thing – it would mean that she'd got over their argument and decided to go out and have fun. It was fine, he would try her mobile again later, much later, when dinner with the aunt was over, when Jennah had calmed down and wasn't so upset any more.

Flynn sat back and switched on the TV. But he couldn't sit still, his foot kept drumming against the coffee table. He chewed his thumbnail down to the quick, made himself a cup of coffee, went to the loo, had another cup of coffee . . . Behind the window, the sky was darkening and the streetlamps were coming on. He didn't bother to switch on the light but paced the length of the floor, the living room lit only by the flickering television screen. He stared at the phone, willing it to ring and checked the reception on his mobile over and over again. But both phones remained silent.

Would Jennah be too angry to call him? Would her mother remember to pass on the message? Would she call him to let him know Jennah had returned? Probably not. Why should she? Especially if Jennah came home saying she hated him and never wanted to see him again. Should he call back? But they would be in the middle of dinner and maybe Jennah would have told her mother what he had said and she would be furious with him and tell him never to call again . . . But he had to talk to her. He had to explain! Maybe he should go round. No, that would be worse. He had visions of Jennah's mother screaming at him through the letter box . . .

He drummed his fingers against the cushion, spun the remote round and round on the coffee table, got up and went over to the window, circled the room, sat back down, got up again. He watched two episodes of *Friends* and didn't even smile. He tried to watch the ten o'clock news but nothing made sense. It was past ten already! Why hadn't Jennah phoned?

Come on, he reasoned, she wasn't about to phone him, he had just yelled at her to go away. Jennah's mother was no more likely to phone either. He was going to have to call again. Perhaps he could write her a letter . . . No, this was ridiculous! All he had to do was pick up the phone! Elbows on knees, breathing hard, he fixed the innocent white handset with a desperate stare. It began to ring.

It took him a moment to react. For a second he thought that he had willed it into life. Then he sprang up.

'Flynn?' Jennah's mother. She didn't sound angry at all. He ached with relief.

'Yes!'

'Did you say that Jennah left you at about quarter past eight?'

Flynn's heart started to pound. 'Yes.'

'And she didn't say where she was going next?'

'No.'

There was a pause. 'Did she seem upset?'

Flynn felt his throat constrict. 'We – we had a bit of an argument.'

'Was it serious?'

'No,' Flynn said desperately. 'I mean yes, maybe. She – she was upset that I'd been avoiding her recently and – and I lost my temper and kind of shouted at her.'

'So when she left you, she was upset?'

Flynn felt his face burn. 'Yes, she – she was crying.'

There was another long silence. Flynn was sure that the pounding in his chest must be audible.

'Right,' Jennah's mother said finally. 'Stay by the phone, would you? I'm going to have to call all her friends. She seems to have disappeared.'

'You still up?' Harry crashed through the front door, shaking his damp curls and tramping into the living room. 'It's pissing down outside – typical British summer. What have you been up to?' He stopped in the doorway, illuminated in the light of the flickering television screen. 'Anything good on?'

There was a silence. Harry switched on the light.

'What's up? Why are you looking at me like that?'

Flynn released his thumb from between his teeth. 'Jennah's gone missing.'

Harry shrugged. 'Yeah, I got a call on my mobile a

280

couple of hours ago from Jennah's mum. She said Jennah was late for dinner or something.'

'You don't get it. She came to see me at eight and never went home.'

'So? It's only – what – quarter to twelve? She's probably out with some friends. Have you tried her mobile?'

'Yes, it's switched off. I've left about six messages. She promised her mum she'd go straight home. Her aunt was coming round for dinner.'

'Oh.' A silence. 'Well, she must have forgotten . . .'

'Her mum called everyone she knows. No one's seen her.'

Harry chewed his lower lip and sat down on the arm of the couch. 'OK . . . well . . . let's be reasonable . . . She's only been missing a few hours . . . It's Saturday night, she's probably gone clubbing—'

'She hasn't gone clubbing!' Flynn startled himself as he began to shout. 'She was upset – something might have happened to her. I'm going to look for her—'

Harry grabbed him by the arm. 'Hold on, hold on. You have no idea where she is. Let's figure out where she might have gone, at least.'

Flynn stopped, breathing hard. 'All right,' he said desperately.

'Did she say what she was upset about?'

'Yes – no – it was me – I shouted at her!'

Harry looked at him askance. 'What? Why?'

'I don't know! I don't know!' Flynn jumped up from

the sofa and ran his hands through his hair as if he were about to pull it out. He walked over to the window and banged his forehead against the pane.

'Well this is great,' Harry said wryly, straddling the arm of the sofa and peeling off his denim jacket. 'First you give her sleepless nights before her exams, then you chase her away when she comes over to see you!'

Flynn turned slowly from the window, one hand still clutching the frame. 'Why would my not speaking to her for a few days make her so upset? Something else must have happened.'

'Oh, for God's sake.' Harry began to kick off his shoes, looking irritated. 'Of course it's because of you. You know damn well she's crazy about you.'

Flynn felt his heart begin to pound. 'Very funny.'

'Jesus, Flynn!' Harry rolled his eyes. 'Everyone knows it! She's been crazy about you for ages!'

'You don't know what you're talking about—' Flynn began.

'You can stop playing the fool,' Harry snapped. 'She told me she tried to kiss you.'

Flynn felt the blood rush to his face. 'Ha ha, very funny, that was just a mistake—'

'A mistake?' Harry, standing with only one shoe, looked as if he might start to laugh. 'Tell me, how does one *accidentally* kiss someone?'

Flynn looked at him, his cheeks burning, breathing hard. 'Just shut up. You know that was out of pity. It was only because *you told her*!'

Harry stared at him, the whites of his eyes gleaming in the half-light. 'Told her what? What the hell are you talking about?'

'You *told* her.' Flynn turned round slowly, back pressed against the window pane. 'You went and told her that I'd fancied her for ages, and she felt sorry for me, with my illness and stuff, and so she kissed me, out of pity—'

'Out of pity?' Harry groaned and clutched at his curls and bent over, as if getting ready to pull his own head off. 'Oh my God, I can't take any more of this. You really are completely and utterly out of your mind!'

'OK.' Flynn sobered suddenly. 'What then?' His voice dropped, and he leaned against the windowsill for support.

Harry straightened up slowly, his damp hair sticking up comically, and took a deep breath. 'I don't really know how many ways there are to say this, Flynn,' he began, 'but Jennah's crazy about you. You're the reason she broke up with Charlie. Everyone knows it. People at uni call her the smitten kitten. When you're not around, you're all she talks about.'

Flynn stared at him. 'But—' he protested weakly.

Harry held up his hand. 'No, listen! I never even *hinted* that you used to fancy her. And, believe me, after the way you reacted to her kiss in the pub, that's the last thing she suspects!'

Flynn stared down at the threadbare carpet. The television continued to flicker. A car drove by in the street below. A long silence passed.

283

'Oh, fuck,' Flynn said in a whisper.

'Yes, yes, I completely agree.' Harry flung himself onto the sofa, rolling his eyes dramatically. 'For the last two weeks she's been trying to patch things up with you, and now she thinks she's not only made a fool of herself, but gone and lost you as a friend as well.'

A door slammed somewhere below, making Flynn jump. 'Shit. Oh, shit, I've got to find her—' He crashed into the hall and shoved on his shoes.

'Wait, we still don't know where she is!'

Flynn shoved him off. 'I'm going to find her! She's got to be out there somewhere! I'll find her!'

Flynn raced down the stairs and burst out into the street. The orange glow of the streetlamps was reflected on the slick, wet pavement; the parked cars and black railings glistened. The rain was falling thick and steady – within seconds his T-shirt was stuck to his skin. The bottoms of his jeans soon clung wetly to his calves and by the time he had reached the main road he could feel the damp seeping into his socks and pants. He ran through the next set of lights and splashed his way through two enormous puddles that took up half the road. He almost lost his footing on the slimy pavement and, on one corner, bumped hard into a woman who shrieked. He was hooted at by a night bus as he sprinted blindly across the road before heading down towards Notting Hill Gate. He had no idea where he was going. All he knew was that he needed to get through as many streets in as little time as possible.

It was difficult to grasp the enormity of what Harry had said. There had been no grin, no snort of laughter, no sudden confession that it had all been some kind of hoax. Harry had been serious. The kiss had been serious. Jennah had broken up with Charlie before she even knew Flynn was ill. That couldn't have been out of pity . . . He had to find Jennah. He could hardly imagine what she must be feeling right now – angry, hurt, humiliated, betrayed?

It was so late now. Where the hell could she be? If she'd gone to a friend's then she'd have called home. It didn't make sense. She always had her mobile on her. Unless – unless something had happened . . . Unless she had been attacked. Girls went missing all the time, only to be found in woodland weeks later, raped and murdered. The thought of that happening to Jennah made his mouth fill with bile and a sob tore at his throat. He would carry on running till he found her. He would find her, he would.

It was increasingly hard to see. Two dark red blotches pulsated in front of his eyes. A sharp stabbing pain started in his chest and it hurt to breathe. At one point, he skidded to a halt, thinking he could see a great river lapping at the pavement ahead of him. But it was just his imagination; the wavelets were made out of concrete, and he ran across the river to the other side. He bit his tongue against the pain in his chest and tasted blood. The only sound was the drum of his heartbeat and his great, rasping breaths. He kept thinking he was going to have to stop, kept thinking there was no way he was going to be able to run at this pace for another second, but then he made it to the corner of another street and he told himself one more, just one more . . .

Sometime later he was sick. Tipped forwards onto his hands and knees and threw up on the pavement. He couldn't run again after that. It was an excruciating effort just to get back onto his feet. He couldn't breathe fast enough and his throat was making these weird heaving noises. He was walking like a drunk, zigzagging across the puddles. He slipped on some wet leaves and the pavement came up to slap him. He staggered back to his feet again, his body pulsating with pain. He kept thinking he could see a bench ahead but, when he got closer, it turned out to be nothing more than a shadow between the trees. His whole body screamed at him to lie down, but he thought of Jennah and kept on going . . .

After a while he realized that he had come full circle. He was back on Bayswater Road. He couldn't even remember which way he'd been . . . It was an effort just to stay on his feet. And somewhere he was aware of a voice, a voice that kept saying his name, somewhere to his left, somewhere from the car that was crawling along the side of the road. There was a kind of static in the air and he was afraid he was imagining things again. But the voice kept on and on.

'Flynn, get in the car, just get in the car—'

He allowed himself to turn his head and saw Rami, head stuck out of his car window, arm outstretched, crawling along beside him. He wanted to collapse with relief and stopped, the ground tilting in every direction.

Rami jumped out of the car and grabbed him. 'Come on, I've got you. Get in, get in!'

He felt as if he were floating. His body seemed weightless as he collapsed into the front seat. Rami got back behind the wheel and pulled Flynn's seatbelt across him.

The air inside the car was warm and steamy. Rami had turned the heating up high but within seconds the windows had fogged up and Rami was leaning forwards in an effort to see through the windscreen. As the car glided effortlessly through the wet streets, Flynn was aware of his brother muttering to himself. 'Jesus Christ, here we go again . . .'

By the time the gasping noises had stopped, they were in Watford. The rain was still falling as Flynn stumbled out of the car. It took Rami a moment to find his keys and by the time they stepped into the warm, bright entrance hall Flynn was shivering so violently it felt as if a giant hand was rattling him by the neck. Suddenly there was the sofa and towels and hot-water bottles and more towels and a hot drink that he sloshed all over the carpet. Sophie and Rami's voices talking loudly, then more softly, then whispering, then louder again. Clothes being dragged off, dry clothes being shoved on, a hairdryer burning his ears, bleeding grazes down his arms, Sophie brandishing cotton wool, and voices, voices, voices, and the telephone ringing. Coughing, coughing, coughing. And finally a strange feeling – a tingling, a prickling, soft dry clothes against his skin, a glowing feeling surrounding him . . . Warmth.

5:17 a.m. He wondered where those luminous digits were coming from. Too small to be his alarm and the wrong colour too – blue instead of green. He turned his head on the pillow towards another light and saw a crack in the door, a yellow glow seeping in from the hallway outside. He stretched out and his foot hit the arm of the sofa. He had fallen asleep on Rami's living-room couch and there seemed to be a weight on top of him . . .

Groggily, he struggled to sit up and beat back the covers – one, two, three layers covering him. He pushed the blankets to the floor and spent a few seconds fumbling about in the dark for the lamp. He yawned, blinking blearily and looking down with surprise at the UCL tracksuit and thick socks he was now wearing. Then his grazed arms began to throb and he remembered Jennah.

He knew exactly where the car keys were – in the pocket of Rami's jacket. But Rami's jacket was not on its usual peg by the front door. Nor was it slung over the back of one of the kitchen chairs. After wasting a good five minutes wandering aimlessly back and forth between the living room and kitchen, Flynn realized the jacket had to be in Rami's bedroom.

The stupid door creaked, which wasn't a good start. Then the light from the landing fell directly over Rami's gently snoring face. Flynn darted over to what looked like a pile of clothes by the window and banged his toes against the foot of the bed. A small sound escaped him. Rami began to stir. Flynn crouched down, gripping his bruised toes. Then he straightened up slowly and began to go through Rami's pockets.

'Oh Jesus, Flynn, what now?'

Flynn span round. Rami was propped up on his elbows, looking straight at him.

'I need the keys!' Flynn whispered urgently.

'What keys?' Rami hissed, reaching for his T-shirt. 'Come on, let's get out of here before we wake Soph.'

Downstairs, Rami put the kettle on. Flynn paced the floor, biting his nails.

'I really need to borrow your car, Rami. I'll be careful, I promise. I'll bring it back before tonight but you've got to lend it to me—'

'Flynn, there's no way I'm lending you my car at this time in the morning, especially after the state I found you in. And I'm not too impressed that you were going to take the keys and help yourself to it, either.'

'You don't understand – it's an emergency!'

'I spoke to Harry. I know about Jennah. But you are

289

not going to be able to find her by combing the streets in the car any more than you were going to find her by running through the streets in the dark. Christ, Flynn, what were you thinking? You could have—'

'But *you* found me, didn't you?'

'Only because Harry told me you were running around Bayswater like a maniac!' Rami looked angry. 'Look, I'm sure Jennah's got a lot more sense than you and won't have been walking the streets all night. She's most likely just gone to stay with a friend and forgotten to tell her mother.'

Flynn ran his hands through his hair in desperation, a dreadful wave of panic rising in his stomach. 'Rami, you've got to believe me. She's been missing for nearly twelve hours. Something bad has happened to her, I know it has, I know it has. I *know* Jennah, she's my best friend – at – at least she used to be – and I know she wouldn't stay out all night just for fun. Something's happened to her. I want to find her, I've got to find to her, Rami, *please*!' He hated the frantic, imploring tone of his voice but couldn't manage anything else.

'I'm not lending you the car, Flynn, and that's that.' Rami filled the mugs with hot water, and Flynn knew by his tone that he meant it. A crushing wave of guilt and helplessness washed over him.

'Damn it, Rami, you've got to help me! It was all my fault! Everything was my fault! I wouldn't talk to her for two weeks and she kept on trying and I kept on ignoring her and then she got upset and came round to talk to

290

me and I yelled at her. Rami, I yelled at her! I told her to leave me alone and to go away and that I didn't want to talk to her and then she started to cry and I didn't even go after her—'

'Look, stop shouting and calm down. Sit down for a minute.'

Flynn threw himself furiously onto a chair and bit his thumb to fight back the rising tears. Rami placed a mug beside him and joined him at the kitchen table.

'I was horrible to her!' Flynn burst out. 'I was really horrible to her and – and now she's disappeared and – and it's all my fault!' He clenched his teeth until his jaw hurt.

Rami wrapped his hands around his mug and leaned forwards. 'Listen. It's not your fault that Jennah's disappeared for a while. Yes, it sounds like you didn't handle the situation very well and it probably *was* your fault that you ended up having a row. But that doesn't mean you're responsible for her disappearance. If somebody attacked her, which is *really* unlikely, then the attacker is the one to blame. If Jennah has decided to lie low for a while and lick her wounds, which is far more likely, then that's her decision and her fault for causing her mother and friends to worry. But you didn't *make* Jennah disappear.'

Flynn rubbed his fingers up and down his burning cheeks. 'But don't you see? It doesn't matter whose fault this is! She's missing, that's all that matters! Something terrible could have happened!' He slammed his fist down on the table. 'I might never see her again!'

There was a silence. Rami stared across the table at him. Flynn pressed his fist to his mouth to muffle his ragged breathing. He mustn't lose it, he mustn't start crying – he would never persuade Rami to lend him the car if he did.

But something in Rami's expression seemed to change. 'All this stuff between you two started because Jennah kissed you one day in the pub?'

'How do you know? Yes, yes!'

Rami's eyes didn't leave Flynn's face. He seemed to be thinking hard. 'Why did that make you so angry?'

'What? I don't know! I was just embarrassed. But, Rami, about the car—'

'Hold on. So because you were embarrassed, you started ignoring her. And she got upset and came over wanting to go back to being friends . . .'

'Yes! But that's not the point! The point is—'

'And her asking whether you could just be friends made you so angry that you started yelling . . .'

'Yes, I told you! So can I just borrow—?'

'Flynn, do you fancy Jennah?'

Flynn stared at him. 'What? What are you talking about? She could be anywhere! She could be dead and you're talking about—'

'Why don't you answer the question?'

'Because I'm not – I don't—'

'Think about it for a second.'

292

Flynn felt the blood pound in his face. 'I don't want to talk about this!'

The flicker of a smile passed over Rami's face. 'Tough luck, I do.'

Flynn scraped his chair back. 'What are you talking about?' he shouted. 'All I want to do is borrow your car! I ask you for one tiny little thing—'

'Just answer the question.'

'Leave me alone!'

'Do you fancy her?'

'Stop asking me that!'

'Oh my God.' Rami was trying not to smile. 'You're *in love with her*, aren't you?'

'I don't know!'

'Of course you know. Are you?'

'I hate you!'

'*Are you?*'

'Yes!' Flynn yelled at the top of his voice. 'I am! Happy now? Satisfied? Since I first met her. I've been in love with her since we first met! What the hell did you *think*?'

CHAPTER FOURTEEN

Flynn lay face down on the sofa, a burning cigarette between his fingers. He felt wrung out, exhausted; the sleeve of Rami's UCL sweatshirt was soaked with tears.

'I hope you realize that Sophie has a nose like a bloodhound,' Rami said, a smile in his voice.

'Are you going to give me some Valium then?' Flynn said thickly.

'No.'

'Then I'll smoke every last cigarette you've got.'

Rami laughed. Then there was a silence. 'What do you think you're afraid of?'

Flynn just shook his head.

'It's being vulnerable, isn't it? It's admitting that you want something, someone, and that you might not get her.'

Flynn dragged his sleeve across his face. 'I *have* wanted someone, for seven fucking years. Do you have any idea what that's like?'

'I can imagine,' Rami said. 'But now that she wants you, it's too late?'

'She's gonna find another Charlie.'

'Not if you ask her out, she won't.'

'I can't go through that again.'

'Wanting but not getting? Do you honestly think that's the answer, to go through life never wanting anyone, just in order to avoid getting hurt?'

'It's worked so far, hasn't it?'

'Has it? *Has it*?' Rami's gaze was hard, almost fierce.

Flynn looked down at the floor.

Rami said, 'You won't find happiness by hiding from life, Flynn.'

After a while, Rami got up and went into the kitchen to make some more coffee. When he returned, he handed Flynn a steaming mug and a small, chipped pill.

'What the hell's this?'

'Three hundred milligrams of lithium,' Rami said. 'Half your usual dose. We can do this the easy way or the hard way.' He smiled.

'I'd rather have some Valium,' Flynn said.

'But I'm the doctor.'

Defeated, Flynn put the pill on the back of his tongue and swallowed it with a mouthful of scalding coffee. 'Here's to never wanting to get out of bed again,' he said.

'No,' Rami countered. 'Here's to getting reacquainted with your own feelings. Here's to being able to want, without being sure you're going to get. To risk being hurt and to risk being rejected. Here's to *life*.'

Flynn raised his mug with a small, tired smile. 'Cheers,' he said.

Half an hour later, the phone sprang into life. Rami went to answer it in the kitchen. When he returned, a pale dawn was beginning to touch the living-room curtains.

Rami said, 'You'd better have a shower and make yourself look respectable. We're going into London. Someone spent the night with a friend and is now safely back home. And I think you owe her an explanation.'

Jennah lived with her mother in Aldgate in a house that looked smaller than Flynn remembered. He had chewed off most of his thumbnail by the time they had crossed London and the sun was already high in the sky, drying out the puddles from the night before. Rami pulled up without turning off the engine and looked at Flynn expectantly.

'How can I explain—?' Flynn began.

'You'll find a way.'

'What if she never wants to see me again?'

'I don't think she's one to give up so easily.'

Jennah's mother opened the door, looking tired. 'I was half expecting you.'

Flynn felt the heat rush to his cheeks. 'Can I talk to her?'

'You can, though I should warn you that we've

just had words, so she won't be in the best of moods.'

Flynn went upstairs and knocked on Jennah's bedroom door.

The door opened halfway and Jennah stood there, leaning against the wall. She looked pale and calm and painfully pretty.

'Oh, it's you.'

Flynn took a deep breath to speak, but she cut him off. 'Flynn, I tried to talk to you yesterday. I'm all out of words now . . .'

'I know,' he said quickly, desperately. 'But – but I'm not.'

Her expression didn't change.

'It's my turn now,' Flynn said.

There was a moment's hesitation. Then Jennah stepped back from the doorway. 'OK,' she said.

Jennah sat cross-legged on her bed. Flynn sat on the chair, hands on his knees, fighting the urge to bite his nails. Jennah just looked at him. There was a long silence. He didn't know where to start.

Jennah finally gave him a hint of a smile. 'Don't look so scared.'

He gave a small, embarrassed laugh.

'I'm sorry if I worried you last night,' Jennah kicked off helpfully. 'It was childish and stupid, I know.'

'You really did worry me,' Flynn said without looking up.

'Sorry.'

'OK, well I'm sorry too. I shouldn't have shouted at you. I behaved like an idiot.'

Jennah gave a wry smile. 'You're right about that.'

Another long silence. 'Well at least we've cleared that up,' Jennah said brightly.

Flynn looked up desperately. 'There are some other things I need to tell you too.'

'What?'

'You know this – this thing I've got?'

'Bipolar disorder? That's manic depression, isn't it?'

He nodded. 'There's this medicine I'm supposed to be taking,' he began awkwardly. 'It was making me feel really crap. So I stopped taking it and I sort of got ill again and I was feeling really shitty when you came round.'

'You stopped taking the lithium?'

He looked at her in surprise. 'Yes.'

'And now?'

'Now I'm taking it again. I guess – I guess I do need it. I thought—' He took a deep breath. 'For a while I thought maybe it was all a mistake – maybe I was just overreacting to things and just needed to exercise a little more self-control. And . . . well . . . it turned out it was bigger than that. It turned out that I needed the medicine after all.'

She gave him a long look. 'Are you going to keep taking it?'

'I suppose I am.'

'Are you going to get better?'

'I honestly don't know.'

There was a silence. 'It's bad luck,' Jennah said suddenly.

'What d'you mean?'

'The bipolar. I mean, it could have happened to anyone. It could have happened to any of us. But it happened to you.'

'Yes.'

She smiled suddenly. 'Shall we go downstairs and have something to drink?'

He looked at her. Say yes and he would be off the hook. Say yes and they would be back where they started, just good friends, safe and comfortable, the way it had always been. Say yes and they could put all this messy business behind them and relax. Say yes and he could breathe again and life would be easy . . .

'No.'

Jennah looked at him in surprise.

'I – I – you know that thing that happened in the pub?'

'When I kissed you?' Jennah gave a wry smile. 'Couldn't we just put that behind us now?'

'Well no – well, the thing is, I actually made a mistake. I mean that— What I mean is, I reacted the opposite to how I felt— In other words I reacted to it in a way that wasn't exactly in line with—' He broke off, breathing rather fast.

Jennah was looking at him, a small smile hovering on her lips. 'What are you talking about?'

299

Flynn looked at her, his face burning. 'Can I – can I just try explaining that again?'

Jennah smiled uncertainly. 'OK.'

He looked at her and took a deep breath. His heart was going like a sledgehammer. 'What I was trying to say was just that – was just that I – um – despite my reaction, I really liked the fact that you kissed me and I really wish that you would do it again, or – or that maybe I could . . .' He looked at her dizzily. *God, if I'm supposed to die, now would be a good time.*

Jennah stared at him. Then she bit her lip, holding back a smile, her eyes very bright. 'Really?'

He nodded, reeling.

'Well then,' she said and swallowed. There was a pause. 'Well then,' she said again. 'I think that this time it's only fair to point out that it's your turn.'

'OK.' He looked at her, frozen. 'OK.'

Jennah smiled. 'OK,' she echoed.

He got up. Went over to the bed and sat down next to her. Cupped her cheek in his hand. Leaned forwards. Closed his eyes. And kissed her.

EPILOGUE

Jennah twisted a strand of hair tightly around her little finger and looked anxiously at the slowing traffic ahead. She took Flynn's hand off the steering wheel to look at his watch for the third time.

'We're OK,' he said.

'I know.' She wrinkled her nose and turned away, drumming her fingers on the armrest.

'Stop it,' Flynn said with a smile.

She gave a small laugh. 'Sorry.'

Flynn released the clutch and edged a few inches closer to the brake lights in front.

Two months had passed, the summer was drawing to an end and already the days were getting shorter. Jennah glanced at the suit on the back seat.

'Shoes?' she asked suddenly.

He gave her a meaningful look.

'OK, OK, I'll stop!'

He put his hand over hers.

They swung into the car park. Flynn flashed his pass at the attendant and they were waved through. As they pulled up under the shadow of the London Eye, Jennah got out, pulling her shawl around her. Flynn gazed at her over the bonnet of the car. She looked breathtaking in her long crimson dress, her hair pinned up, tiny pearls hanging from her ears. Her black shawl fluttered in the early evening breeze.

Flynn took his suit and shoes from the back seat and slammed the car door shut with his foot. Jennah held out her hand, her eyes sparkling once again with excitement. They made their way under the bridge, towards the long flight of steps, and Flynn suddenly stopped dead, staring up at the huge mass of grey-stone building towering above them.

Jennah squeezed his hand. 'OK?'

'Mm.'

'Terrified?'

He nodded, his mouth dry.

She smiled. 'Then you're fine. That's exactly how you're supposed to be feeling. I must confess, I'm a little terrified myself!'

He took a shaky breath, still staring at the long flight of steps ahead. 'Here goes.'

'Wait – did you remember to take your meds?'

'Right before we left.'

'OK.' She let her breath out slowly and then surprised him with a kiss. 'You're so cute with your hair all gelled and spiky. You know, all I'm going to be thinking when you're on that stage is that *I* get to take you home with me tonight.'

He smiled. 'Really?'

'Really.'

He laughed. And took her hand and went up the steps to the Royal Festival Hall.

The applause was heavy and went on for a long time. When André finally came off the stage his face was pale, beads of sweat lining the creases on his forehead.

'Thank God that's over,' he mumbled to no one in particular.

Flynn stood up and offered his hand. 'Well done.'

André accepted the handshake with a wry smile. 'Were all sixty-three split notes noticeable?'

'Not to me.'

'Oh well then, perhaps there's still hope. When are you playing?'

'After this one.'

'Well, good luck. Oh, and in case I don't see you before the end, I was wondering if you and Jennah wanted to come out for a drink with me and Rachel afterwards.'

Flynn raised his eyebrows in surprise. 'OK.'

'Great. See you later.'

Flynn sat, elbows on knees, squeezing his stress ball to warm up his fingers and staring at the ground. His heart began to hammer again as he realized that the Chetham's girl, Amelia, had already started the second movement. He tugged at his bow tie and tried to swallow. He noticed a scratch on the side of his well-polished shoe and rubbed at it distractedly with a bitten-down fingernail. *Dear God, I've changed my mind. I don't need to win – I just want to get through this . . . Just get me through this . . .*

He was jolted by the sound of applause. *Already?* The guy with the headset had his hand on the red curtain, ready to let Amelia through. Flynn gripped his knees, his fingertips with their bitten-down nails white against his black trousers. He tried not to look up as she came in, long dress rustling.

'Do I have to go back out?' she asked the headset guy, sounding flustered.

'Yes, just one more bow. Ready? One, two and—' The red curtain was twitched back again and Amelia stepped back out into the bright lights.

A shiver of terror rushed through Flynn and he inhaled deeply and tilted his head back against the wall. The applause died and Amelia rustled back in, her cheeks aglow, and disappeared down the corridor.

'Ready?' the headset guy said to Flynn.

Flynn looked at him and nodded numbly.

The guy beckoned him over. 'OK, nothing to worry about,' he said, taking hold of the top of Flynn's arm with an iron grip. 'There's no rush. Take your time walking on and remember to adjust the stool. And try to enjoy it out there!'

The tuning was beginning to die away. Flynn stared down at the floor. The headset guy peered through the gap in the curtain. 'OK, here we go. One, two and—'

The red curtain disappeared. Strong, hot lights blinding him. Five polished wooden steps to the stage. A mass of black backs and black music stands in front of him. A narrow pathway ahead of him through the orchestra, leading to the conductor's rostrum and the piano. He went up the steps. Made his way between the chairs and stands. The conductor smiled at him as he approached. He reached the piano. To his right was the dark mass of audience, stretching back and up, further than his eyes could see. Somewhere out there were Mum and Dad and Rami and Sophie and Harry and Jennah.

He sat down at the piano. Adjusted the stool. Felt for the pedal with his right foot. Touched the keys. The applause died away. Nothing but the pounding of his heart. He sat still, resting his hands in his lap. Then looked up at the conductor and nodded. The conductor turned back to face the orchestra and raised his arms. A moment of screaming silence, then the music started. The soft, simple, two-note introduction to Rachmaninov's Third Piano Concerto rose from the orchestra. Flynn returned his gaze to the piano. He lifted his hands and started to play.

The
Book Thief

by

MARKUS ZUSAK

It is 1939. Nazi Germany. The country is holding its breath.
Death has never been busier, and will become busier still.

By her brother's graveside, Liesel Meminger's life is changed when
she picks up a single object, partially hidden in the snow.
It is *The Gravedigger's Handbook*, left there by accident, and it is
her first act of book thievery. So begins a love affair
with books and words, as Liesel, with the help of her foster
father, learns to read.

Soon she is stealing books from Nazi book-burnings, the mayor's
wife's library, wherever there are books to be found.
But these are dangerous times. When Liesel's foster family hides
a Jew in their basement, Liesel's world is both opened up,
and closed down.

The Book Thief is a story about the power of words and the
ability of books to feed the soul. In superbly crafted writing
that burns with intensity, award-winning author Markus Zusak
has given us one of the most enduring stories of our time.

ISBN: 978 0 370 32921 5

MONKEY TAMING

by

JUDITH FATHALLAH

When Jessica was thirteen years old, she met the Monkey.

The Monkey lived inside her: a driving, fiery voice telling her that
thinness was the only way. The only way to be safe, to be good,
to be acceptable and above all, to escape from the cold, looming
threat of approaching adulthood. Jessica listened to the Monkey,
and it consumed her.

This is the illuminating story of a teenage girl's wanderings in
darkness: the spiral down into madness, the terrible
realities of an adolescent psychiatric unit, and the stark choice
that she must either tame her monster – or die.

Through memory, reflection, and enduring black humour, Jessica makes
a tenuous peace with the world and with her emerging adult self.

ISBN: 978 0 099 48845 3

The Fearful

by

KEITH GRAY

For those who want to believe, no proof is needed. But for those
who can't believe, no evidence is enough.

The legend says that in 1699 schoolteacher William Milmullen
and his five pupils visited Lake Mou, but only William returned.
He claimed that a terrifying creature had risen from the lake and
devoured the boys. But had it? And if it all happened so long
ago, does it really matter to anyone nowadays anyway?

The legacy of that tragedy lives on in the town of Moutonby.
A town divided between those who believe that something
terrible still lurks deep down in the lake, and those who don't.

Tim Milmullen wishes he knew. Every day he watches the dark water,
looking for a sign. Because if the stories are true, if 'the dragon'
in the lake is real, then according to the legend he's the only one who
can stop it from killing again.

ISBN: 978 0 099 45656 8

this is all

by

Aidan Chambers

Subtitled 'The Pillow Book of Cordelia Kenn' this is the story of
Cordelia from the time she is 15 until she is 20. She is pregnant
and plans to give this account to her daughter on her 16th birthday
so that they can share their youth together.

She tells of her mother (who died when Cordelia was 5), of her
father and her aunt Doris, of her love for William Blacklin,
the first boy with whom she chooses to have sex - and with whom
she falls deeply in love. She writes about Julie Martin,
her teacher who helps her spiritually, describes her love affair with
an older married man and her terrifying sexual experience with
an unbalanced young man who is obsessed with her. The book includes
thoughts on being a woman, on poetry, music, reading and
writing, on being pregnant, and finally, on her marriage to William.

This Is All is an anthology, written in six 'books', of Cordelia's
adolescent life, by turns funny, poignant, sad, exciting,
fascinating, ironic and truthful about topics that parents often do
not tell their children. It is a richly entertaining and challenging read.

Out now in paperback

ISBN: 978 0 099 41776

postcards
from no man's land

by

Aidan Chambers

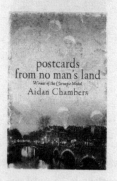

Jacob Todd is abroad on his own for the first time, visiting his grandfather's grave at the annual commemoration of the Battle of Arnhem in Amsterdam. There, he meets Geertrui, a terminally ill old lady, who tells an extraordinary story of love and betrayal, which completely overturns Jacob's view of himself and his country, and leads him to question his place in the world. Jacob's story is paralled in time by the events of the dramatic day in World War II when retreating troops were sheltered by Geertrui's family.

An intensely moving and richly layered novel, spanning 50 years, which powerfully evokes the atmosphere of war while brilliantly interweaving Jacob's exploration of new relationships in contemporary Amsterdam.

ISBN: 978 1 862 30284 6